What In Hell Does God Want

Carmon Green

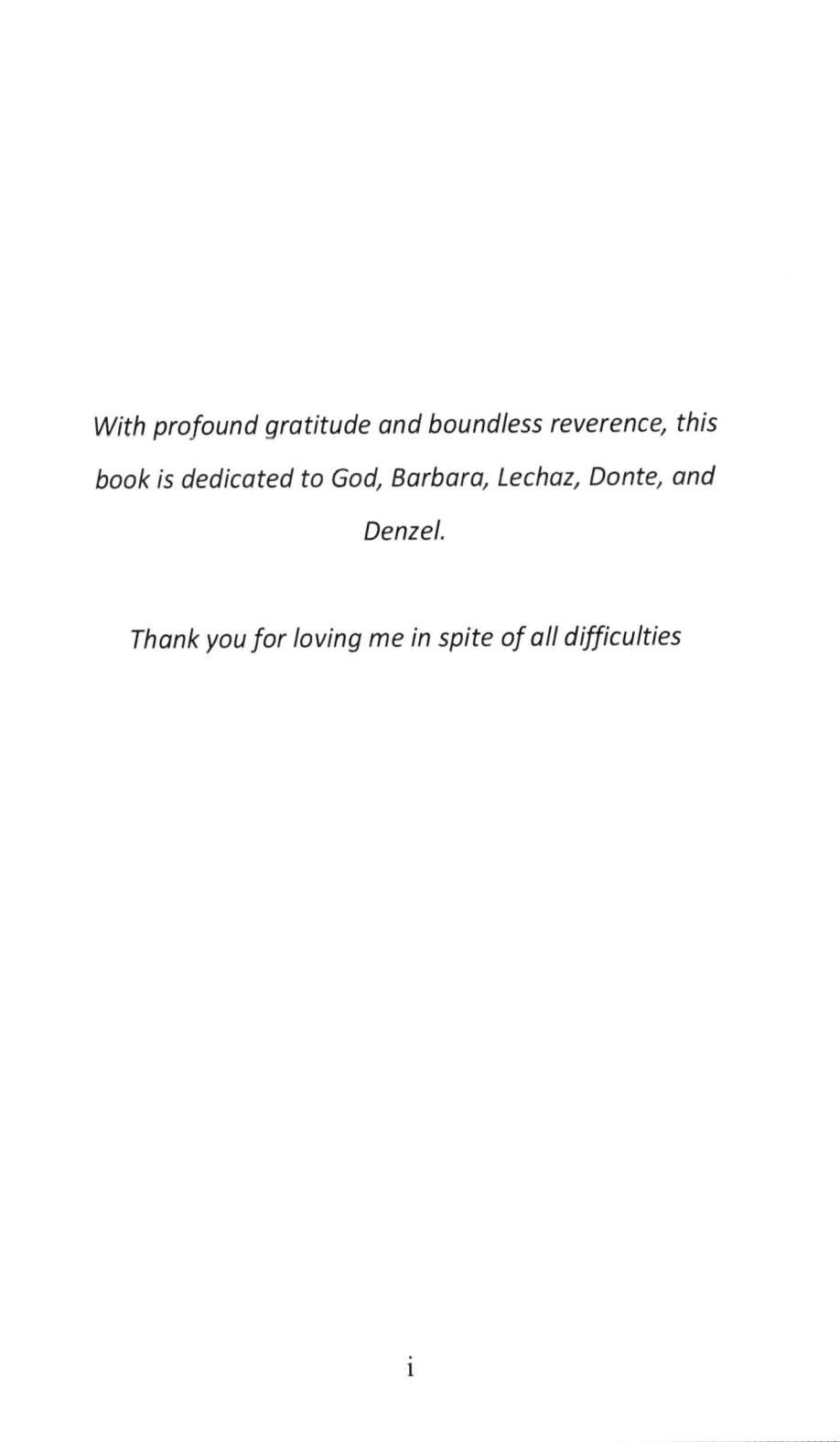

With profound gratitude and boundless reverence, this book is dedicated to God, Barbara, Lechaz, Donte, and Denzel.

Thank you for loving me in spite of all difficulties

With heartfelt appreciation, I extend my deepest gratitude to my beloved family and steadfast circle of friends, whose unwavering presence has been my solace through every trial and triumph. Your love sustains me, and for that, I am eternally grateful.

I am especially indebted to the following individuals for enriching the soil of my life with their unwavering support and encouragement: Khalilah (La-La), Bonita Locus, Noel, Charles D., Saleem, Mom and Pop Green, Ebony, The Johnson and the Carr Family, and The Pritchette Family.

Your contributions have nourished my growth and filled my heart with profound gratitude.

CONTENTS

About the Author

My name is Carmon Green. I proudly identify as a Black woman, a devoted follower of Christ, and a dedicated wife. My greatest joys stem from nurturing my two biological adult sons, cherishing my beautiful stepdaughter, and guiding my two intelligent stepsons through their formative years.

Raised in Philadelphia, Pa., by a resilient single mother alongside three siblings, my early years were marked by humble beginnings and formidable challenges. Seeking solace, I found refuge and purpose within my community church, where I was called to serve as an ordained deaconess for a decade, offering spiritual support to those in need.

Guided by faith, I embarked on a 25-year journey in law enforcement, answering God's call to serve and protect. Later in life, I pursued higher education, delving into the realms of psychology and criminal justice, culminating in the attainment of a bachelor's degree in science.

My background and experiences have given me a

taste of the good, bad, and unstable aspects of society.

I have encountered numerous forks on the road, made friends for life, and encountered unfavorable people on my travels.

Nevertheless, I value and treasure them all, for they are a part of errors, but they've all taught me something: the blueprint of my growth.

To you, my newfound friend, I extend my heartfelt gratitude for choosing to share in the laughter, smiles, and tears of my creative journey. Your unwavering support means the world to me.

REMEMBER THIS:

We all weave through life with events that test our emotional and mental resilience. Even though we might not have chosen the difficulties we encounter, the healing process is uniquely ours.

We frequently internalize our suffering, letting it fester and contaminate our entire existence. But facing our inner selves and making the painful but necessary journey toward genuine healing is where true power resides.

May we embrace the essence of "Self" and aspire to greatness with purposeful intent.

May God's blessings guide and sustain us on our journey.

Warm regards,

Carmon Green

Introduction

The tan SUV rolls to a stop in the driveway, Sasha's apprehension palpable as she gazes at her home from the back seat. The sight of the borrowed car, snatched by her husband three nights ago, only adds to her unease. "Thank you for putting up with me," she murmurs, her gratitude tinged with guilt, before slipping out of the car without waiting for Nikay and Torri's response.

Nikay's forced "anytime, girl!" Earns a strained smile from Sasha, though inside, she seethes at their judgment. "To hell with both of y'all for judging me," she thinks bitterly, closing the rear passenger's door behind her. With a heavy heart, she unloads her plastic shopping bags and the Gucci duffle bag overflowing with clothes as the trunk pops open.

Entering her house, Sasha punches in the front door code, praying that no drama lurks beyond the unlocked threshold. Stepping into the grand living room, she takes in the neatly arranged furniture, a stark contrast to the chaos within her mind. As she deposits her bags in a corner, the sounds of her husband's slumber echo from the master bedroom—a sleeping bear, temporarily at peace.

Moving through the house, Sasha enters the kitchen, surprised to find the Friday night dinner dishes cleared away. His act of cleaning hints at a rare moment of respite from their turbulent emotions, stirring a mix of hope and apprehension within her.

Quietly slipping off her shoes, Sasha tiptoes towards the bedroom, her heart heavy with the weight of shame and guilt. With cautious steps, she seeks confirmation of his slumber, hoping for a reprieve from the storm brewing within them both.

There he lies, stretched out, his stocking cap snug on his head, one hand nestled inside his sweatpants, finding solace in each rumbling breath. Sasha returns to the living room, her gaze falling on the disorganized bags. Tears well in her eyes as she realizes she can't risk unpacking, fearing what might transpire if he wakes.

"Okay, now what?" She whispers to herself, the weight of uncertainty pressing down on her. Suddenly, she remembers the urgency of finding the car key. With cautious steps, she ventures into the master bedroom, craning her neck to peek around.

Nothing.

She hurries downstairs to the second guest bedroom,

heart racing. As she entered, a mix of confusion and disbelief washed over her. The room is adorned with her stepchildren's baby photographs, meticulously placed on the dressers. His shoes stand in regimented lines against the wall as if he has claimed the space as his own. Sasha's emotions swirl, torn between anger at his calculated detachment and a flicker of relief at the prospect of reclaiming a fragment of autonomy.

Regardless of her conflicting feelings, the scene before her defies description. It's a tableau of manipulation and estrangement, where words fail to capture the depth of emotion. Only sharp, dagger-like words could pierce through the layers, reaching the heart of the matter.

With a sudden movement, the key catches Sasha's eye, perched at the edge of the dresser as if forgotten in haste. Snatching it up like a prized possession, she searches for a hiding spot, already bracing herself for the tumultuous aftermath. The coat pocket seems a safe bet—inside it goes, hanging innocuously in the closet. If he searches, he won't suspect the coat she rarely wears, and if he finds it, a plausible explanation can be conjured to quell his potential rage and insults.

Taking a deep breath, Sasha attempts to navigate the whirlwind of thoughts swirling in her mind. A hot bath seems like a sanctuary, a gesture to signal her desire to avoid conflict. With determined steps, she retraces her path to the master bedroom, only to find the once-open door now firmly shut. Turning the doorknob—locked.

Frustration boils within her as she heads to the adjoining office room, hoping for an alternative route into the master bedroom. But as she tries the door to the master bathroom, her agitation peaks—locked.

"What the fuck!?" She exclaims, her voice tinged with a mix of anger and desperation, trapped in a maze of closed doors and unanswered questions.

"He has got some nerve," Sasha mutters under her breath as she knocks on the door, a humble request for him to unlock it.

But after three rounds of consecutive knocks, the volume on the flat-screen television spikes, signaling the onset of the silent treatment. Recognizing the futility of her attempts to gain his attention, Sasha retreats to the study, choosing silence over further confrontation.

Seated in the quiet confines of the study, Sasha wrestles with the bewildering cascade of emotions triggered by his passive-aggressive reaction. What did she do wrong, if anything, to deserve this treatment yet again?

Her mind drifts back to Thursday, the day Rashaun had taken her car, leaving his own on empty in the garage—a routine occurrence. She had sat nervously, praying for his safe return from his nights of drinking and smoking pounds of weed. Then, the dreaded phone call came. "Bae, your Escalade is messed up," he had said, his explanation dripping with indifference.

The irony wasn't lost on Sasha—a man on probation for two DUIs, branded a reckless driver with six thousand dollars in moving violations, now blaming a nonexistent bicyclist for his misfortune.

"Who rides a bike in a rural area, with no city light poles and nothing in sight for 10 miles, at 3 AM?" She ponders, the absurdity of his excuse amplifying her frustration.

After five agonizing hours of waiting for the tow truck provided by her insurance company, he finally strolled through the door, seemingly unscathed. "That man was pissed, cold, and high as a damn kite," Sasha recounts, her voice tinged with a mixture of frustration and resignation. "He had a mean look on his face, ensuring he didn't make eye contact with me."

Sasha's anxiety forces a nervous smile as she imagines his thoughts, playing out the scenario in her mind. "I know she can see straight through my bullshit," she imagines him thinking.

"The meaner I look, the less likely she'll inquire further. I'll just walk past her, ignoring her with my 'don't-fuck-with-me' energy."

It worked, too, Sasha acknowledges, begrudgingly admiring his ability to manipulate the situation to his advantage. "His tactics always deter me from confronting him," she reflects, a hint of defeat in her tone.

Slightly shaking her head, Sasha reminds herself, "It's all cap. His tactics never change." Despite her acknowledgment, she knows she'll continue to navigate the intricate dance of their relationship, each step fraught with tension and uncertainty.

Sasha's mind races as she recaps the events of the evening. After what seemed like a night of normalcy, with him sleeping off his burden of explanation, he had transformed into an unusually soft and polite version of himself. He even took the initiative to prepare dinner, taking into account her preferences, and engaged in enjoyable conversation.

But then, the moment shattered. As he finished his shower, preparing to head out, he casually requested the key to the borrowed car. Summoning her courage, Sasha bravely uttered, "No, Rashaun, I don't trust you." Before she could even finish her statement, he sucked his teeth with aggression and stormed out of the room, his steps echoing on the stairs leading to the front door.

Moments later, Sasha's unease grew as she noticed the absence of the familiar sound of the garage door opening, where his truck usually resided. Peering out the window, her heart sank as she watched two red brake lights retreat into the darkness, moving backward out of the driveway.

Panic seized her as she rushed to the bedroom, her eyes scanning her untouched pocketbook. That bastard, she seethed inwardly, realization dawning upon her. He had premeditatedly stolen the car, manipulating her with his deceptive calm before the storm.

The bitter truth hit Sasha like a wave—she had fallen for his manipulations time and time again. And in that moment, she swore she wouldn't let herself be fooled by his facade of tranquility any longer.

Admitting the truth to myself, panic instantly gripped me as I realized he was off to meet his drinking buddies in the hood. That meant I wouldn't see him until morning—a prospect that filled me with dread. Frantically, I bombarded his phone with texts, pleading for him to bring the car back. But, as expected, he ignored me, his silence confirming my worst fears.

In a desperate attempt to instill fear in him, I threatened to report the car stolen. But deep down, I knew it was futile. Nothing scares him; he knows I'd go to great lengths to avoid social embarrassment and drama, even if it means enduring his torment.

Rashaun needs a wake-up call. He needs to understand that I won't continue to be a doormat for his whims. Let him miss me for once! So, without hesitation, I called Nikkay to pick me up, deciding to spend the weekend away from the chaos. "Now," I thought bitterly, "you can worry about where I am for a change!"

As I made my escape, doubts gnawed at me. Did my plan work? Or have I unwittingly invited another storm into my life, one I can't see my way through? Only time will tell.

Chapter 1

Sasha Wright sits on the steps, casting her gaze over the neighborhood she longs to escape. There's a complex mix of emotions—a love-hate relationship, she muses. Philadelphia: a city of hundred-thousand-dollar homes with no backyards. The Wright family knows this landscape all too well, entrenched in the middle-to-low-income culture that defines their existence. They've grown accustomed to the scent of struggle and the low water pressure from open-fire hydrants—it's become their norm.

An urban family in an urban neighborhood can't help but feel like statistics, boxed into societal categories beyond their control. Yet, amidst the challenges, there's a sense of resilience, a determination to defy the odds and carve out a path of their own.

The vibrant activities of children playing hopscotch and double dutch in the street momentarily interrupt Sasha's thoughts. "I miss it," she murmurs wistfully, a football whizzing past her from a touch football game played by the older kids.

Under the blazing sun, its rays beat down on her

moist caramel-colored skin, causing her carefully curled shoulder-length hair to slowly succumb to the heat. Hours spent styling vanish as the curls loosen. Sasha always ensures her wardrobe matches the current trends, finding affordable makeup from Rite-Aid that she applies flawlessly. Her bamboo earrings, sourced from the Ave, always dangle neatly from her ears, emitting the perfect sound when disturbed.

Despite being an all-star athlete and one of the most popular students at Dobbins High School, Sasha knows that her past successes don't guarantee her future.

I always made the honor roll and was accepted to Temple University on a basketball scholarship! One little mistake changed everything," she reminisced bitterly. "That damn Vick! Two misdemeanors and a hot drug test killed everything! I never knew selling food stamps as a family could be considered an enterprise for welfare fraud!" Rolling with Vick was fun, though. The blunts and coronas were free, and he always got us into the speakeasies and clubs on Erie Ave. Vick's house was the neighborhood's hangout spot. I just happened to be there when his family was busted. I got caught with three dime bags in my pocket. Them jawns were fat too," she chuckled, the memory surprising her.

"Why did you get my shirt on!" An angry voice yelled from behind her. Startled, Sasha turned around and saw her sister Tasha, the second oldest triplet, standing in the doorway. It was like looking in a mirror. Tasha was soft-spoken, a mother's helper, searching for her own identity. Annoyed that Tasha would yell this outside for everyone to hear, Sasha replied, "This is not your shirt!" The unaware self-entitlement forced Sasha to lie. Tasha screamed, "Take it off, it's my shirt! I bought it from The Banana Republic 2 weeks ago, and you know it!" Knowing it wasn't going to happen, Tasha walked back into the house, feeling the pressure to stand up for herself more.

Tasha steps into the kitchen, greeted by the comforting aroma of collard greens and baked chicken wafting through the air. For a moment, she's drawn away from her urge to vent as she opens the refrigerator, confirming her mother's famous potato salad is indeed there.

"Shut my door, girl, and get out my bowl," Cookie scolds, her tone both firm and familiar. Tasha quickly complies, closing the refrigerator door with a smile. "Dag, Mom, I just wanted to taste it," she jests, her irritation momentarily forgotten.

"Mom? Are you going to cook the crabs?" Tasha inquires, noticing the crustaceans wrestling around in the sink.

"Don't you see them wrestling around in the sink?" Cookie replies with a chuckle.

Speaking of wrestling, Tasha can't help but broach the topic of the ongoing argument with her sister. "Shasha has my shirt on. She always takes my things without asking. The part that bothers me is she'll claim it as her own and want to fight as if I don't have the right to it."

Cookie chuckles softly, a hint of amusement in her voice. "Y'all been doing this for years," she remarks, a testament to the enduring sibling dynamics in their household.

Frustrated, Tasha raises her voice, "It's not funny, Mom. She's been bullying me for years. I'm sick of it."

Cookie responds calmly, "All siblings go through fussing and fighting, but she loves you, Tasha."

Greg enters the kitchen, catching wind of the conversation. Playfully, he taps Tasha on the head, advising, "Just fight it out like y'all always do."

Tasha swats his hand away, exclaiming, "Stop, boy!"

Greg laughs, teasing, "I heard you can't beat Shasha anyway."

"Mom, tell Greg to shut up!" Tasha demands, annoyed by his instigating.

"Stop instigating, Greg, and come fix you and your father's plate," Cookie interjects, redirecting his attention.

Greg reassures, "She knows I'm only playing, Mom."

"Well, I got to go work tonight. Are you staying?" Cookie asks Greg.

"Yeah, I'll be back," he responded.

Greg removes the lid from the crab pot, inhaling the aroma of the perfectly seasoned boiling water. With precision, he retrieves the large tongs from the drawer and begins to pick up the live crabs from the sink, gently placing them into the boiling water. As Greg tends to the crabs, Cookie exits the kitchen.

Greg turns to Tasha, his brow furrowed with concern. "You and Shasha at it again?" He inquires gently.

Tasha sighs heavily, her frustration evident in the lines etched on her face. "She's always taking my stuff," she begins, her voice tinged with exhaustion. "Ever since we were small, she'd bully me, embarrass me in front of my friends, and lie to me just to get out of trouble. It's getting old." The weight of years of sibling rivalry and resentment hangs heavily in the air as Tasha shares her grievances with Greg.

"You were no better, Greg," she continued. "You instigated everything just to see us physically fight like we were your personal entertainment."

Greg chuckles a feeble attempt to mask his guilt. "But it was fun," he offers weakly, trying to justify his actions.

"That ain't funny!" Tasha stamps her foot in frustration. "Stop being so sensitive. You know I'm only playing," Greg responds, brushing off her concerns.

Tasha shoots Greg a look of disdain, silently waiting for an apology. Greg, unfazed, continues to smile as he places the crabs into the pot, the tension between them palpable in the air.

Greg stood tall at 6'3, his dark complexion adding an air of mystery to his handsome features. He was a ladies' man, unapologetic about his charm. The age gap between Greg and the triplets was evident, with him being 11 years their senior. Born from Cookie's first marriage to Gregory Wright Sr., they were high school sweethearts who tied the knot shortly after graduating from Lincoln High School. Their love story was the talk of the town, with many believing they were destined to grow old together, as foretold by the yearbook's prophecies. Yet, the bliss didn't last.

Shortly after saying their "I Do's," Cookie gave birth to Greg. However, rumors and gossip swirled about the timing of her pregnancy. Despite the whispers, Cookie and Gregory Wright Sr. were married just three months after their high school graduation, and Greg arrived six months later. The taboo topic surrounding the timing of Greg's birth remained unspoken, lingering in the air like a secret no one dared to confront.

Sadly, their marriage dissolved when Greg Jr. turned 11, the victim of infidelity and the strain of early parenthood. Cookie, burdened by the responsibilities of being a wife and mother at such a young age, found herself overwhelmed. A fleeting moment of feeling desired led to an encounter with the father of her triplets, a night of passion that shattered her marriage irreparably.

Unfortunately, she was left to navigate the challenges of motherhood alone; Cookie's babies were born fatherless. Despite this, they were perfect in her eyes. Little Greg lived with his father, visiting Cookie and his baby sisters often, a reminder of the fractured family dynamic that defined their lives.

Greg emerged from the kitchen, a plate laden with food cradled in a bulging plastic bag from Super Fresh Market.

"Mom!" His voice echoed upstairs from the living room. "I'm heading out. I'll be back soon!"

Cookie's response, a gentle "Alright, baby, love you," drifted down to meet him.

As Greg stepped towards the door, he encountered Sasha on the front steps.

"You doing alright?" He inquired.

Sasha offered a nod, replying, "Yeah, I'm good.

Where you off to?"

Greg's response came easily, "Just going to see pops, be back in a bit."

"Aye bet. Don't forget to bring me something back." Sasha uttered.

Greg's grin widened as he responded, "I might. Give Tash back her shirt, and I'll think about it."

Sasha, unimpressed, sucked her teeth and retorted, "Whatever," her hand gesturing dismissively, ending with an extended middle finger.

With a flick of his wrist, Greg cranked up the volume of his black Mustang's engine, the red leather interior gleaming under the sunlight. He revved the accelerator unnecessarily, the sound echoing through the neighborhood. Turning up the CD player, the beats of Eric B and Rakim's "Make Em' Clap to This" filled the air, drowning out the engine's roar.

As the bass mix intro played, Greg bobbed his head in rhythm, eagerly awaiting the first verse. Right on cue, he glanced at Sasha and began to rap along with the song.

"I came in the door. I said it before,

I never let the mic magnetize me no more.

But it's biting me. Fighting me. Inviting me to rhyme.

I can't hold back. I'm looking for the line."

With a roar, Greg pulled away, his black Mustang disappearing down the street. Sasha's gaze lingered until the sound of his music faded into the distance, swallowed by the city's noise.

Chapter 2

As the day transitions into the evening and the streetlights flicker to life, the neighborhood children scatter to play in front of their homes. Greg reclines on the porch, savoring the last crab leg while his cold beer sweats in the evening air. Sasha emerges from the house, the screen door banging shut behind her—a delicate fragrance of white diamond perfume and dove soap trails in her wake as she passes Greg. Settling into the weathered cushion swing, a cherished relic from her childhood, Sasha absentmindedly swings back and forth, engrossed in her flip phone.

"Where are you off to?" Greg inquires, curiosity lacing his voice.

"Just figuring things out," Sasha replies, her attention still focused on her phone. "Did you bring something?"

Greg chuckles. "I brought myself something," he quips, a playful glint in his eyes.

Cookie walked out onto the porch, adjusting to the warm climate in her dog print scrubs. "On your way to work, Mom?" Greg inquired.

"Yeah," Cookie replied, turning to face Greg. "Get them stinky crab shells off my porch, and Sasha, get your tail in there and help your sister with the dishes!"

Cookie paused to retrieve her keys from her pocketbook, pulling out a set adorned with her nurse's key chain and a rubber stress ball while Sasha remained engrossed in her cell phone.

"Sasha, now!" Cookie demanded.

Reluctantly, Sasha rose from the swing, attempting to save her face amidst embarrassment. She headed into the house to assist Tasha.

"Have a good night, Mom. I'll be here," Greg offered.

"Okay, Greg. Thank you. I'll see y'all in the morning," Cookie responded before heading off to work.

Night had fallen, casting its dark cloak over the surroundings. Greg lounged on the porch, deeply engaged in a phone conversation with one of his girlfriends, relishing his fourth beer. Tasha ventured outside, escaping Greg's bothersome antics. She switched on the dim porch light and delved into the novel she had been trying to complete for days. Meanwhile, Sasha swiftly emerged from the house and took her place at the edge of the porch. Her gaze fixated on the street as if anticipating someone's arrival.

Interrupting his phone call, Greg inquired, "Where were you heading?"

Sasha responded succinctly, "Out."

Vick turned the corner, his rap music booming as he approached Sasha's home. Sasha stepped out to the curb, watching the Volvo as it navigated the narrow street with caution, avoiding the parked cars that lined the curb on one side. Despite not owning a car himself, Vick managed a fleet of vehicles belonging to his siblings and cousins. It was easy to be drawn to Vick; he was a popular figure in the neighborhood, with striking features and a charismatic charm that belied his fast-talking nature. Despite being only three years older than Sasha, Vick looked out for her like a protective older brother.

Known as a "go-getter" in the community, Vick often overestimated his worth with women. He believed that he was deserving of women who were way out of his league. However, Sasha remained by his side, providing him with a rare sense of trust and camaraderie. In Vick, Sasha found not just a friend but a confidant who embraced her quirks and peculiarities without reservation. Their bond, forged through shared experiences and mutual trust, transcended the superficiality of many relationships in their neighborhood. Vick's genuine acceptance of Sasha allowed her to be her true self, unencumbered by societal expectations or preconceived notions.

As Vick's car pulled up, Sasha swiftly made her way to the passenger door.

"Yō, what's up, man?" Vick's voice rang out to greet Greg, who offered a brief nod in response.

"Aye, Sash... act like you know," Greg warned Sasha before she got into the car.

"Okay. I won't be back too late," Sasha reassured him.

Sliding into the passenger seat, Sasha greeted Vick with a smile, the scent of weed lingering in the air, confirming it was going to be a memorable night. With confidence, Vick steered the car away from the curb.

Their first stop was Lou Choo Bar, a hotspot for the older crowd. Vick double parked on the crowded street, eager to assess the bar's atmosphere. He had hoped to find more women than men inside, knowing it would increase his chances of getting laid that night. Sasha remained in the car, indulging in the half-consumed joint that rested in the ashtray, waiting for Vick's return.

Moments later, Vick walked out of the bar with a beautiful, tall Latina woman by his side. As they approached the car, the woman smiled upon seeing Sasha in the front passenger seat.

"Look who I found," Vick said with a grin.

Sasha turned towards Vick, delighted to see her friend Ava.

"Ava, what's up, girl? I've been calling you all night!" She exclaimed.

"Hey girl," Ava replied, "what are you up to?"

"Chilling. Come on, get in," Sasha offered.

Ava reluctantly got into the weed-scented vehicle. As she settled in the back seat, waiting for Vick, she couldn't help but remember the last time she was with Sasha when she was high. Sasha had punched a girl and broken her nose because she accidentally touched Sasha's glass of beer. The situation worsened as Sasha assumed a starkly different persona, akin to Ms. Hyde, even exhibiting hostility towards those around her.

The driver's door opened, and Vick got into the driver's seat, bragging about the phone number he had obtained from a woman he had tried to impress. They pulled off and arrived at the Yellow Bird, the Jamaican dance hall, where Sasha was loved by the regular patrons.

Sasha swung the passenger door open and stepped out as if she was about to greet a crowd of adoring fans. Ava followed behind her, a loyal sidekick in the night's adventures. They scanned the scene outside: folks hanging around, sipping Genesis Stout and swaying to the Jamaican beats echoing from the building.

An island voice called out to Sasha, "Sassy girl, come over here; where you have been hiding?"

"Miste', what's good?" Sasha shot back with a smile.

Miste' couldn't help but admire Sasha's bold outfit – the tight red skirt, flashy Pumas, and that pink tee with "H o t t y" stamped across her chest in red letters. Her clothes hugged her curves just right, and Miste' couldn't look away.

Having arrived from Haiti to the States back in 1980 for business, Miste' embraced the culture and quickly realized the plethora of business and personal opportunities available to him. Hence, Miste' made the choice to remain in the States after his arrival from Haiti in 1980. His occupation remained a mystery to most, but his reputation as someone not to be trifled with was well-established on the streets. With his goatee and meticulously kept dreads, the 34-year-old possessed a natural charm that drew women to him effortlessly.

His demeanor, coupled with his unwavering respect for women, was palpable to all who encountered him. It was a quality he wore on his sleeves, along with the bankroll he kept, which didn't hurt.

Wrapping Sasha in an affectionate embrace, Miste' pulled her close, his arm extending down her back as he drew her into his embrace. "Miss you, girl. Where have you been hiding?" He teased.

Sasha, breaking away with a smile, responded, "I've been home, but I'm out now, just to see you."

"Miste' chuckled in response, dismissing the matter with a nonchalant 'Whatever!'

As they chuckled together, Sasha strolled alongside Miste' to his storefront next door, where a cold Corona and the finest island marijuana awaited them. Standing on the stoop, Sasha peered through the empty store, its shelves sparsely populated with outdated groceries. Miste' disappeared inside briefly and returned bearing gifts, which Sasha accepted with gratitude. Settling in, Sasha and Miste' savored each other's company over their drinks and the soothing island rhythms.

Miste' had always seen something special in Sasha, something different from other women. Her resilience, strength, and potential as a successful black woman captivated him, drawing him closer to her.

Meanwhile, Ava sipped on her Heineken at the crowded bar while Vick enjoyed the company of a female stranger rubbing against his genitals. Sasha walked into the bar an hour after they had arrived and joined Ava at the bar.

"Damn! You couldn't share?" Ava said, teasing Sasha, who smiled with her eyes slightly closed from the herb.

As Sasha adjusted herself on the stool next to Ava, she replied, "I got some more; stop sweating me."

Sasha waited for the bartender amidst the pulsating rhythms of reggae mixes and rounds of drinks. After a few rotations, a man approached Sasha from behind. "You're just gonna take my seat," he joked, removing his jacket from her stool.

"Does it look like I am sitting on your lap? The chair was empty, so I sat down," Sasha retorted.

"Aye, Ma... I don't want no trouble," the man replied.

Sensing the tension, a female approached, ready to take over the man's troubles. Sasha impulsively confronted the female, leaving Ava to turn her head away, knowing any intervention might escalate Sasha's urge to fight.

Vick spotted the dispute and hurried over to Sasha and the irate woman. Both were shoving people aside, gearing up for a brawl.

"What's going on?" Vick interjected, stepping between them.

Sasha, seething with anger, shot back, "She started it, Vick! She's got a problem with me!"

Vick, sensing the escalating tension, took Sasha by the arm and led her away from the confrontation. "Let's go, Sasha. This isn't worth it."

Ava settled the tab and trailed behind, trying to calm the situation. "Come on, let's just leave. It's not worth the trouble."

"Shut the fuck up! You just sat there, didn't say anything," Sasha snapped at Ava as they headed towards the car.

"Because it was stupid! Fighting over a chair, Sasha!" Ava retorted, exasperated.

As they got into the car, Vick swiftly drove off, hoping to diffuse the tension. Inside the car, Sasha's anger still simmered, while Ava regretted getting involved in the first place.

Tension thickened as silence filled the car. Vick drove quietly, hoping for the atmosphere to ease. Despite the strain, he remained steadfast in his role as Sasha's protector, ready to shield her from the fallout of her actions.

Hungry, Vick steers into the parking lot of the Eagles Bar and Max's at Broad and Erie Avenue. He hops out of the car, leaving the girls to their own devices, hoping they might resolve their differences in his absence. Inside the car, Sasha and Ava sit in silence, each lost in her own thoughts, gazing out their respective windows.

Ava steps out of the car and lights a cigarette, seeking solace from the tension that hangs in the air like a heavy cloud. The minutes tick by slowly, and after what seems like an eternity, Vick reappears, his hands laden with a bag of goodies. As he slides back into the driver's seat, he eagerly inspects his purchase, a wide grin spreading across his face. With a flourish, he presents Sasha and Ava with a 12-foot-long tightly rolled sandwich, its tantalizing aroma filling the car with the promise of the best cheesesteak in the hood.

"You'll good?" Vick asks, his eyes alight with anticipation.

"Always," Ava replies with a smile, her earlier tension easing at the sight of the delicious treat.

However, Sasha remained silent. Her attention focused on the wafting scent of the savory sandwich in her hands as she eagerly unwrapped her portion.

After finishing their meal, Vick drives to the after-hours spot called "The Chicken Coup," which is just three blocks away. This dive was carved out in the basement of a row home. Inside, the space has been transformed into a bar. Despite its emptiness, the watering hole has the ability to make its patrons forget that there are small family apartments located upstairs.

Entering the dimly lit space, Sasha, Ava, and Vick feel a sense of familiarity wash over them. With only a few people lingering, they're pleased to arrive early and secure three of the five stools at the bar. Sasha boldly orders two shots of Hennesy, purposefully ignoring Ava's expectant glance. Inwardly, she murmurs to herself, "Déjà vu," sensing the beginning of the silent treatment. Nonetheless, she quietly orders a rum and coke, determined not to let Sasha's demeanor affect her enjoyment of the evening.

They indulged in the smooth sounds of 90's R&B drifting from the speakers placed strategically in the corners of the dimly lit space. Ava retrieved her drink from the bar and ventured into the room, eager to mingle. Approaching a man who clearly wasn't from the neighborhood, they engaged in flirtatious banter as Ava savored her rum.

Meanwhile, Sasha observed from afar, feeling the effects of the Hennesy taking hold. A battle waged within her as she wrestled with her annoyance at Ava's reaction to her silent treatment and the judgment she felt for her past behavior. Seeking solace, Sasha ordered another drink, hoping to drown out her internal conflict.

As Vick launched into a lengthy discourse about his romantic conquests, Sasha couldn't help but notice the attention Ava was drawing from the men in the room. Unable to contain her jealousy, Sasha abruptly excused herself and clumsily rose from her bar stool.

"Where are you going?" Vick asked, his concern evident in his voice.

"To the bathroom," Sasha slurred, unable to hide her inebriation.

Driven by her envy, Sasha stumbled past Ava, accidentally spilling alcohol on her favorite shirt.

"Dag!" Ava exclaimed, her disappointment evident.

Nearby men quickly offered napkins to help clean up the mess, sensing the tension between the two women.

Sasha initially felt proud of potentially embarrassing Ava, but her pride quickly dissipated when the men came to her aid.

"What's up?" Sasha retorted.

"You spilled my drink all over me, Sasha!"

"So what?" Sasha replied. "What are you going to do about it!?"

Ava rolled her eyes and muttered to herself, "Bitch, you tripping!"

Unaware of the whispered insults, Sasha seized a handful of Ava's hair and forcefully brought her down, preparing to strike. Precision uppercuts rained down on Ava, who struggled to defend herself. With each failed attempt to retaliate, Sasha's fury intensified. She continued the assault, eventually pushing Ava to the ground and delivering a final blow with her sneaker.

Vick tried to reach Sasha through the crowd, but his efforts were in vain until he finally managed to pull her away from Ava. In a desperate move, Sasha grabbed a glass ashtray and struck Ava's forehead, causing a gash. As blood spurted from the wound, Vick intervened, shoving Sasha out the door in a flurry of confusion and dropping his keys in the process. Sasha retrieved them without hesitation, uttering curses as she headed to the car, unfazed by the altercation.

"Fuck that Bitch," she shouted. "Vick, let's go, bunk that hoe."

"Leave her ass there!" Vick exclaimed.

Overwhelmed by the situation, he hesitated before reluctantly following Sasha to the car, snatching his car keys from her.

As they approached the car and finally settled in, tension hung heavy in the air, suffocating the atmosphere with its weight. Vick's voice broke through the silence, filled with disbelief and concern."What the hell, Sash!?" His words echoed in the dimly lit parking lot.

Sasha met Vick's gaze with a nonchalant shrug as if the chaos of moments before had evaporated into thin air. With practiced ease, she reached for the stash of weed Miste' had given her earlier and began rolling.

Chapter 3

As the blinding lights of the hospital hallway flashed by, they cast stark shadows against the walls, amplifying the screams of agony that reverberated through the sterile corridors. Ms. Wright was rushed into the surgery room, where an atmosphere of uncertainty greeted her like a chilling draft. Alone and scared, she trembled with worry, the weight of fear pressing down upon her like a suffocating blanket.

In the midst of her anguish, she couldn't help but reflect on her first pregnancy, a time when the pain seemed bearable compared to the searing agony she now endured. Peeking down at the pool of blood between her legs, a cry of despair tore from her throat, echoing in the stark room.

Then, amidst the chaos, a voice cut through the darkness like a beacon of hope. "Ms. Wright, I know it hurts, but you have to push now," the voice urged gently, a soft hand reaching out to grasp hers in a comforting gesture. Drawing strength from the touch, Ms. Wright felt a surge of determination wash over her.

"Breathe," the soft voice near her ear instructed. "On

the count of three, I want you to push as hard as you can."

With every ounce of strength she possessed, Ms. Wright summoned her resolve and pushed, each moment stretching into eternity as she fought against the waves of pain crashing over her.

After what felt like an eternity, the room was filled with the sound of newborn cries, three beautiful baby girls entering the world in a chorus of life. Exhausted beyond measure, Ms. Wright succumbed to sleep, the weight of her ordeal lifting as the peaceful stillness of rest enveloped her weary body.

Six hours later, Cookie stirred from her exhausted slumber, greeted by the soft murmur of a nurse and the plaintive cries of two newborns.

"Hello, mom," the nurse whispered, her voice a gentle reassurance in the dimly lit room. Anxious to finally meet the tiny beings who had occupied her womb for nine long months, Cookie's heart raced with anticipation.

The nurse paused, her gaze shifting to the armband Cookie wore, ensuring it matched those of the babies. "Yup. Cynthia Wright," the nurse confirmed with a warm smile.

Cookie said, "Oh my God... They are beautiful," her eyes glistened with happy tears as she saw her beloved infants for the first time. However, in the middle of the intense surge of feeling, a twinge of dread stole into her heart, clouding the historic moment.

Cookie stopped, her mind rushing to the inquiry that was there, unsaid but clearly felt. Her voice trailed off. She started, "Well... where is..." but stopped short as doubt bit her.

Before she could voice her fears, the nurse gently interjected, her tone both comforting and evasive. "The doctor will be in to speak with you," she said, offering a small measure of reassurance amidst the swirling uncertainty.

As if on cue, the door swung open, and the doctor entered the room.

"How's mommy doing?" The doctor asked, his tone gentle yet firm as he inspected Cookie's incisions. "Your C-section scar looks good. The first two babies came out smoothly. However, we had to perform a C-section for the third baby because she was in breach. She's in the ICU undergoing tests as a precaution."

Three days later, Cookie was discharged from the hospital with her three girls, stepping out of the sterile hospital room into the welcoming embrace of home. They left with the reassurance of pending test results and the relief of being together under one roof.

Raising three babies simultaneously came naturally to Cookie. From the outside, it appeared easy, but inside, she felt lonely and longed for her ex-husband. Lil Gregory visited on weekends when Greg had to work longer hours, offering a helpful hand. Despite his small size, he proved to be a great assistant.

Cookie had minimal support; she was the youngest of her adoptive siblings and was treated like an outsider by her adoptive mother. The reasons were unclear, leaving Cookie feeling isolated within her own family. Fostering and adopting children had become a trend to gain more financial support from the state, supplementing earned wages.

What cruelty on the child's face. They are treated as outsiders within their family and potentially seen as a means to financial gain rather than being valued and loved for who they are. It is heartbreaking to realize the negative impact on their emotional well-being and sense of belonging, and so was the case with her.

Growing up, she endured the pain of being ignored and bullied by her siblings without being able to reason what in the world she did to deserve such mistreatment. The revolving door of foster care taught her the value of silence, as the chances of being adopted were slim after five years. Yet, even the slightest glimmer of being wanted brought her immense joy. Despite her attempts to seek solace by confiding in her mother about her sisters' relentless pranks and teasing, she received dismissive responses like "That's what siblings do; your sisters love you." These words failed to provide comfort, leaving her feeling isolated and misunderstood. The close proximity in age only intensified the torment she endured, turning her childhood into a relentless struggle for acceptance and belonging.

As she matured, her long silk hair, Indian features, and statuesque legs made her beauty stand out among her sisters. Walking the halls of her high school, every boy's gaze lingered on Cookie, though she remained oblivious, her focus dedicated to her studies. Then, one day, a note was passed to her by a student she didn't know. It read, "I really like you, Greg." She recognized the name but needed to be more certain. The Greg she knew was the most popular boy in school, a football player who seemed to date all the popular girls.

After school, she found Greg waiting for her at the bus stop. "Did you get my note?" He asked. Ignoring his question, Cookie replied, "Don't you have football practice?" "It's a light workout today; I skipped practice just to walk you home," Greg explained. Cookie smiled, feeling pretty for the first time. It marked the beginning of a high school romance, though it wasn't without its challenges, especially within Cookie's household.

Rumors circulated that she had stolen one of her sister's boyfriends, a hurtful accusation that Cookie was determined to dispel. Suspecting her sisters' involvement in spreading the rumor, she approached them directly, seeking answers and hoping to put an end to the malicious gossip.

"It isn't a rumor; you did take my boyfriend," Clara, the middle child, vehemently claimed, her voice filled with accusation and hurt.

"I did not! You and Greg never went together!" Cookie retorted, her own voice rising in defense.

"We did so!" She shouted back, frustration evident in

her tone.

Standing amidst the tension, Cookie felt a whirlwind of confusion and frustration engulfing her. As Nancy, the oldest sister, pulled Clara out of the room, Cookie turned to her cousin with bewilderment. "What is happening?" She asked, her voice tinged with uncertainty.

Nancy reappeared, accusing and resentful in her face. She implied that Cookie had known about her sister's attempts to earn Greg's favor for months and accused Cookie of purposefully interfering with their sister's long-standing crush on him.

Fighting back against the unjust accusations, Cookie vehemently defended herself, asserting her innocence in the matter. "I am tired of being the scapegoat for your insecurities!" She yelled, her frustration boiling over. "I am not going to stop dating him because of your jealousy! I finally found someone who doesn't treat me like shit, and I am not dumping him so you can feel better about yourself!"

The phone rang, slicing through the quiet of the kitchen. Cookie hurried to answer, her heart pounding with apprehension, her hand trembling as she lifted the receiver.

"Hello?" She said tentatively, her voice laced with uncertainty. "This is she."

"Hi, Doctor Taylor," came the voice on the other end of the line. "I'm glad you returned my call. I'm having the darndest time with Sade. She has been crying uncontrollably, and I can't get her to eat. I can't get her to latch on to...."

Cookie's breath caught in her throat as she was abruptly interrupted by the gravity of the situation. Atticism?! The word hung heavy in the air, sending a chill down Cookie's spine. Her eyes filled with tears as she listened intently to the doctor's words, bracing herself for the terrifying news that she feared would come. As the conversation unfolded, Cookie's heart pounded with fear and uncertainty. With trembling hands, she made her way to Sade's crib, her mind racing with worry. She scooped up her precious blessing, holding her close as unstoppable tears streamed down her cheeks.

***

Cookie looked around the comedy club. Years had flown by, and Cookie was finally finding some much-needed time for herself, a rare opportunity to paint the town red. It felt tense like something exciting was about to happen. The room was a bit dark, and it smelled like stale popcorn and something weird, like burnt rubber. People were laughing and talking, making a constant noise in the air. Juanita, ever the social butterfly, squeezed Cookie's hand reassuringly.

"Relax, Cookie," Juanita whispered, her voice barely audible over the din. "It'll be fun to get out after all these years."

Cookie wasn't so convinced. Stepping out of her comfort zone had always been difficult, and tonight seemed particularly daunting. Her fingers traced the worn leather of her purse, her gaze flickering to the stage where a spotlight illuminated a lone microphone and a stool. Soon, the emcee would appear, and the night's entertainment would begin.

Suddenly, a boisterous laugh erupted from a table directly across the room. Cookie instinctively turned her head, locking her gaze with a pair of warm brown eyes across the crowded space. He was handsome, no doubt about it, with a charmingly crooked smile that crinkled the corners of his eyes. He nudged the man beside him, gesturing towards the stage with excitement. The man, along with two other women, joined in the laughter, carefree and happy.

A blush crept up Cookie's cheeks, catching Juanita's

attention.

"Someone seems smitten," Juanita teased, raising an eyebrow suggestively.

"No way," Cookie dismissed the notion, averting her gaze. "I don't even know him."

"Well, maybe you should," Juanita said, nudging Cookie playfully. "He seems like your type."

Cookie rolled her eyes, but a small, involuntary smile played on her lips. The man, seemingly oblivious to their exchange, leaned back in his chair and laughed. There was something about his easygoing nature, his effortless confidence, that intrigued her.

As if sensing her scrutiny, the man's gaze met hers again. A flicker of surprise crossed his face, quickly replaced by a warm smile. He raised his glass in a silent toast. His gesture seemed both playful and charming.

Cookie felt a flutter in her chest as if a mixture of nervousness and unexpected excitement brewed under her skin. For the first time in a long time that evening, she found herself genuinely looking forward to the night. Perhaps, just perhaps, Juanita was right. Maybe a little fun was exactly what she needed.

Cookie turned her gaze away from him and began enjoying the show. After some time, Cookie leaned into Juanita as her eyes watered from the side-splitting performance on the stage. The comedian's sharp wit had them in stitches, momentarily erasing the anxieties of daily life.

Right then, Juanita caught the man looking at Cookie again. Juanita, noticing John's gaze, nudged Cookie playfully. "Check out our admirer over there," she teased, following Cookie's line of sight.

Cookie's cheeks flushed a light pink. "Oh, come on," she scoffed playfully, though a secret thrill danced in her stomach. She stole another glance at John, pretending to be disinterested as she ran a hand through her hair.

The comedian's set ended. The man leaned towards his friends, whispering something that elicited a chorus of chuckles. He stood, stretching his tall frame, and scanned the room once more before making his way towards the bar. As he passed Cookie's table, their eyes met again. This time, he offered a confident as if trying to initiate a conversation.

Cookie returned the smile, adding a playful wink that sent a jolt through the man's system. He reached the bar and ordered a drink. Moments later, he found himself back at their table, clearing his throat sheepishly.

"Excuse me, ladies," he began. "I couldn't help but notice you were enjoying the show as much as I was. I'm John Bradshaw."

Cookie extended her hand. "I'm Cookie, and this is Juanita."

Juanita scooted over, making room for John. "He's been giving you the eye all night," she teased, winking at Cookie.

John's cheeks flushed again. "Well, the comedian was pretty funny," he stammered, earning a laugh from both women.

As the night progressed, John drew himself into conversation with Cookie. He was captivated by her intelligence, her quick wit, and the way her eyes sparkled when she laughed. They discussed everything from the terrible weather outside to their hopes and dreams for the future. Juanita, sensing the growing connection between them, gracefully excused herself, leaving the two alone.

When the club lights finally dimmed, signaling the end of the night, John walked Cookie and Juanita to their car. Under the soft glow of the streetlamp, he mustered the courage to ask, "Would you like to get coffee sometime? Maybe catch another show?"

Cookie's heart skipped a beat. This man, with his kind eyes and nervous smile, had sparked an unexpected flame within her. "I'd like that," she replied with a smile.

As Cookie and Juanita drove away, Cookie's heart soared. She knew there was something special about him. John swept her off her feet effortlessly, igniting a spark that felt like love at first sight. She couldn't wait to see where this unexpected encounter would lead.

***

As Cookie got to know John better, she discovered his military background and ownership of a tow truck company. He had always dreamed of starting a family, and his nurturing nature shone through in everything he did. When he wasn't busy with work, he could be found tinkering at the car lot or showcasing his talent on the drums at his church.

Cookie quickly found herself drawn to John's warmth and kindness. What started as casual dating soon evolved into spending quality time together with Cookie's daughters and little Greg. John effortlessly stepped into the role of a father figure, displaying remarkable patience and affection, especially towards Sade. He even took the time to teach her how to whistle, a skill that brought endless joy to the household.

Before they knew it, John had seamlessly integrated into their lives, his presence becoming a natural part of their daily routines. With his unwavering support and assistance in babysitting, Cookie found the opportunity to pursue her dream of finishing nursing school while raising her children without the struggles she had once feared would overwhelm her.

Cookie heard a knock at the door and quickly opened it, her voice filled with excitement as she greeted Juanita. "Hey, sis! Come on in," she said, ushering Juanita inside with a warm smile.

Juanita noticed the concern in Cookie's demeanor and asked, "What's wrong?"

"John is sleeping; he has to go to church shortly," Cookie replied softly.

"Are the girls asleep too?" Juanita inquired.

"No, they are across the street playing at a neighbor's," Cookie explained as she strolled into the kitchen. "Five-year-olds never get tired of playing," Juanita observed her every move.

"I see you are sticking to your workout vow," Juanita remarked, noting Cookie's deliberate movements.

"Yup, I am going to get this body back yet," Cookie responded with determination in her voice.

After an hour of catching up, Juanita gave Cookie a hug and vowed to visit more frequently. Following her departure from the residence, Cookie tidied up and reflected on her enjoyable time with her pal. She climbed the stairs to see how John was doing. John gave her a deep kiss while grabbing her by the waist. She graciously yielded as his tongue gently prodded her lips open. The hug became closer. John's erections got stronger as he put his hand down Cookie's sweatpants. Cookie's eyes rolled behind her head as she enjoyed having her clitoris gently caressed again and again. He tugged her hair and tilted her head back, kissing her neck and putting his tongue all the way up to her ear.

"Call Juanita over again to join us," he whispered, sticking his tongue in her ear.

Cookie pulled away from him and turned to go.

"Don't act like you ain't wit it," John chuckled. "You enjoy it; in the past four years, you haven't complained." John brings it up to her.

"John, fuck you!" Cookie responded.

"What did you just say?" John approaches Cookie, who is cowering in the corner.

"Who the fuck are you talking to?" John dared Cookie. "I didn't hear you. Say it again," he demanded.

"Please, John!" Cookie begged.

John punched Cookie in her left eye, causing her to let out a blood-curdling scream as she felt her eye socket break. With one hand glued to her injured eye, the other scattered back and forth in hopes of hitting John. Unfazed, John punched Cookie in the head and then picked up a wooden TV tray, using it to beat her all over her body until she blanked out.

Exhausted from his work, he took a brief respite to use the bathroom. As Cookie gradually woke up, she became aware of the long stream of urine hitting the water at the bottom of the toilet, a sound that penetrated her subconscious. Summoning every ounce of strength, she attempted to rise and make her way to the stairs. With great effort, she crawled on her knees, dragging her bleeding, lifeless body inches from the stairway.

After washing his hands, John encountered Cookie in the hallway. Irritated by her attempt to leave, he seized her by the hair and assisted her down the hardwood stairs, one agonizing step at a time. Each movement jolted Cookie's bruised body, a painful reminder of the countless beatings she endured. Despite her desperate attempts to scream, exhaustion renders her voice feeble, her throat ablaze with each effort as though her voice box were ripped from her throat.

After descending the stairs, he callously leaves Cookie on the floor, and she lies there, consumed by a fervent prayer that the torment would finally cease. The sound of him picking up his keys and exiting the door echoes through the silent house. Waiting anxiously for a few agonizing minutes, straining her ears for the telltale sound of his car pulling away, she mustered all her strength to crawl towards the phone.

With trembling hands, she dialed the number of the neighbor where her children were playing and timidly asked if they could stay longer than planned. The neighbor's voice, filled with concern and compassion, is all too familiar to Cookie.

"Do you need me to come over, Cookie?" The neighbor asks kindly.

"No, I'm okay," Cookie replies, masking the pain in her voice. With a heavy heart, she hung up the phone and dragged herself to the sofa, collapsing in exhaustion as sleep claimed her once more.

Five hours had passed when she opened her eyes. Her body was still heavy with exhaustion. As she stumbled off the sofa, her eyes searched for the clock on the wall.

With one good eye and only 50 percent vision in the other, she finally located the time. "8:00 o'clock. John will be home soon," she murmured to herself, a sense of dread creeping over her.

Hurrying to the bathroom as fast as her battered body allowed her, she inspected her injuries, tears streaming down her face with each new wound discovered. Once all the tears had been shed, she gathered what little strength remained and made her way to the girls' room. Standing in the doorway, she gazed at the toys scattered on the floor. Closing her eyes, she allows herself a moment of respite, a brief escape from the pain and turmoil that engulfed her. In the stillness of that moment, it felt as though all her fears had been purged from her body, dissolving into nothingness with each exhale.

Cookie hastily grabbed the children's backpacks, stuffing them with as many clothes as they could hold. In her bedroom, she located the largest duffle bag she could find and proceeded to fill it with her own clothes, shoes, and important documents. Donning a sweatsuit, sneakers, and dark glasses, she prepared herself for what lay ahead. Before leaving the house, Cookie paused to retrieve the shoe box from the shelf in the closet. Inside lay John's gun, a heavy reminder of the danger she was leaving behind.

Bang! Bang! Bang! The sound of Cookie's urgent

knocks echoed through the neighbor's door.

"Who is it!?" The neighbor's voice echoed from behind the door, peering through the spy hole. As soon as she recognized Cookie, she swiftly opened the door.

"I'm here to get the girls," Cookie declared, her tone hurried and tense.

"Come on, girls, get your things, hurry," the neighbor urged, her voice filled with concern. Sade rushed to her mother's side, whistling and patting her ear uncontrollably, unaware of the tension in the air.

Observing Cookie's injuries and the packed bags, the neighbor handed Cookie Sade's jacket and asked, "Do you need help? You seem a bit shaken."

"I'll be okay. I just need to get the girls out of here," replied Cookie.

As soon as the girls approached her, she strapped the backpack on each child and slung the duffle bag across her body.

As she took the hands of her children, just before leading them down the steps, she whispered, "Thank you," to her neighbor.

The trio started walking, their destination uncertain. After two hours of walking, Cookie, realizing she had no ATM card, stopped to count the money in her wallet. Only $13 in cash and $37 in food stamps stared back at her.

"Not enough for a cab," she muttered to herself, feeling the weight of their situation.

Meanwhile, Sasha, Tasha, and Sade play tag as they run around their mom to avoid being "it." Sade, who did not fully comprehend the game, simply followed whoever was running and shrieked with excitement.

Cookie couldn't shake the feeling that John was aware she had left, especially now that darkness had settled. She hoisted Sade onto her back and took each of her children by the hand, setting off on foot for another two hours. They ventured out of the neighborhood, aiming to make themselves less recognizable. With each passing car, Cookie ducked behind parked vehicles, her heart pounding with the fear that John would scour the entire area all night looking for them.

Seeking refuge, Cookie hid behind buildings to rest,

attend to the children's needs, and feed them pop-tarts. With nowhere else to go, desperation settled in.

Soon, she reached the Fern Rock Subway station in the Olney section of Philadelphia. It was the farthest train and bus station from her home in Germantown. Weary, Cookie found a bench and gently placed her children on it, hoping they could sleep for a while. They were sleepy, hungry, and crying, but Cookie knew she had to do whatever she could for her children. Spotting a pay phone nearby, she fumbled for the coins in her sweatpants pocket. Despite the pain she was in, fueled by adrenaline, she walked as fast as she could, inserting the quarter into the slot and struggling to recall them from memory; she finally dialed the numbers.

After several rings, someone finally picked up on the other end. Without hesitation, Cookie spoke, her voice trembling with emotion. "Hello... Momma Wright?"

Chapter 4

"Good morning. Are the girls still sleeping?" Momma Wright, Greg Wright's mother and Cookie's former mother-in-law, inquired of Cookie.

"Yes, Ma'am, they are," Cookie replied.

Though Greg and Cookie had ended their marriage years ago, the bond between Cookie and the Wrights remained strong. Sonya and Raymond Wright, Greg's parents, had raised Greg in a loving middle-class home, instilling in him the same warmth and kindness that also shone in Momma Wright's eyes. Sadly, Raymond passed away just a year after Greg and Cookie's divorce, but Momma Wright's love for Cookie remained the same despite her husband's death.

"Well, the coffee is hot; have some," Momma Wright offered.

Cookie poured herself a cup, sensing a conversation brewing.

"Come on over here and sit down with me, child," Momma Wright beckoned.

Cookie carefully carried the condiment tray to the small kitchenette, where the morning sunlight streamed through the window, casting a warm glow over the space that overlooked the quiet rear driveway.

"How do you feel? Your wounds are healing nicely," Momma Wright observed with a mixture of concern and relief etched on her face. "I still think you should have gone to the hospital. He could have killed you!" She exclaimed, her voice brimming with concern.

Taking a sip of her coffee, Cookie met Momma Wright's gaze, "I feel fine, Momma," she assured her, her voice steady despite the memories still lingering. "Plus, they would have called the police, who would have called DHS, and I don't need my benefits in jeopardy right now," she explained, acknowledging the complex web of consequences that could have unfolded had she sought medical attention.

"I actually have good news," Cookie said with excitement.

"Well, tell me, 'cause I ain't gonna play no guessing games," Momma Wright insisted.

Cookie blurted out, "I got the job at Jefferson Hospital."

Momma Wright joined in her excitement. "That's fantastic news.

"The girls and I can finally get out of here. It's been three months since John moved out. I am looking at another house this afternoon. I am really looking forward to having a brand-new start."

"I sure hope so because you babies deserve it," Momma Wright said warmly as she gave Cookie a big hug.

"Thank you so much for being there for me," Cookie said sincerely, tears welled up in her eyes. "In these six months, I will never forget what you did for me."

"Greg and I will always be there for you. You are family, Cookie, don't ever forget that," Momma Wright reassured her, taking her hands in hers.

In less than a year, Cookie thrived in her role as a nurse at Jefferson Hospital. She found solace in a spacious new home for her children and embraced a supportive church community. With her steady income, she bid farewell to welfare assistance and focused on building a brighter future for her family. The children's joy and contentment radiated in their newfound stability.

***

It had been a year since Cookie fled with her daughters. At first, it was a phantom, a shadow of the abuse she had escaped. But doubts crept in with every sleepless night. She'd convinced herself he'd changed – surely, the shame and exposure of her leaving would be enough. Besides, deep down, despite everything, a flicker of that old love stubbornly refused to die. She wanted to feel the tingle in her heart once again that came every time he touched her.

One day, a message from John arrived. An apology, a confession, a plea to see her. Cookie knew it was foolish and a dangerous gamble, but something in her moved. Perhaps it was desperation for closure or the naive hope that this time, after all she had been through, things could be different.

Cookie stared at the message typed on her phone as the pixelated letters burned into her retinas. It was short, just a few lines, an apology veiled in self-pity, a desperate plea for a meeting. Every part of her screamed "no."

This was exactly what she'd feared, the emotional manipulation disguised as remorse. But beneath the anger and hurt, a remnant of the love she'd once held for John whispered things into her head.

She'd spent the past year painstakingly building a new life for herself and her daughters. They were safe, finally, protected in the normalcy she'd craved. But the normalcy came with a suffocating silence, an absence of the warmth John's touch, however tainted, had once offered. She'd convinced herself love had died in the face of his actions, but the ember refused to be extinguished.

Perhaps it wasn't just love that remained, but a sliver of hope and desperation. Word had spread through their small community. His outburst, the way she'd left – the whispers and the knowing looks had surely reached him. The shame, the exposure... that, more than anything, was what made her believe he might have changed.

The man who'd always craved approval, who'd lashed out in fear of his own failings being revealed, would be mortified. And desperation, she had learned, could be a potent motivator for change... or for further manipulation.

With a trembling hand, she silenced the phone. The hope that

John had truly changed, that their fractured love could somehow be mended, was a dangerous thought. But the possibility, however remote, was enough to sow a seed of doubt. The familiar fear bothered her as a reminder of why she'd left in the first place.

Days turned into weeks. The flicker of hope refused to be ignored, and finally, with a deep breath and a heart filled with trepidation, Cookie typed a single word in response: "Where?"

***

As Cookie stirred from her sleep, she buried her head in the pillow, relishing the last moments of comfort before the day began. The soft patter of little feet in the hallway drew her attention, and she opened her eyes to the gentle glow of sunlight filtering through the blinds. Stretching her arm towards the nightstand, she admired the rock adorning her ring finger, its brilliance contrasting with the gentle sunbeams filtering through the mini blinds.

Turning on the lamp, Cookie was greeted by the joyful faces of Sasha, Tasha, and Sade as they rushed in to give their morning kisses.

"Good morning, sweethearts," she greeted them warmly, enveloping each child in a loving embrace. "Wash your face and brush your teeth. I'll be down in a minute," she added.

With laughter and chatter, all three scampered into the bathroom to begin their morning routine.

Sasha got Sade's toothbrush and applied toothpaste to it while Tasha reached up to turn on the water. She grabbed a small square facecloth to wipe away the bubble gum-flavored toothpaste dripping down Sade's chin. Cookie soon walked into the bathroom to check on their progress.

"Bae? Do you want grilled toast?" She asked her fiancé, who was reluctant to get out of bed. John grunted in agreement as he made his way to the bathroom door.

Sasha, Tasha, and Sade darted past him, giggling as they rushed to their room, eager to retrieve their matching Barbie slippers and bathrobes. Sade, clutching her favorite Cabbage Patch doll, happily whistled while dressing the doll in its robe, her laughter filling the room with joy.

As the family gathered around the breakfast table, John's voice broke the morning calm. "I think I'll pass on church today," he said, his tone resolute.

"Why?" Cookie queried, spooning more scrambled eggs onto his plate. "You know I have to work tonight, John. Are you sure you don't mind having them all day?"

"Absolutely sure," John reassured Cookie, his voice filled with conviction. "I don't mind having them all day. It's a chance for some quality time together." He grinned.

Cookie's smile widened, a sense of warmth and appreciation washing over her as she observed John's changed attitude and his eagerness to spend time with their daughters.

As the sun dipped low on the horizon, Cookie returned from church, her spirits lifted by the fellowship and camaraderie of the service. With a smile brightening her face, she approached John, who sat on the porch with a burning cigarette resting in the ashtray.

"Hey, handsome," she greeted him, leaning down to plant a kiss on his cheek. "Did you eat?"

"We just finished," John replied, his tone relaxed. "Fried up the wings that were in there."

"Sorry, I'm late," Cookie said, a hint of apology in her voice. "I had to drop little Greg off. We had dinner at the church after service." She gestured toward the bags hanging from her hands. "I brought home plates."

"Thanks," John mumbled as he eyed the bags dangling from Cookie's hands. Being too lazy to get up and help with the bags, he leaned over and opened the screen door for Cookie, allowing her to enter the house.

The three sprinted toward Cookie, their voices filled with excitement. "Mom!" They screamed, wrapping their arms around her waist and legs. "We missed you," Tasha exclaimed.

Cookie returned the embrace, giving Tasha an extra squeeze. "Y'all clean this mess up," she chuckled, gesturing to the scattered game pieces, toys, and dolls littering the floor. Soon after, the girls cheerfully dashed off to tackle the organized chaos and began tidying up.

Feeling the weariness of the day settle in, Cookie made her way upstairs for a well-deserved nap before her shift at work.

Following a rejuvenating slumber, Cookie walked

down the stairs, kissed her family goodbye, and left the house for the hospital.

"Come on, girls, all of you, go put your pajamas on," John instructed the six-year-old girls. After enjoying a round of applesauce and their cherished movie, "The Wizard of Oz," John tenderly picked up each of the girls, one by one, since they had dozed off.

Ensuring Sasha and Tasha were snugly tucked into their mom's bed, he arranged them carefully. Then, with gentle care, he settled Sade in her room on the plush, adorned futon. With the television flickering to life, John meticulously adjusted the pillows until they felt just right. Finally, settling into his spot with legs crossed and remote in hand, he sank into the cushions, ready to unwind with his favorite HBO channel.

John's show ended, and he idly flipped through channels, his fifth beer in hand. After glancing at Sasha and Tasha to confirm they were asleep, he turned to the Playboy channel. Two Caucasian women filled the screen, moaning as they engaged in intimate acts. John's hands slipped into his sweatpants, stroking back and forth in frustration as he struggled to find release. Growing increasingly frustrated, he reached over to Tasha, gently lifting up her nightgown.

As he continued to stroke Tasha between her legs, his arousal heightened with each touch. Tasha woke up feeling confused and frightened, but a sense of danger prevented her from screaming and waking Sasha. Meanwhile, the scene of the two women on the TV screen failed to satisfy him. Determined for more gratification, John lifted Sasha's nightgown, positioning her sleeping body on his lap for better access. Sasha awoke to the discomfort and intrusion, crying out in fear as John's fingers entered her young body while he continued to stroke between the legs of Tasha. His breath catches in his throat as he opens Sasha's legs and presses his penis against her tender flesh. He reaches the opening and ejaculates by forcing the tip of his penis inside her vagina.

For days on end, none of the girls revealed his unsettling secret, and with each passing day, John's confidence in remaining undetected grew, which led him to continue for a whole year.

From occurring once a month to every other day, the beatings intensified. Cookie grew resistant, yet she couldn't muster the courage to walk out of the relationship she had portrayed as perfect to her loved ones. She lay beneath the blankets, naked with her sore lip, while the scent of his smoking cigarette irritated her senses. As Cookie prayed, John put out the cigarette.

"Please, Lord, not tonight," she pleaded silently. "Please, please, let my babies be safe tonight."

Cookie feigned sleep, lying still and silent as John lay close, indulging in his preferred porn. Not more than a few minutes later, slipping on his beloved Woolworth slippers, he got out of bed. Tears trickled down Cookie's cheek as she heard John walk into Sasha and Tasha's room, yet she stayed motionless despite hearing the muffled screams.

The next day, John fired up the grill, a small gesture to alleviate the tension he had caused. As the scent of barbecue filled the air, Sasha and Tasha played hide and seek upstairs, seeking refuge from any potential conflicts between their parents. Meanwhile, Sade lay peacefully asleep on her futon, unaware of the turmoil around her.

After finishing his cooking duties, John settled onto the sofa to relax. "I'm going to lay down, Cookie. Wake me when the mac and cheese is ready," he said, his tone surprisingly calm.

Cookie nodded, grateful for the momentary peace, and replied, "Okay, bae." As John disappeared into the bedroom, Cookie sighed, hoping for a brief respite from the chaos of their daily life.

The timer on the oven rang after thirty minutes, signaling that the bubbling, cheesy dish was ready. But before Cookie could attend to the meal, she heard the most terrifying blast followed by a thump that shook the entire house.

The house became silent all of a sudden. For a moment, Cookie went into a trance. Right then, her bubble burst by the soft whimpering from Sade's bedroom. Her heart pounded in her chest. She hadn't felt this uneasy in a long time. Without losing a single minute, she ran up the stairs. Cold sweats covered her face as if she had washed it. *Something is terribly wrong. Oh God, Oh God, s*he was mumbling more loudly than she thought as she ascended her way up.

She approached the door of Sade's room cautiously, knuckles rapping against the aged wood.

"Sade?" Her voice wavered into a whisper.

No answer.

The stench hit Cookie before she even opened the door. The doorknob twisted under her fingers, and the door creaked open. A whimper, the faintest of sounds, drew her further inside. And then she saw them - a sight that froze the blood in Cookie's veins. A flash of bare skin. The unnatural angle of a too-small limb. John splayed like a broken doll. Not across Sade... but on top of her.

He lay sprawled out with his bare back marred by a gruesome wound. His blood was staining the fabric beneath him. The sight stole the air from her lungs, leaving her gasping for breath. Right then, Cookie's gaze darted from the lifeless bodies to Tasha and Sasha, who were holding each other, tears streaming down their faces like rivers. Sasha stood rigid with her eyes vacant, mirroring the emptiness that felt to be swallowing Cookie whole.

Cookie didn't scream. The sound froze in her chest as her world imploded. It wasn't the first time she saw John naked, but in this sickening tableau, her husband was transformed. Every rumor, every sideways glance from the neighbors - it all crystallized into this one horrific image.

This was worse than any nightmare. This was the first time she fully registered the truth – this wasn't an affair; this wasn't just betrayal. It was something far more sinister. *My autistic child! My child! This animal didn't even leave my youngest angel?* A stream of thoughts and screams ran through her head, but nothing came out of her mouth.

John...on Sade... but Sade was so small... it doesn't make sense...

She lunged forward, not towards Sade, but John. Her fingers clawed at his limp flesh, trying to peel him off her baby. All she wanted at that moment was to confirm Sade was alright.

No. No, this isn't real. A nightmare. Just a nightmare, wake up, wake up...

She wanted to deny the reality, but the reality was all too clear to deny. As if a current of energy jolted in her body, she kicked his body from the top of her child. His weight was a dead stone, his skin clammy and cold. The stench of him, not sweat but something foul and feral, gagged her. His eyes were open yet unseeing. His body had fallen off the futon, but his hand was still on Sade's delicate skin. She pressed her fingers against his arm to remove his hand from the top

70

of Sade.

As soon as she removed the body, horror washed over her.

Bile rose in her throat...

Her knees gave way, but the floor didn't meet her, the world started spinning faster and faster...

A choked sob escaped her lips…

She saw blood spurting from Sade's head where a bullet had intercepted its path from John's body. In that moment, the world around Cookie shattered. Her body froze; her thoughts seized.

Moments later, she turned around to face Tasha and Sasha. She wanted to ask what had happened. Part of her didn't want to know; another part had to.

What had happened here? How could I have been so blind? All this time, the animal had been raping my autistic child, and I had not known?

Tears began to cascade down Cookie's face, her body shaking uncontrollably. This was her daughter, her baby. Every fiber of Cookie wanted to scream in outrage.

Cookie's breath hitched in her throat as she saw the gun resting innocuously at Sasha's feet. Every piece of the incomprehensible puzzle began to click into place. The locked door of Sade's room, the frantic whispers emanating from within, the muffled screams...Sasha and Tasha witnessing the horrific scene of their sister being raped...getting their hands on the weapon and then...

A vision of a few months back flooded her mind. Back when John swept her off her feet once again and went down on his knees. He seemed different then, genuinely remorseful for past mistakes, eager to build a new life together. Hope, a fragile flame, had flickered within her, fueled by his apparent change and the promise of a happy family.

The hopeful image shattered against the horrifying reality before her. The weight of her inaction crashed down with the force of a tidal wave. Shame coiled in her gut.

She had known, deep down, the whispers reaching her ears, the flinching she saw in Tasha's eyes, the withdrawn silence of Sasha. But fear had kept her tongue tethered and her gaze averted. Fear of confronting John, of the potential for violence, of losing the fragile semblance of a family she'd desperately clung to. Fear of judgment, of whispers turning into accusations, of being labeled an unfit mother for not seeing the signs, for not protecting her daughters enough.

Embarrassment at her own naivety, at believing John could truly change, at letting her hope blind her to the truth festering beneath the surface. Embarrassment at failing her daughters, at prioritizing her own fear and insecurities over their safety.

A tsunami of guilt took over her entire being, so thick and suffocating it threatened to consume her. The "what ifs" echoed in her mind, a relentless chorus of self-recrimination. *What if she had spoken up? What if she had fought harder? Could she have prevented this tragedy?*

With trembling hands, Cookie approached Sasha, enveloping her daughters in a tight, protective embrace. Tears streamed down her face as she shielded their innocent eyes from the harrowing scene, whispering soothing words of reassurance amidst the chaos, promising them that everything would eventually be alright.

Chapter 5

The scent of pine mingled with the aroma of baking spices, filling Miles and Tasha's home. Soft Motown carols played in the background, and the Christmas tree, adorned with lights and sparkling ornaments, cast a warm glow on the room. Tasha, dressed in a festive red and white pencil dress that matched the table's festive decor, emerged from the back office, tucking her Bible back onto the garland-trimmed bookshelf. She surveyed the twelve-seat dining table, her fingers gliding over the silver, ensuring everything sat in perfect alignment. The polished cutlery mirrored the gleaming China setting.

"Pastor, did you check the turkey?" Tasha asked while removing a speck of dust from the table.

Miles came from behind and kissed his wife, "Yes, I did, evangelist." He then went inside.

Suddenly, the gentle melody rose to a short chime. "Honey, they're here!" Tasha called over to her husband. She reached the door as it swung open, revealing Greg with a large bag held tightly in his arms.

"Hey, big Bro!" She boomed.

Greg pulled her into a warm embrace. "What's up, baby sis?"

"Need help with that?" Tasha asked, gesturing to the bag.

Greg chuckled. "Nah, I need this within reach, none of that 'fruity bougie wine' you like." They laughed as Miles entered the room. His face lightened up at the sight of his brother-in-law. A handshake and a bro-hug followed, punctuated by Miles' friendly, "Come on, man!"

The two men disappeared into the man cave to have a game of pool and cigars before dinner. The soft melody chimed again, this time eliciting a smile from Tasha. "Mom!" She exclaimed, hurrying towards the door.

Cookie stood there enveloped in a winter coat. "Oh my my!" Tasha breathed.

"Your lights are beautiful outside, Tash," Cookie complemented Tasha as she kissed her on the cheek.

"But you, you're even more beautiful," Tasha replied. "Let me get your coat."

Taking Cookie's coat, Tasha hung it carefully before ushering her inside. Just then, the doorbell rang once more, and Sasha entered with Mise' in tow.

"Hello?" Sasha called out as Tasha greeted her with a warm hug.

"Hey, Sis, come on in! Hello, Mise', it's good to see you both," Tasha added warmly. "Are Vick and Ava still coming?"

"Yes, Ava went to pick him up," Sasha explained. "Vick's car battery died in this freezing weather."

As they chatted, the doorbell continued to chime, welcoming more guests from the church. Finally, Ava and a slightly disgruntled Vick rounded out the group, completing the evening.

Tasha and Cookie orchestrated the feast on the dining table. Turkey, stuffing, collard greens, candy yams, cranberries, and steaming corn on the cob formed a colorful tableau. Murmurs of appreciation rose as guests took their seats, preparing to indulge in the culinary bounty.

With their bellies full and chatting, the group migrated to the living room with beverages and homemade pies in hand. The fireplace's soft crackle added a nice touch to the conversations that continued to spark and flow. Sister Mary, taking a bite of Tasha's sweet potato pie, exclaimed, "This is heavenly! What's your secret ingredient? It's unbelievably sweet without the taste of any sugar."

"It's my little secret," Tasha replied with a playful chuckle.

"Why are you saying 'It's your little secret' as if you use something different than what we all use," Sasha jumped into the conversation and mocked.

Tasha, aware of the history Sasha carried and the way alcohol fueled her insecurities, opted for silence. Sasha stared at Tasha, and jealousy began to brew like a pot of water. Her gaze flickered around the room, taking in the expensive decorations that draped her home and the genuine happiness on Tasha's face. It all felt like a personal attack on her.

The evening wore on as the guest ignored Sasha's attempt to embarrass Tasha and continued to enjoy their time at her house. As Tasha began the cleanup, she extended an olive branch to Sasha, "Sash, I made your favorite chocolate cake. I'll pack it for you to take home."

Sasha, deploying her silent treatment, coldly ignores the gesture. Mise', sensing Sasha's internal struggle, placed a hand on hers. Across the room, Deaconess Mary looked at the plethora of trophies and medals displayed in the glass cases.

Cookie reminisced and bragged about her girl's successful performance on their high school debate team. This particular memory was a sore spot for Sasha, the one sport where she'd always placed second to Tasha. As if sensing an opportunity to reclaim some misplaced glory, Sasha pivoted the conversation towards a specific medal in the case.

Tasha began to recount the victory story but made the mistake of mentioning that Sasha had been the alternate debater for that particular competition.

"Tasha, why are you lying!?" Sasha's voice spiked. "You were the alternate, and I was the primary!"

Knowing Sasha's desperate need for recognition, Tasha attempted to diffuse the situation. "Not this particular contest, Sasha; remember I received this gold medal arguing 'Nature vs Nurture'?

Sasha stood up and aggressively walked towards Tasha. "Bitch! You know your ass is lying! Most of the trophies in there are mine. You always gotta front when you get around people!"

"Okay, Sasha," Tasha calmly responded, trying to defuse the tension.

"What? Say something else!?" Sasha dared, escalating the confrontation. Mise' finally intervened, standing up to stop Sasha from physically hurting Tasha. Vick and Ava quickly grabbed their coats, sensing they might become Sasha's next targets.

Greg rushed towards Sasha. "Sasha, stop!" He boomed. "It's clear you're upset, but this isn't the way to handle it. Both of you were excellent debaters; that's all there is to it."

Pastor Miles walked all the guests to the door, sensing the rising tension. Sasha ignored the comments and turned to Cookie and Greg. "This is what I'm talking about! You all act like she's some saint!" She accused, "You've always treated her better than me!"

Greg's face hardened. "Are you even serious right

now? You're tripping! No one owes you anything, Sash! Mom never treated anyone better than you; that's your own insecurities!"

Cookie's voice, usually warm and gentle, now carried a note of sadness. "Sasha, honey, I was there for everything. I supported you through every game and practice after calling out from work. It wasn't always easy, but I did it because I love you."

"I don't want to hear that shit!" Sasha snapped back. Pastor Miles, re-entering the room, heard her comment. "Sasha, I understand you're hurting, but the way you're talking and using that language is unacceptable, especially towards your mother. Come with me to the study for a minute, and let's talk about things calmly."

Sasha followed Miles without further protest. As they entered the study, she began a torrent of accusations. "I know that's your wife, but you don't know her. She has judged me my entire life. She thinks she looks better than me and slept with all my boyfriends."

Miles listened but remained neutral. Sasha continued, "'She can't do anything wrong!' my foot! I bet she hasn't told you she got pregnant at fourteen and had an abortion. And Missus, strict disciplinarian, hasn't said a word to her little princess!"

Miles knew this wasn't a moment for sermons. He had to be a pillar of support for his hurting family members. Miles took a deep breath, setting aside his role as pastor for the moment. He knew Sasha's accusations about Tasha were unfounded and a cruel twist of the truth rooted in Sasha's own past actions. The rumors about Tasha were not only untrue, but they were also the opposite of reality.

Miles himself lived in the same neighborhood as the Wrights, and everyone knew Tasha's character; the rumors Sasha spread were like whispers in a hurricane. Sasha, unfortunately, had a habit of creating and spreading gossip, but that only countered back. Sasha was known in the street and developed rumors about herself. If, by chance, Tasha happened to make a friendly acquaintance on her way home from the store, Sasha would later intercept the phone call and arrange a meeting with the same person, all while posing as Tasha.

Miles then remembered the unspoken secret, the rape that led to Tasha's pregnancy at a young age. Shame and a desire to protect Tasha, Cookie, and Tasha had kept it hidden from most of the family. Although Greg and Sasha knew, they allowed them to think she was pregnant by another underage boy she was dating due to Tasha's overwhelming feeling of shame and embarrassment. Tasha, years later, had finally confided in her husband about the trauma and the isolation she felt as a teenager. Now, witnessing Sasha's unraveling, Miles recognized the need for action.

"Listen, Sasha," he began gently, "I'm not here to preach or belittle what you're feeling. Sometimes, all we need is a reminder of what truly matters, especially in moments like this."

He continued, "Life sends us on unique paths, Sasha. You are just as successful and beautiful as your sister, just in different ways. You excel in your career as a physical therapist."

Miles paused for a moment and then acknowledged. "I understand the past hurts, and we can't change it. But we can choose to move forward. This is the reason time and choices are important. But we can harness something powerful enough to transform our lives and move forward in any direction we want it to go."

Sasha looked at him with a flicker of confusion.

"Forgiveness!" Miles stated. He then picked up a small card from his desk and placed it in her hand before leaving the room.

Sasha looked down at her palm and read the card that had written on it: Mathew 18:21-22 (NIV).

"Then Peter came to Jesus and asked, 'Lord, how many times shall I forgive my brother or sister who sins against me? Up to seven times?' [21] *Jesus answered, "I tell you, not seven times, but seventy-seven times"* [22]

Chapter 6

The air thrummed with a rhythmic pulse of reggae music that pulsed through 'The Yellow Bird' club. Hand in hand, Mise' and Sasha entered with an air of effortless grace, like seasoned performers gracing their familiar stage. Sasha, adorned in glistening gold bangles and a dazzling diamond watch, moved to the music with an infectious joy that drew smiles from every corner of the room. Sasha and Mise's bond was undeniable. They had confidence in each other, which made clear they were each other's priority. Sasha didn't mind if other women looked at Mise'; she knew he loved her the most.

Sasha's eyes then landed on Vick. She walked through the crowd, and with a playful lilt in her voice, she glided over and greeted him with a "Hey Boo."

Vick's response was a simple, "I see you," followed by a hug.

"You good?" Vick inquired, concern flickering in his eyes.

Sasha responded with a question on top of a question,

"Why do you ask?"

"Last time I saw you," Vick began, his voice low over the music, "you were…wilding out. You gotta stop that, okay?"

Sasha's reply was a dismissive, "Whatever."

"For real, Sash!" Vick's voice rose slightly, but the music drowned out his words. "I haven't called because I wanted to give you space, but you need to know your family and friends love you. We put up with a lot of shit, Sasha, especially Ava."

Sasha, lost in the rhythm of her favorite song, ignored him and swayed the music with practiced ease.

Frustrated, Vick raised his voice to get her attention, "For real, Shasha!"

His persistence paid off. Sasha paused, and her gaze met his. "Alright, alright, alright," she conceded, "I hear you." She paused, then leaned in and kissed Vick on the cheek, "You know I love y'all too."

Mise' approached Sasha and whispered something in her ear. Sasha pulled back with a flash of defiance crossing her face. "I don't feel like going, bae," she said firmly.

Mise' leaned in again, his voice low.

Sasha hesitated, then shrugged. "Okay," she muttered. Turning to Vick, she said, "I'll be right back."

"Need me to come with you?" Vick asked.

"Nah, I'm good. Be back in a bit," Sasha replied before slipping out of the bar. Meanwhile, Mise' disappeared into the back office with the owner of The Yellow Bird.

An hour later, Sasha returned. She dialed Mise's number, but ten minutes passed with no response. Finally, he emerged from the crowd. She handed him a small, festively wrapped box with a ribbon on top. He kissed her cheek and vanished into the night.

"I know you ain't making drops for him," Vick said, suspicion lacing his voice.

Sasha flashed him a playful grin. "Relax, Vick. Just did him a favor and picked up some cash while I was at it. No big deal," she said with a nonchalant shrug.

Vick narrowed his eyes slightly. "Just be careful, Sasha," he warned.

Chapter 7

Sunlight streamed through the cherry oak desk of Pastor Miles' office at Glory World Mission Church. He was working on the baptism schedule when a knock on the door interrupted him. He looked up and saw Sasha walking in after a knock.

"Hey, Sis!" He greeted. "Come in, have a seat," Miles replied, gesturing towards a chair.

Surprised to see her mother there, Sasha took a seat next to her in front of Miles' desk. "What are you doing here?" She asked Cookie.

Miles, sensing Sasha's surprise, added, "I'm glad you could make it. I asked Cookie to come because your mother is getting baptized again this Sunday, and I'd like the whole family to be there."

Sasha nodded, a simple "Yeah, of course" escaping her lips.

Just then, Tasha's gentle knock on the door drew their attention. "Pastor, you needed me?" She inquired.

"Yes, Hun, come in," Miles invited, motioning her to the assistant chair. "I wanted us to have a pre-meeting before your mother's baptism on Sunday."

Tasha stepped into the purple-themed office and sat on the chair adjacent to Miles's.

"Okay," Sasha and Tasha responded at the same time.

"Let's bow our heads for a moment of prayer," Miles directed, leading them in a short opening prayer.

Once finished, Miles turned to Cookie. "Cookie, the floor is yours."

Cookie spoke directly to her daughters. "Girls, I love you both more than words can express. I'm proud of you both. Every day, I'm so grateful for both of you. The day you were born was one of the happiest of my life. It pains me to think that I've ever caused you any pain. That's why I'm here today, to ask for your forgiveness."

Tasha reached out and squeezed her mother's hand. "We love you too, Mom."

Sasha's gaze remained fixed on her lap and then echoed her sister's sentiment with a quieter "Yeah, we love you too, Mom. But what are you apologizing for?"

Cookie's voice trembled as tears flowed from her eyes. "For putting you in that situation with my cousin, John." Her voice choked.

Sasha recoiled in her chair, her voice raw, "Huh? Wait, what? Your cousin?"

Tasha echoed Sasha's shock, "Mom, what do you mean, your cousin?"

Cookie struggled to find words. "We didn't know until... until after we started dating…"

"And y'all still kept sleeping with each other! That's disgusting!" Sasha lashed back.

"Sasha, wait, hear your mother out," Pastor Miles interjected.

"After we started dating," Cookie choked out, "we discovered the connection... it was distant. John is my mama's uncle's grandchild. He grew up in Cincinnati—that's why we never met him."

"That's why you kept us away? Depriving us of a real family?" Tasha's voice carried hurt.

"You kept us away from family so you could continue sleeping with that… that pedophile! That rapist!?" Sasha's voice rose in a mix of disgust and fury.

Tasha's voice quivered. "And all that stuff about your evil step-sister and wicked mother, was that some made-up story too?"

Cookie shook her head desperately. "No, Tasha, all that was true. I was so young... We were both young and... I was so unhappy with myself. And he... he was the only one who seemed to want me. I just wanted to feel wanted."

Sasha's anger blazed. "Adopted cousin or not, that's wrong! You robbed us of a real family. Just like you always wanted to be adopted, we wanted grandparents, cousins, and aunts! And you took that away! How could you do this?"

Pastor Miles got up from his table and walked around to Sasha's chair. He gently placed a hand on Sasha's shoulder as she continued to address her mother. "Let's take a deep breath. We're facing sensitive truths, and it's good these are coming to light. This was hard for your mother to admit. Your mother has opened up about something painful from her past. That took courage, and she asked for your forgiveness."

90

Pastor Miles instructed, "Let's take a moment. Breathe deeply, in through your nose, out slowly through your mouth. Repeat it a few times and let go of any tension you hold."

As the women followed his instructions, their rapid breaths gradually shifted into a slower rhythm. "Now, close your eyes," Miles continued. "Tasha...Sasha, I want you to dig in the roller decks of your minds and find the darkest secret you can find that would hurt someone in this room if they were to learn of it."

A tear escaped Sasha's eye as she kept her eyes closed, a nervous laugh catching in her throat.

Miles chuckled softly. "It seems someone has found something."

He shifted his gaze to Tasha. "Tasha, have you found anything in your mind's roller decks?"

"Yes," she replied quietly.

"Take another deep breath, then release it slowly. Repeat it a couple more times."

As the final breath escaped their lungs, Miles asked,

"Do you feel slightly calmer now compared to the first breath?"

"Yes," both women responded, their voices barely above a whisper.

"Open your eyes," he instructed.

Gazing into Sasha's eyes, Miles continued, "Sasha, I want you to look at the person your deepest dark secret offended. Look them in the eye and picture yourself saying the words and then picture asking for forgiveness."

Sasha met Miles' gaze as soft pearls formed in her eyes.

"It's not as simple as it seems, is it?" Miles acknowledged.

Without waiting for a response, he turned to Tasha. "Tasha, do the same. Picture yourself facing this person, offering your apology."

Tasha looked down at her lap, unable to meet his gaze.

"Vulnerability and forgiveness are complex," Miles explained gently. "They can evoke feelings of victimization, vulnerability, and even misplaced weakness. Sometimes, forgiveness makes you feel as if you are a wimp, and the receiver of the forgiveness is in control and just wants you to feel soft. So, we decide not to forgive, to show them whose balls are bigger. 'Pride:' That's the devil's trick to keep our understanding clouded. Feelings! They're what the enemy exploits if we lack a full comprehension of them and ourselves. Take love and forgiveness, for instance – they're the pillars that uphold the devil's schemes."

The women listened intently as Pastor Miles continued, "They are the weapons that the devil employs most frequently against us. Love and forgiveness, when misunderstood or misused, can be wielded against our own well-being."

"Why?" Tasha's voice trembled as she spoke.

Pastor Miles said, "I'll give you three reasons. Firstly, because negative emotions often stem from or are overcome by love and forgiveness. Secondly, these are some of the most challenging emotions for us to confront. Thirdly, forgiveness is a fundamental human value." Miles continued in his solemn voice, "Asking forgiveness requires immense love, courage, and selflessness. It is hard to sit in front of a person, let alone two persons, and ask them to forgive you. If you ask me, I would say it is one of the most difficult things to do, and someone asking for forgiveness is one of the most courageous beings. So, girls, can you find it in your hearts to offer your mother some understanding?"

Sasha snatched her Gucci bag and, in a voice tight with anger, said, "I ask for your forgiveness because I'm walking out! I don't want to hear anything she has to say." Before anyone could react, she stood up to storm out of the office.

Cookie's voice broke down into sobs. "Sasha, please, baby... I'm so sorry. I'm so sorry for what... for what John did to you both. I can't even express how many times I wanted to confront him myself. You know how many times I wanted to get up and walk behind him with a gun and shoot him myself." Her voice choked, unable to finish the sentence.

Sasha's scream tore through the air, echoing through the church and reaching the parking lot. "You knew?!" She wailed. "Oh my God, YOU KNEW?"

Tasha's composure shattered. "You knew? You knew all along you're telling us now?!" Tears welled up in her eyes as she yelled.

Cookie pulled Tasha close, trying to hug her. Tears streamed down their faces, mixing with their makeup.

Sasha's legs seemed to give way beneath her, sending her crashing to the floor. She let out a heart-wrenching cry, her body rocking back and forth. "Oh my God, Sade, I'm so sorry…I'm so sorry!" She repeated.

Tasha joined her sister on the floor, and their bodies were wracked with sobs. "It wasn't your fault, Sash," she whispered. "It wasn't your fault. It was an accident, baby…it was an accident!"

Cookie, tears streaming down her face, struggled to find words. "There were times... I was too weak to resist... too terrified to fight back. I knew he could have hurt you even more." Her voice fractured as she whispered, "Sasha, it was all my fault. I failed to protect Sade..."

The words seemed to break a dam within Sasha. A primal scream erupted from her as she screamed, "NO! SHUT UP! SHUT UP! SHUT UPPP!" She shrieked as tears blurred her vision.

Tasha reached out, her own voice breaking. "Sasha,

please..."

With a jolt, Sasha pulled away. "Let me go, Tasha! I need to get out of here before I lose control and hurt her." She trailed off, her eyes darting around the room as if trapped. She snatched her bag in a frantic movement. She mimicked Cookie's words through gritted teeth, "I caused Sade's death," the words dripping with bitter sarcasm.

She stood up, and before turning toward the door, she walked toward Cookie and, in a raw, anguished cry, screamed at her face, "You took Sade away! YOU MURDERED MY SISTER!"

Stepping closer, she leaned into Cookie's face as her rage barely contained. "MURDERER!" She screamed.

With a final, furious shove of the door, Sasha stormed out, leaving behind a room soaked in tears. Pastor Miles rushed to comfort the sobbing women. He gently offered, "Tasha, I'll drive Sasha home and then come back to the church in Uber. Is that alright?"

Tasha, her eyes red-rimmed, nodded in silent agreement as Pastor Miles rushed out to catch Sasha.

Chapter 8

Downtown, the center heartbeat of the city of brotherly love, the beautiful sky scrapers stood as it's pillars, where the well-to-do played. Sasha glided on it's streets with confidence, saturating her mind with the feeling of importance. She enjoyed the brief escape of norm, as she fit right in to the bougie surroundings.

The clinking of glasses and murmur filled the air of the Marriot Hotel Restaurant as Sasha pushed open the heavy glass doors. Her eyes scanned the space, searching for a familiar face. A smile bloomed on her face as she spotted Mise' perched at the bar with a cognac glass swirling between his fingers.

"There goes my Sassy," he spoke in a voice thick with a Jamaican lilt as he caught sight of her.

"Hey, Mise'," Sasha replied, her smile widening.

He held out a cognac glass, condensation clinging to the sides. Inside, amber liquid swirled over ice cubes. "Hennessey, just the way you like it," he winked. Sasha took the proffered glass as Mise' led her past the bar. His hand found hers, guiding her towards a waiting table already set for two.

As they settled into their plush chairs, Mise' inquired, "How's my girl?" His gaze held a genuine concern.

Sasha sighed. "It's been a trying week," she admitted.

"Talk to me," Mise' urged.

"I just need to take my focus off of me for a minute," she confessed, sinking into the chair.

A waitress materialized beside them with a professional smile. Mise', ever the charmer, flashed the waitress a smile as he ordered the lamb with garlic mashed potatoes. Sasha, opting for something lighter, requested the cobb salad with strips of rib eye, cooked medium rare.

As the waitress disappeared, Sasha blurted out, "Mise', why do you keep me around?"

Mise' raised an eyebrow with a playful glint in his eyes. "Because it's fun to be around you, Sassy. Plus, you make me look good," he added with a chuckle. Sasha's expression turned serious. "Seriously, though. You have a lot of women chasing after you, and you never married."

Mise' leaned back in his chair, steepling his fingers. "What do you want to know, Sassy? I have family back home," he said.

Sasha asked, "Children?"

Mise' shook her head. "No children. I do have five siblings; I'm the oldest. We grew up in poverty, and our mother died young."

Sasha listened intently, her expression unreadable. "I'm so sorry to hear that, Mise'," she said finally and then offered a small smile. "What made you come to the States?" She asked.

Mise' swirled the amber liquid in his glass. His expression turned serious. "Let's just say I had to make ends meet back home. There weren't a lot of options for someone in my situation."

He paused, taking a sip of his cognac. "There were these guys in the neighborhood, all struggling just like me. Then, there was this other guy, a big shot in the neighborhood. Everyone looked up to him. He'd always be passing out money to people who were down on their luck, like me and my crew. He could get you anything you needed - medicine, groceries, even if you were in some kind of trouble, he'd take care of it. He was powerful. Seemed too good to be true, you know?"

Mise' leaned closer, his voice dropping to a low murmur. "It wasn't until much later that we found out he was playing both sides. Turns out, he was way more politically connected than anyone knew. He wasn't so interested in helping people as he was using them. We were pawns in his game, doing his dirty work to further his own agenda."

He hesitated, then continued, "I ran errands for him, his 'Arons' as you might say. Didn't matter if it was good or bad as long as the job got done. He paid well, and frankly, I didn't have much choice. He was my only way out of that situation, or you can say, my only way of making money."

A flicker of a smile played on Mise's lips. "Then came the States. His political favors started reaching across the ocean, and he needed someone to handle them. He, well, 'voluntold' me for the job."

Sasha let out a soft chuckle. "Voluntold, huh?" She corrected playfully.

Mise' shook his head with a hint of amusement in his eyes. "Exactly. He'd tell you to do something but frame it like a question. Saying no wasn't an option, for retaliation was his unwritten rule. Still, being his guy here meant he trusted me, right? And let's be honest, coming to America was a dream come true for me."

He took another sip, looking into the distance. "He set everything up, got me here, and here I've been ever since. Any money I make, it all goes back home."

Mise' left the details hanging, trusting Sasha to connect the dots. The peek into his past had only piqued her curiosity further, but for now, she simply nodded. The man behind the easy smile was shrouded in a veil of mystery, and Sasha knew there was more to this story than Mise' was letting on.

Sasha nibbled on her salad. She knew it wouldn't be appropriate to pry further. Nevertheless, she couldn't ignore the unease gnawing at her.

"Mise'," she began, her voice hesitant, "There is something I wanted to talk to you about."

Mise' paused mid-chew, his gaze flitting up briefly

before returning to his plate. He offered a silent nod, acknowledging her words without interrupting his meal.

Taking a deep breath, Sasha continued, "It's about the last few runs I made for you. The men... they made me very uncomfortable. They would flirt and try to touch me. The more I stopped them and let them know I was not wit-dat, the more aggressive they became. I even told them that you sent me. They all began to speak Creole to each other. I don't know what they were saying, but one of them laughed and asked me, 'Was that supposed to scare me?' I... I really don't feel comfortable going over there anymore," she concluded.

Mise' finally finished chewing but his expression remained unreadable. He took a long sip of his cognac. After a moment of silence, he simply nodded in agreement. "I have a meeting to go to; I'll call you later," he said, wiping his mouth with the crisp napkin.

Sasha managed a weak smile, "Okay."

Mise' reached into his pocket, pulling out a thick wad of cash. He peeled off ten crisp hundred-dollar bills, folded them neatly, and slid them discreetly under her salad bowl. He leaned in and planted a brief, impersonal kiss on her head before turning and striding out of the restaurant.

Sasha stared after him, the unease morphing into a bitter taste in her mouth. Sasha sighed, picking at her salad as she scrolled through her phone. A message from Ada popped up, suggesting a trip to the mall. It was a welcome distraction. With a tap on the screen, she replied, "I'll meet you at Franklin Mills Mall, in front of the orange section, in an hour. Leaving now."

Chapter 9

The long shopping trip with Ada had left Sasha with a pleasant exhaustion. Laden with shopping bags from her mall trip with Ada, she pulled into Tasha's driveway. Pulling into Tasha's driveway to share the day's spoils with her sister. But the peace was shattered the moment she stepped out of the car. Loud, familiar voices, raised in argument, spilled from the open windows.

Sasha paused, a surprised laugh escaping her lips. *Tasha and Miles arguing?* It was practically unheard of. She became curious, so she crept closer as the voices grew clearer. The bickering, however, lacked the usual venom. Instead, it was a comical back-and-forth, devoid of the colorful language that usually peppered arguments.

Just then, a shadow flickered across the distorted glass of the front door. Tasha's voice boomed, "Who is it!?"

"It's me, Sasha. Open the door," Sasha called back, amusement dancing in her voice.

A few seconds later, the rhythmic click-clack of Tasha's stilettos echoed across the polished marble floor as she marched towards the door. The door swung open, revealing a flustered Tasha. Her usually pristine face was a mask of annoyance.

"Looks like I came at a bad time," Sasha remarked with a playful smile on her lips.

Miles, caught in the act of marital discord, offered a sheepish grin. "Oh, Pastor, you in the doghouse?" Sasha teased.

Tasha, however, wasn't in the mood for jokes. "Sasha, this is a bad time," she muttered.

Unfazed, Sasha winked. "It looks like I came at the perfect time then," she countered, her gaze flickering between the two. "I've never seen a pastor look like a dog with his tail between his legs."

Instead of calming the situation, Sasha's playful jab seemed to irritate Tasha further. "Come on, Tash," Sasha persisted, reaching out to usher her sister towards the bedroom. "In the room with me, I brought you something. You could use a break."

With a resigned sigh, Tasha allowed herself to be led away. As they settled onto the plush bed, Sasha's gaze fell on the glistening tears welling up in Tasha's eyes. Gone was the fiery Tasha, replaced by a woman with a secret sorrow. Sasha realized that this wasn't a playful spat – it was something deeper, more serious. A knot of helplessness formed in Sasha's stomach as her sister's unspoken pain settled in.

Sasha became worried as she watched Tasha struggle to compose herself. "What's wrong, Tash? What's going on?" She pressed gently.

Tasha took a deep, shaky breath. The urge to confide in her sister warred with the instinct to protect Miles' image. A single tear escaped, tracing a glistening path down her cheek and landing with a soft plop on her tightly clasped hands in her lap.

"Let it out, Tash," Sasha coaxed. "Talk to me. Everyone knows you're human, no matter how perfect you try to make things look from the outside. It's okay to be human," she reassured, reaching out to rub soothing circles on Tasha's back.

Suddenly, a sound from outside the room pierced the heavy silence. Tasha's head snapped up. "Wait a minute, Sash," she muttered in a whisper and hurried out of the room, returning a moment later. Sasha could see a flicker of anger replacing the despair in Tasha's eyes.

"He left," she announced. "That was his car I heard starting up."

"Where is he going?" Sasha inquired.

"Probably to see that Jezabel!" Tasha spat out with a venomous edge creeping into her tone.

Sasha's brow furrowed in confusion. "Who? What Jezabel?"

"Sasha," Tasha hissed. "That bum is cheating on me!"

The revelation slammed into Sasha like a physical blow. "What!?" She exclaimed in disbelief and shock. "No, not Miles." For a moment, she didn't know if she heard it right. "Sis, are you overreacting? What happened? Sit down, Tash," Sasha said firmly, ushering her sister back onto the bed. "Let's figure this out."

But Tasha, fueled by a torrent of emotions, ignored Sasha's request. With a burst of pent-up frustration, she blurted out her secret, the carefully constructed facade of her seemingly perfect marriage crumbling around her. "It first started off with me noticing money missing from our accounts," she confessed. "At first, I didn't think much of it. The bills were paid, and the amounts were small. But as time went on, it became more frequent, and the sums got larger."

A bitter edge crept into her voice as she continued. "He began lying to me. He'd tell me a bill was paid, but later, I'd find out it was only partially covered, leaving us with late fees every month. Or the bill collectors would call, demanding payment for bills neglected for months!"

Tears welled in her eyes as she choked out, "Receipts... I kept finding receipts from restaurants, bars..." Her voice trailed off as the pain became evident in her clenched fists.

"One time, he went to a church conference in Rio," Tasha continued. "He said it was for five days, but the conference was only a weekend event. Turns out, the lying snake used our timeshare to save money! And guess what? A bill came from the hotel demanding payment for room service – dinners for two! Three nights in a row, Sasha! Apparently, his precious credit card declined after they returned home."

A fresh wave of hurt washed over her face. "I even found texts, emails, pictures! Proof of affairs with three different women! Sasha," her voice broke, "do you know how difficult it is to walk into church and put on a fake smile? Like we're the walking-talking example of what we preach?"

The anger returned. "I sit there looking stupid, front row, listening to this freaking phony preach to people! Every Sunday, Sasha I go to church trying to keep a good face. Hugging everyone, saying 'God bless you,' encouraging them, while I'm drowning in his lies! Playing the good little wife! Who's going to encourage me, Sasha?"

Sasha listened, her heart breaking for her sister. A choked sob escaped Tasha's lips. "' It's lust, it's just a stronghold,' I kept telling myself," she whispered. "I just keep praying for my husband, and while I'm on my knees praying, another woman is on her knees doing every disgusting thing with my husband that I don't even want to mention."

Tasha paused for a moment as she wiped the tear from her face. "The deacon board had the nerve to have a meeting about me!" Tasha continued. "They think I'm standoffish and mean! They told Miles to 'sit me down' instead of sticking up for me! And that coward, he tells them I'm jealous of the time he spends at church! That he'll deal with me!"

Sasha's heart ached for her sister. The picture-perfect life Tasha had projected was shattered. In that moment, the shopping bags and the mall trip faded into insignificance. All that remained was the raw need to be there for her sister.

Suddenly, a surge of anger flared in Sasha's eyes. She rose abruptly from the bed and stormed out of the room. Tasha watched her go, momentarily stunned. Moments later, Sasha reappeared, carrying a black leather binder and a loose stack of papers. They looked official, filled with handwritten notes. "Do these belong to Miles?" She asked.

Tasha was bewildered. "Yes, why?"

Without further explanation, Sasha marched back out of the room and disappeared into the hallway. Tasha, worried about her sister's sudden outburst, followed cautiously. She could hear the sound of running water coming from the bathroom.

Hesitantly, Tasha peeked through the open door.

Sasha stood facing the tub with a single sheet of paper clutched in her hand. A mischievous glint flickered in Sasha's eyes as she ripped the paper into small pieces, letting them flutter down into the swirling water.

"Oh, my goodness, Sasha!" Tasha cried, her hand flying to her mouth. "That was Miles's study and sermon for the upcoming baptism and Sunday service!"

Sasha looked up. "Didn't you tell me once – 'God equips the call'?" She said. "Well, I guess Pastor Miles just has to go off his personal testimony. God just equipped him with..." she trailed off, letting out a dramatic sigh.

The absurdity of the situation, coupled with the relief of finally venting her anger, struck Tasha. The absurdity of the situation hit them both at once, and they burst into laughter. It was a raw, cathartic release of tension. After a few minutes, the laughter subsided.

"You feel a little better?" Sasha asked gently.

Tasha wiped a tear from her eye. "Weirdly, I do," she admitted. They both giggled again. The sisters walked back to the bedroom holding each other's hand. As they sat down again, Tasha steered the conversation in a different direction.

"So," she chirped. "What did you get me?"

"Oh yes!" Sasha grinned, reaching into her purse and pulling out a small gift bag. "Voila!" She exclaimed, handing it over.

Tasha eagerly took the bag as her earlier anxieties momentarily vanished. With a flourish, she tore off the wrapping paper and revealed a familiar box. Her eyes widened in delight.

"Infinity!" She squealed, recognizing her favorite perfume. "Oh, Sasha, you shouldn't have!"

"But I did," Sasha countered, a knowing smile gracing her lips. "After all, it is your go-to."

Tasha wrapped her arms around Sasha in a quick hug. "You always know just what to get me," she murmured.

She carefully unwrapped the box. Holding the bottle aloft, she took a moment to appreciate the sleek design before spritzing a touch onto her pulse points. With her eyes closed, she inhaled deeply, the sweet, rich aroma instantly transporting her to a place of calm serenity.

"Mmm, I love this smell," she sighed contentedly.

"Thank you, Sis. Not just for the perfume, but for everything."

"Anytime, Tasha," Sasha replied, squeezing her sister's hand. "You know I've always got your back."

Tasha returned the squeeze. "I know you do," she whispered. Taking a deep breath, she decided to shift the focus. "So, how have you been?" She asked.

Sasha's eyes sparkled with excitement. "Good! Really good, actually. Guess what? I got voted VP of my homeowners' association at the complex." "Wow, congratulations!" Tasha exclaimed, genuinely impressed. "That's fantastic news, Sasha!"

"And there's more," Sasha continued with a mischievous grin spreading across her face. "I met a guy today. At the mall, of all places."

Tasha's eyebrows shot up. "A guy? That's amazing! Tell me everything!"

Sasha settled back in the plush chair and began talking like a teenager about their crush. "Oh, Tasha, he is fine!" She gushed. "He is 6'2, big chest and arms. He drives a Lincoln SUV, and he moved here from Texas. We ended up talking for like two hours after he walked Ava and me to our cars," she concluded.

"That's wonderful, Sash! I'm so happy for you," Tasha exclaimed. "So, what does this mystery man do for a living?" She inquired.

Sasha's smile widened as she leaned forward. "Guess what? He's a professional wrestler!"

Tasha's eyes widened in surprise. "A wrestler? Really?"

"Yep," Sasha confirmed. "His stage name is 'Ultimate Pain.'"

A flicker of recognition crossed Tasha's face. "As in... WWF Ultimate Pain?" She asked.

"The one and only!" Sasha declared. "His real name is Rashaun Russell, and he wants to take me out next weekend."

"Wow, that's amazing, Sash!" Tasha exclaimed, genuinely thrilled for her sister.

"He has some crazy strict practice schedule this week before his fight at the Spectrum Center, but guess who scored free tickets?" Sasha wiggled her eyebrows playfully. "ME!" She squealed triumphantly.

"And guess who's going with you?" Tasha declared, a mischievous glint mirroring her sister's.

"Of course you are!" Sasha exclaimed, throwing her arms around Tasha in a grateful hug.

"Are you staying for dinner, then?" Tasha asked, pulling back from the hug. Her stomach was growling softly.

"Of course I am," Sasha replied.

Chapter 10

Tasha stood by the stove, listening to the low hum of the gas flame. It was the only sound besides the clinking of silverware against porcelain as Sasha set the table. Reaching for the pot handle, she let out a quiet sigh. The aroma of Sasha's favorite mashed potatoes, fragrant with garlic and simmered for hours, filled the air. It was a dish that held years of memories, each steaming bite evoking a different chapter in their shared history since it was Sasha's favorite.

Gently, almost reverently, Tasha turned off the burner. The flame sputtered out, leaving behind a faint orange glow that cast long shadows across the kitchen countertop. Picking up the pot, she came to the lounge and set it on the table.

"Did you manage to reach Greg?" Tasha inquired.

Sasha nodded, devoid of enthusiasm. "He's still out of town. Says the construction contract will take another month." A faint smile flickered across her lips. "He's doing okay, though. Sent his love."

A playful glint entered Tasha's eyes. "Well, I know

who to hit up for some extra cash when he gets back then," she teased, and they both shared a laugh.

As they settled around the dinner table, Tasha felt a familiar knot of apprehension tighten in her stomach. This, she knew, was the opportune moment to address the elephant in the room: the incident at the church. Yet, the fear of Sasha shutting down, erecting walls of emotional stone, held her tongue hostage.

She wanted to approach it delicately, so taking a fortifying sip of water, Tasha met Sasha's gaze. "I spoke with Mom," she began in a gentle voice.

Sasha continued eating her short ribs as her body language touted with suppressed emotions.

"Everyone's worried. They think you should call her," Tasha continued.

The mere mention of Mom seemed to steal Sasha's appetite. Finally, she placed her fork down, and a defeated sigh escaped her lips.

"Tasha," she began, her voice tight with barely concealed anger, "I appreciate your concern, but I'm truly alright. I just…. I don't have anything left to say to her." A pained expression flickered across her face. She wanted to stop right there, but her anger grew larger. "How can you still have her in your life, Tasha, after what she allowed to happen to us!?"

Tasha's voice rose slightly, a tremor of hurt and betrayal making itself evident. "I get it, Sasha," she said, her eyes welling up.

"She was supposed to protect us! She chose him, that coward, over the safety of her own children!"

Unable to hold back any longer, tears streamed down Sasha's face as she rose from the table and began to pace. The years of pent-up hurt and anger spilled forth with a torrent of raw emotion that threatened to drown them both.

"Sash," Tasha's voice softened, "she was being beaten. Every day, she didn't know if she'd survive. I'm not excusing her. But for forgiveness, there has to be some understanding, a sliver of it." Tasha's plea was laced with desperation.

"You would say that," Sasha mocked.

"What's that supposed to mean?" Tasha demanded.

"She always put you first," Sasha's voice dripped with bitterness. "It was always 'Tasha this,' 'Tasha that.' You were her mini-me," she said with a humorless laugh. "Did she ever care about me, about what I was going through?"

"Why didn't you say anything, Sash?" Tasha countered gently.

"She should have asked me!" Sasha's voice rose. "I was her daughter! While she endured him, I was being violated by the same monster! I was being raped by that animal who penetrated her every day and then would penetrate her daughter too! The same man who made me shoot my sister! And he was her own cousin!"

"She is sick, Sasha. She has been seeing a therapist for about a year now," Tasha informed her.

"What about our mental health? She didn't even put us in therapy!" Sasha responded.

Tasha held her silence, allowing the storm of emotions to rage within Sasha. She wanted her to vent and let it all out.

Tears streamed down Sasha's face. "She is so selfish, Tasha! So selfish! My nightmares, the chills, a desperate prayer occasionally – that was my therapy!"

Tasha crossed the room and held Sasha close. Sasha met her gaze, searching for answers. "How can I forgive her? That's what everyone says, right? Move on and forgive her? My life is hell, Tasha," Sasha choked out.

Tasha reached out and wiped away the tears that streamed down Sasha's face. She knew there weren't any easy answers, no quick fixes. Sasha's pain ran deep.

"I can't answer why these things happen, Sash," Tasha said softly. She chose to stay silent and then offered a gentle reminder of some forgotten memories. "Sasha, remember when you were little and how you used to talk for hours in your sleep and wake up screaming in the night?" She began softly. "Mom would hold you close and rock you for what felt like forever. And remember, growing up, you could seemingly do no wrong. Remember that time you put glue in my hair, and Mom yelled at me for having it."

A faint smile touched Sasha's lips.

"She always told me to leave you alone," Tasha continued. She closed her eyes briefly, remembering. "She did protect you. Maybe not in the way we needed her to at the time, but she kept you close. It might have been too late, but it's true."

A hurt began to creep up in Tasha's voice now. "Sometimes, I felt so left out, like my pain didn't matter. I held the guilt for many years and secluded myself, barring myself in books. I even started blaming myself more, thinking I was being punished because I handed you the gun to play with before it accidentally went off." Tears welled up in Tasha's eyes.

"Tasha, please," Sasha whispered. "The gun accident wasn't your fault. You were just a child."

Tasha looked away, tears silently slipping down her cheeks. Sasha wrapped her arms around her sister, holding her close. They sat in silence for a long time until Tasha looked at her sister's face and said, "Sasha, I was wondering... would you consider coming to Mom's baptism?"

Sasha's response was a humorless chuckle devoid of warmth. "A baptism, huh? Seems convenient. A cheater washes a murderer of all her sins."

Tasha's heart ached for her sister. "Sash, please."

"Nah, I'm not coming to that circus. I'm good," Sasha replied. "If I went, I may just jump in and drown them both."

Tasha reached out, wanting to offer comfort but unsure if it would be welcome. "I understand your anger, Sasha. But I won't push you. However, I will continue to pray for you, for Mom, and for us."

"Yeah, you do that," Sasha responded and then moved toward the table. Picking her plate up, she went towards the kitchen. She stared down at the remnants of the meal, the garlic mashed potatoes and short ribs.

"Tell pastor cheater to find another girlfriend's house to dine at," she announced. "Because these leftovers are coming home with me."

Chapter 11

Sasha sprawled across her plush, pink chaise lounge. The worn velvet felt cool against her bare arms. Her thumb scrolled listlessly through the feed of Facebook updates, each filtered photo and curated story failing to spark any real interest. A shrill trill shattered the silence, jolting her out of her mental fog. Glancing at the screen, she saw Vick's name flash, a warmth blooming in her chest.

"Hey, Vick," she answered.

A throaty chuckle came through the receiver. "Hey you, stranger!"

"Where have you been hiding? Haven't seen you in a while," Sasha asked.

Vick let out a snort. "Since you met Mr. Pain-in-the-Neck, you don't know anybody." he teased.

"Oh, shut up, Vick," Sasha replied.

"Just pulling your leg, girl. What's on the agenda for tonight?"

"Nothing much, really."

"Really? You're not going to your mom's baptism?" Vick asked with a hint of surprise in his voice.

"Nope," Sasha said, popping the 'p' defensively.

"Okay, okay, I won't pry," Vick conceded. "But seriously, Sasha, you should go. You only get one mother, you know."

"We're all going over to her house for dinner afterwards anyway," Vick continued, his voice taking on a cajoling tone. "At least show your face, even if it's just for a little while."

Sasha bit her lip, torn between her stubborn resolve and the faint tug of obligation. "Nope," she mumbled, the word leaving her lips more out of habit than conviction.

Vick chuckled, a soft, knowing sound. "You're stubborn as a mule, you know that?"

"Yup," Sasha admitted.

"Well, at least you're honest," Vick conceded. "Alright, I'll let you go. I'm finishing getting ready, and I'll call you when I get over to your mom's house."

"Okay, talk later," Sasha replied, hanging up the phone.

The silence returned. Sasha's gaze drifted towards the window as she saw the sun casting long shadows across the cityscape. But her mind was far from the present. It was consumed by the ghost of Russell. She began to reminisce about their last few dates. Her heart pounded with the memories of the special moments. The long romantic walks and being treated as a VIP at his matches gave her hope that he was Mr. right.

Russell confided in her about his last girlfriend. He explained how she was unappreciative of his success and just wanted to party all the time. He wanted a family, and she was in rebellion to live as anyone's wife or mother. As Sasha remained optimistic, butterflies entered her stomach fantasizing about their future together. She smiled, as she continued to gaze out the window. *'I'm falling fast for him,'* she admitted to herself.

Picking up her phone once more, she dialed his number. The rings echoed in the emptiness, met only by a voicemail beep. Deflation washed over her as she ended the call, the phone falling limply back onto the chaise lounge.

Restlessness gnawed at her. She rose from the chaise lounge and began pacing the room, her bare feet whispering against the hardwood floor. Bored with inaction, her eyes scanned the room, landing on a framed photo on her dresser. It captured a scene from a happier time - Cookie, Tasha, and her smiles were wide and genuine as they frolicked on the beach in Atlantic City. A tiny smile tugged at the corner of her lips, a fleeting memory of simpler times. But just as quickly, the smile vanished and was replaced by a mask of stubbornness. She wouldn't allow herself to be swayed by sentimentality. Not tonight.

Chapter 12

Families streamed in at the Sunday faithful of Glory World Mission Church, awaiting the baptisms. Pastor Miles, usually enthroned in his front-row seat, stood awkwardly at the back with his gaze averted.

Tasha couldn't help but notice her husband's unusual position. It was a familiar pattern, his retreat every time his infidelity came to light. The whispers around her, though subtle, stung nonetheless. The regulars, accustomed to the drama, began to murmur as their narratives had already formed. "Tasha must have done something again," they'd mutter with voices dripping with misplaced sympathy.

But not this time. Tasha wouldn't allow him to escape accountability shrouded in false piety. With quiet determination, she rose and made her way towards the back, closing the distance between her and Pastor Miles. As congregants entered, she greeted them warmly. She forced them to acknowledge her and talk to them both, to realize that this time, the narrative wouldn't be twisted. Her stance was a silent declaration - she wouldn't be silenced, and he wouldn't escape responsibility.

"A warm welcome, Sister Lisa!" Tasha boomed, her voice carrying cheer that bordered on theatricality. Each greeting was delivered with a touch more volume than necessary. This was her performance clearly intended for the watchful deacons stationed nearby. A silent chuckle danced in her head, but Pastor Miles squirmed under the scrutiny. He remained rooted to the spot, feet seemingly glued to the floor. Guilt was pictured all over his face. It seemed to him as if pictures of him cheating were spilling from his pocket with every tentative step.

A deaconess, concerned about the unorthodox setup, approached Pastor Miles. "Pastor, the service is about to begin. Perhaps you'd like to take your place at the front?" She suggested, offering a gentle nudge towards the vacant chair. "I'll be along shortly with your drink and service cloth."

Tasha cut in before the deaconess could finish. "Thank you so much, Sister Mary," she interjected with a dazzling smile. "I'll be happy to take care of the good Pastor today."

Miles shuffled towards his chair, annoyance simmering beneath the surface. He could practically feel

Tasha's breath on his neck as she followed closely behind with a tray of water balanced precariously in her hands.

The church quieted as the baptismal candidates, clad in pristine white gowns, filed in one by one and took their places in the front row. Across the room, Cookie's eyes welled up with tears as she scanned the congregation, searching for Sasha's face. Her gaze met Vick's, and a flicker of recognition passed between them. Sensing Cookie's emotional distress, Vick offered a warm, reassuring smile to her.

As Tasha, now adorned in the formal garb of an Evangelist, approached the podium to affirm the service. A single tear escaped, tracing a glistening path down her cheek as she said her prayers. Pastor Miles, a witness to this display of raw emotion, felt a pang of shame pierce his carefully constructed facade. Yet, the shame remained comfortably numb, failing to ignite the spark necessary for true remorse. He continued the service with the practiced ease of someone reciting a well-worn script. Once concluded, he approached the podium, offering a perfunctory word of thanks to his wife. Publicly declaring his fortune in having Tasha by his side felt like a chore, a routine he mechanically performed, believing it constituted an apology.

Tasha, seated beside him, plastered a smile on her face as the picture of a devoted wife. It was a role she knew well, a performance honed through years of masking her true feelings. The irony of the situation was not lost on her. As Pastor Miles launched into his sermon, grandly titled "Forgiveness Without Conditions," Tasha couldn't help but scoff internally.

As Pastor Miles' sermon droned on, his voice faded into a distant hum in Tasha's mind. A tempestuous internal dialogue was taking place in her head. The words he spoke, "Forgiveness Without Conditions," echoed hollowly in the vast chamber but were a stark counterpoint to the storm brewing within her.

'Why is this becoming such a herculean task?' she thought, frustration gnawing at her composure. *'Is it my duty to lead others to righteousness while my own home crumbles? Is being his helpmate synonymous with shielding his transgressions, a public charade that crumbles behind closed doors? Does shrouding his sins in a cloak of pretense somehow honor him when, in truth, it dishonors me?'*

Her mind churned with questions, each one a searing

indictment of the impossible situation she found herself in. The conflict between the outward display of forgiveness and the festering hurt within her soul felt like a living hell. She yearned for clarity, for a path forward that didn't require her to sacrifice her own integrity.

Chapter 13

Mary J. Blige throbbed through the speakers as Sasha, all curves and confidence, danced around her room, finishing off a blunt. She pauses, checking her reflection in the mirror with a hint of worry flickering across her face. *Is Rashaun ever gonna call?* she thought.

The phone rang, shattering the quiet anticipation. Sasha lunges for it as relief flooded her features. "Hello?"

Static hissed back. "Hello, Mise'?"

She could hear nothing but heavy breathing on the other end. The line went dead. Sasha's brow furrowed. She dialed Mise's number again, but it went straight to voicemail.

"He must have called me by mistake. Haven't heard from him in a while" she muttered, tossing the dead blunt in the ashtray. A shadow of disappointment crossed her eyes.

Sasha plopped down on the edge of the bed, reaching for the blunt she put down earlier. Maybe another hit will chase away the worry gnawing at her. But as she lit it, another image flashed in her mind - Cookie, her mother, her disappointed face at the empty pew at the baptism.

Standing up abruptly, she grabbed her coat. Mixed emotions clouded her face. With a determined sigh, she headed for the door, got in her car, and made her way to the church. As she drove, a battle between guilt and defiance waged within her. At last, she said out aloud as if telling someone, "She doesn't deserve this!"

Halfway down the way, she stopped. Right versus wrong wrestled in her heart. With a screech of tires, she threw the car into reverse, abandoning the route to the church. Instead, she steered towards Mise's store. Maybe another blunt will calm the storm brewing inside. She dialed his number as she drove, but he didn't pick up.

Reaching the store, Sasha slammed the car into park. The store was dark, with a closed sign hanging limply in the window. A look of relief flooded her when she spotted Mise's beat-up Honda parked haphazardly on the sidewalk. "Good, he's here," she muttered to herself.

She approaches the door, rapping on the wood with her knuckles. "Mise'! It's Sassy!" She called out.

Silence.

She waited with a knot of unease forming in her stomach. *Maybe he didn't hear it.* Just as she was about to knock again, a blurry figure materialized through the frosted glass. The figure fumbled with the lock for far too long, and then the door creaked open a sliver. The man stepped behind the door and opened it.

Sasha burst in without hesitation. "Mise'! I called you like ten times!" She threw out, shoving her keys in her purse.

Before she could finish, a hand clamped down on her hair, yanking her head back. A scream died in her throat as the man's voice hissed, rough and reeking of marijuana and cheap beer, "Shut your mouth, girl."

Panic jolted through Sasha. She recognized the second man emerging from the back - the one who harassed her during the cash pick-up she did for Mise'. This wasn't the wrong number. This was a trap.

"Well, well, well," the second man drawled with a sneer, twisting his lips. "Look who decided to join the party, Miss Fancy."

The first man loosened his grip on her locks and

shoved her towards the second. "What the hell is going on? Where is Mise'?" Sasha fought to keep her voice steady as fear clawed at her insides.

The second man threw his head back and laughed. In a harsh, grating sound, he said, "Mise' Mise' Mise…you keep bringing him up as if he can save you. Mise' ain't got nothin' to do with this. This is what got him in trouble in the first place!"

Sasha's blood ran cold. Slowly, she backed away, her eyes darting for an escape. "Mise'!" She called out desperately. "Mise', you back there?!"

The man took Sasha by the arm and shoved through the office door at the back. The shove sent Sasha sprawling through the doorway, landing hard on the slick floor with a sickening thud. As she fought for balance, a bloodcurdling scream ripped from her throat. Blood. It smeared the floor like crimson paint, dripping from the walls in a grotesque tableau. But it was the source that made her scream tear from her throat. Mise'.

He hung limply from the steel pipes in the ceiling, his body contorted at an unnatural angle. His body was a mangled mess, almost unrecognizable. And his hands…they were gone, severed at the wrists, leaving mangled stumps that spoke of unimaginable pain. The sight was enough to turn her scream into a primal howl of terror.

Before she could even process the horror, a hand clamped down on her throat with the force of a vice. The air rushed from her lungs in a strangled gasp. The harassing man, reeking of weed and fermented despair, loomed over her. He had a machete that dripped with a viscous red of blood and flesh that matched the carnage around them.

"Shut your damn Bumbaclot mouth, raasclat!" He roared in a thick Creole accent dripping with malice. His entire hand encased her neck, cutting off her air supply. Sasha clawed at his arm, digging her nails uselessly into the denim.

Just as darkness threatened to claim her, the second man appeared, shutting the door with a sickening thud as if to claim privacy. Just as the world began to fade around the edges, her vision blurred with the impending darkness. Seconds before she could possibly pass out, the man tossed her like a ragdoll. She slammed into the floor, landing with a bone-jarring impact directly beneath Mise's mutilated body.

"Take a good look at your friend," he rasped with a twisted amusement in his voice. Tears streamed down Sasha's face, blurring the horrific scene further. Her legs kicked out in a desperate attempt to crawl away, flinging her shoes across the room like discarded toys.

The man with the machete came closer and settled the tip of it on her chest, right on her heart. "Don't. Move," he snarled in a low growl. For the first time, she met his gaze. It was a chilling sight. Eyes black as coal, a single thick vein throbbing in his forehead like a demonic pulse. Frozen in terror, Sasha stared into the abyss of his eyes. A single thought echoed in her mind: this is where it all ends.

"Please, Sir, please don't kill me," she begged.

"Now you want something from me after you get my partner killed?" Said the man.

"Partner? I didn't kill anyone!" Sasha pleaded.

"You know why they called him Mystery (Mise')?" The man with the machete asked raising her brows.

Sasha shook her head no.

"He made people disappear with orders back home. He is a

legend. Not one body found in 20 years. He let it go to his head. He killed my partner with no orders because you said we want your pum-pum."

A cold dread slithered down Sasha's spine. Her eyes grew wide in shock, but she dared not make a sound.

"Take clothes off," the man ordered her in broken English.

Terror ran through Sasha like a live wire. Her hands and legs trembled so violently she could barely stand. Blood rained down from above on her hair and face from Mise's body. Hearing the man's demand to remove her shirt, her fear solidified into a wall of ice.

She couldn't. Her body wouldn't obey. The man's frustration morphed into rage, seeing her reluctance. In a flash, the machete swung. Sasha flinched back, but it was too late. He slid the sharp blade across her legs from left to right. A searing pain exploded across her flesh. Her scream ripped through the grimy air. She lashed out, kicking blindly with her good leg. The man stumbled back, momentarily surprised. But he recovered quickly, lunging at her with a feral snarl.

Sasha fell backward, and her head fell to the floor with a sickening thud. The world blurred at the edges. Her heart hammered as if it would come out of her chest at any moment.

He was on top of her now. A twisted sense of satisfaction flickered in his eyes. Sasha watched, paralyzed by terror, as his breathing grew ragged, his gaze dropping to his groin. The control he had on Sasha now excited him, and so his erection grew. A primal fear ripped through her. Ignoring the searing pain in her leg, she forced out a choked plea, "Please, please, I never meant to get anyone hurt."

The man ignored her. "Open your mouth."

The stench of sweat and blood filled Sasha's nostrils. Bile rose in her throat, threatening to spill. But she knew defiance would be her death sentence. With trembling hands, she opened her mouth a sliver.

"Wider," he snarled, the blade of the machete glinting inches from her throat.

Tears streamed down Sasha's face, blurring her vision. She opened it wider.

"Stick tongue out," he ordered.

She complied and lolled out her tongue.

"Don't move, or I'll cut it," he warned.

Sasha began to cry now as she sat under Mise's body with a man on top of her, as she kept her mouth wide open and tongue hanging out.

The man then cleaned the tip of the machete on Sasha's tongue, rubbing it from both sides back and forth. Sasha whimpered as the metallic tang of blood and tiny pieces of flesh flooded her mouth. The taste of blood and fear became a suffocating wave. Her stomach lurched, and she vomited, a wet, heaving mess that stained the already blood-soaked floor.

Sasha made her last attempt and cried to the man for her life. But it seemed as if he couldn't hear anything. All he knew at that moment was his lust. Losing his senses to his bizarre desires, he tore Sasha's shirt apart from the chest and ripped her bra off. He then seized the shirt, fashioning it into a makeshift noose. The loop wound tightly around her neck, its reach extending to her hands secured to Mise's ankles and feet. Her toes dangled, grazing the floor in a macabre dance. A bra was then thrust into her mouth, wound securely around her head. Sasha winced as the force tore at the corners of her

He leaned close to Sasha's ear, whispering as he tucked his blood-stained organ back into his pants, "Hang in there, sexy. We'll have more fun when I return." With that, he retrieved the machete and exited the room. Sasha hung there in his seamen and blood. She summoned every ounce of strength and desperately wiggled to loosen the knot around her neck.

Her shirt finally gave way, and Sasha collapsed to the floor, gasping for air. Though her body felt limp, her indomitable spirit surged with determination to escape the horrors she had endured. Snatching her purse, shoes, bra, and shirt, Sasha sprinted out the back door. Hidden between buildings, Sasha held her breath until the city sounds faded. No voices, no car engines, just the chilling silence of her own heartbeat.

When the coast seemed clear of both vehicles and pedestrians, she raced to her car, frantically started the engine, and peeled away, the tires screeching in her wake. Streets blurred into a dizzying kaleidoscope of shock. When the car finally sputtered to a stop, it was behind the familiar, yet strangely ominous, silhouette of the church.

She crawled out of her car, dragging her blood-soaked body along the building. Leaning against the cold brick wall, she caught the faint strains of praise music emanating from within. Peering through the cracks in the imposing stained glass window, she witnessed Pastor Miles immersed in a baptismal ritual with Cookie. He thrashed Cookie's body down in the water, then raised her back up. Overwhelmed by the turmoil within, she saw Tasha succumb to hysteria, a tumultuous mix of laughter and tears that forcibly released the pent-up emotions from childhood.

Returning to her car, Sasha sat with an empty gaze, staring straight ahead as the world finally settled around her. Everything seemed muted, devoid of color. For the first time, the voices in her head were deafeningly clear. They whispered doubts and existential questions, punctuated by flashes of guilt over Mise's fate. "How can this happen!?" She questioned tearfully. Mise's body flashed through her mind. Gripping the steering wheel until her knuckles turned white, Sasha let out a primal scream that echoed into the empty night.

Chapter 14

The day was bright and sunny as sunlight streamed through the windows, illuminating a beautifully decorated home. Cookie bustled around, putting finishing touches on things as she returned home awaiting guests.

Taking a deep breath, she called out, "Tasha, honey, have you spoken to Sasha?"

"No, Ma'am," Tasha replied from the kitchen.

Cookie's smile disappeared completely. She retreated to her bedroom and shut the door gently behind her. A moment of quiet allowed the celebratory mood to settle, replaced by a heavy yearning. Pulling out her phone, she called Sasha several times. The fourth attempt connected to voicemail. Cookie's voice trembled as she spoke,

"Hi, Sash, it's Mom. I missed you today. Honestly, it wasn't the same celebrating this big step without you here. Deep down, I guess I understand. But I wanted you to know; I am so sorry for everything and the pain I caused you. You deserve better. I've loved you since the very moment you were born, and that love will never fade. Please... I hope you find it in your heart to forgive me."

Tears well up in Cookie's eyes. Taking another shaky breath, she finished, "Call me soon, alright? Bye, baby."

Wiping her cheeks, Cookie exited the room, ready to face her guests. The doorbell rang, and a wide smile spread across her face.

"Hey, Mom!" Greg burst through the door, bringing a rush of energy and smiles. Cookie let out a joyous cry.

"Greg! My darling. I wish you made it to service," she exclaimed, wrapping him in a tight hug.

"Of course I did, Mom. I wouldn't miss this for the world. I was just running a bit late getting back into town, so I snuck in at the back." His eyes twinkled playfully. "I saw you and Deaconess Pricilla tearing up the dance floor! You were shouting about 'turkey, potatoes, greens...'"

Greg broke into a mock church shout and danced, mimicking his mother. They both erupted in laughter.

"Oh, you!" Cookie hit him playfully on the arm. "I'm going to get you, boy!"

She pulled him close again, planting a kiss on his

cheek. "Seriously, though, Greg, having you here means the world to me."

"Love you too, Mom, congratulations!" He reached into his coat pocket, pulling out a small card with a handwritten message and five crisp hundred dollar bills tucked inside.

"Just a little something to show how proud I am."

Tears well up in Cookie's eyes again, but this time with pride. She cupped his face and kissed him deeply.

"Thank you, honey. I'm proud of you, too, you and your sisters."

"We know, Mom," Greg said with a grin.

Laughter spilled from the living room as Greg regaled Cookie with stories. Tasha busied herself in the kitchen, finishing up the last of the food. Greg leaned against the doorway with a glass of cognac in his hand.

"Hey, baby girl," he greeted Tasha with a smile.

"Hey, big bro," she replied smiling.

"Where's Miles?" Greg asked, noticing the pastor's

absence.

"Probably still at the church," Tasha said in a falt voice. "He had to take a few elders home. He should be here shortly."

"Okay, cool. Pop said he wants a plate," Greg informed Tasha.

"Sure thing, Greg, remind me before you leave," Tasha said as Greg poured himself a glass of cognac to settle in.

"Where's Sash, Tasha?" Greg inquired.

"I don't know. I haven't spoken to her," Tasha replied. Unfazed, Greg settled into the easy chair and decided to give Sasha a call.

"No answer, got her voicemail," Greg informed Tasha after leaving a message for his sister. "Hey sis, I'm at Mom's house. Hit me back when you get this."

Moments later, Pastor Miles walked in and found Tasha in the kitchen. He approached her from behind as she prepared the food, gently touching her tiny waist in greeting.

Tasha understood that he was merely checking her temperature to ensure a safe passage of communication.

"Mmm, everything smells good," Pastor Miles complimented. Tasha remained silent, focusing on placing each dish on the table as she walked past him.

"Pastor, can you get the chicken on the counter and place it in the center of the table?" Tasha asked.

"My pleasure," Pastor Miles replied, ready to assist with the preparations and assessing a way to lighten the environment.

***

Sasha stumbled into her house. She felt like a hollow shell of the woman who left just hours ago. Every inch of her body throbbed in protest as she peeled off her clothes one by one. The fabric clung to fresh wounds. A crimson stain on her thigh mirrored the violence reflected in the shattered fragments of her self-image.

Entering the shower, Sasha soaked her entire body, from hair to toes. The slashes on her legs burned with the touch of water, and her muscles rebelled against normal movement. Washing between her legs, she screamed upon seeing spots of blood, sliding down to the floor in anguish. Tears mixed with the ice-cold water as Sasha stayed in the tub, crying until the pain subsided.

The icy water finally forced her out. She swallowed two pills of Motrins with a shaky hand. Wrapping herself in a fuzzy robe and slippers, she gathered the bloodied and torn clothing, balled them up, and stuffed them into a trash bag. She hurriedly disposed of the bag in an outdoor trash can, racing back into her home as if chased by unseen horrors.

She carefully slammed the door shut and locked it. Back inside, a primal fear propelled her towards the bedroom. She looked at the mirror, and all she could see was Mise's bloody body hanging from the pipe. Her own reflection in the cracked mirror mocked her. In an outburst, she threw her water glass at the mirror, cracking it.

She quickly grabbed her duct tape and sheets and barricaded all glasses and mirrors that provided any kind of reflection. Only then did she allow herself to sink to the floor?

Her cell phone incessantly rang for 30 minutes, but Sasha heard nothing but her own thoughts and screams. In a desperate cry, she yelled loudly, questioning her existence and the suffering inflicted upon her. Tears flowed freely as Sasha demanded answers.

Tears mingled with rage as she screamed into the emptiness. "Why?!" She shrieked in a raw voice with anguish. "Why me? Why is everything good just beyond my reach? I'm a monster, a murderer, a victim... is that all I am? Why do I even exist!"

Silence. A deafening, suffocating silence. Her thoughts receded into a hollow emptiness. Curled into a fetal position, Sasha rocked herself back and forth until she slept on the floor.

Chapter 15

Three days later, Tasha pulled into the driveway behind her mother's car. Cookie's car sat innocently in the usual spot. She gripped the steering wheel as frustration simmered. All day, unanswered calls to Cookie had gone straight to voicemail. She tried Sasha too but ended up with the same result. Annoyed, she slammed the car door and marched to the porch.

Taking a deep breath, Tasha climbed out and knocked on the door. "Mom? It's me!"

Silence. A sliver of fear sliced through her.

She punched in Greg's number. "Hey, is Mom with you?"

"Nope, I'm still at work," Greg answered.

"Been calling her all day. Need to drop off the baptism papers," Tasha felt worried now.

"You been trying her all day? Maybe she's with Sasha?"

Tasha's frown deepened. "Haven't heard from her either. Four days, no calls." A beat of silence followed her last sentence. "Actually, Greg," she said slowly, "has Sasha called you?"

Another pause came in, followed by Greg's voice. "Now that you mention it, no."

"Alright, I'll use my key. I'll leave the baptism papers on the table. Tell them to call me if they show up, okay?" Tasha ended the call with a sigh.

Unlocking the door, Tasha stepped into the quiet house. "Mom?" She called out, but the silence remained. Placing the papers on the table, she paused. Her lips curled into a soft smile. Looking around the room, she noticed something about the placement didn't feel quite right. With a thoughtful furrow of her brow, she reconsidered. She picked up the certificate again and held it gently between her fingers. Moving across the room, she approached the glass centerpiece and placed the certificate against its smooth surface. She adjusted it until it leaned just so, ensuring it was perfectly displayed. Stepping back, Tasha took a moment to absorb the sight before her as a flicker of pride flashed in her eyes.

Suddenly, she felt exhausted. With a sigh, she moved towards the nearby plush armchair and sank into it heavily, feeling the weight of the past few days pressing down on her shoulders. Sinking deeper into the cushions, she instinctively reached for the worn leather purse resting on the side table. Remembering the long drive and the urgency of the next long grocery drive, she realized she needed a moment to freshen up. With a resigned sigh, she pushed herself up from the chair and made her way towards the guest bathroom discreetly hidden down the hall.

But just as she reached for the door handle, her gaze drew to Cookie's bedroom, where the door stood slightly ajar. Pausing mid-step, Tasha's curiosity piqued. It was unusual for her mother to leave her bedroom door open, especially when she wasn't home.

Unease crept over Tasha as she approached the bedroom door. She hesitated for a moment, listening for any sound from within. She heard nothing but silence.

"Mom?" Tasha called out softly. There was no answer. She pushed the door open a fraction further, peering cautiously into the room. Everything appeared to be in its rightful place – the worn armchair by the window, the framed photos on the dresser – yet she felt an unsettling stillness. The blinds were half-drawn, casting long, distorted shadows across the carpet.

'This isn't right,' her mind screamed, but her feet seemed glued to the floor. Tasha's heart began to thud against her ribs as she moved further into the room. As she reached the center, her gaze fell upon the bed. There, lying on the bed, was Cookie with her body unnaturally still. Her face was pale, her eyes were closed, and her chest was no longer rising and falling with the steady breaths of life.

A strangled gasp escaped Tasha's lips. *'No, no, no,'* her mind chanted in a desperate plea against the brutal reality staring back at her.

Her hands trembled as she reached out to shake her gently. "Mom? Mom, wake up!" She pleaded. But there was no response. Cookie lay motionless. Panic, icy and sharp, clawed its way up Tasha's throat. She reached out again, searching for a pulse, any sign of life. *'Please, please be okay,'* she thought.

With each passing moment, the horrifying truth settled over her like a suffocating fog. Cookie was gone. Tasha collapsed to her knees beside the bed as tears streamed down her cheeks. The world around her seemed to shrink. At that moment, she was adrift in a sea of helplessness.

She could feel panic building up inside her, but she tried hard to stay calm. Her hands were shaking as she reached for her phone. It was difficult to dial Greg's number because her fingers were shaking like a leaf.

The call rang out, but there was no answer. Ten minutes crawled by. The shrill ring of Tasha's phone jolted her.

"Hey, Tasha, everything alright?" Greg's voice, usually booming with life, sounded muted.

A stifled sob escaped Tasha's lips. "Mom," she croaked. "She's..." The familiar lump in her throat choked off the rest.

"She's what? Sorry, I can't hear you," Greg responded, confused.

"Mom is gone, Greg," Tasha replied as a tear escaped her eyes. "Who? Gone where?"

Greg rasped. He pressed the phone tighter to his ear, desperately hoping he'd misunderstood.

"Mom," Tasha managed to reply, tears flooding down her face. "She's... she's in bed. Cold."

A curse, raw and laced with disbelief, ripped from Greg. "Tasha, listen to me. Stay there. I'm coming. Now."

Tasha hung up and stared at the phone, numb, before reaching for it again. Punching in Sasha's number, she held her breath, but it went straight to voicemail, just like the previous attempts.

Alone in the bedroom, Tasha sank onto the bed beside her mother. Cookie lay peacefully with a faint smile playing on her lips. The warmth that had always radiated from Cookie was replaced by a chilling coldness. Tasha stared at her world, her mother, her everything blurring through a veil of tears.

"Why now?" She whispered a ragged plea into the suffocating silence.

No answer came, only the soft sigh of the air conditioner. Tasha tucked a stray curl behind Cookie's ear. "This isn't fair," she choked.

Leaning in, Tasha pressed her lips to her mother's cold cheek. "I love you," she murmured as her words thickened with tears. She squeezed her eyes shut, burying her face in the familiar scent of Cookie's perfume, and prayed. It was her desperate attempt to hold onto the remnants of her mother and relish the last alone time with her.

After a while, Greg tiptoed to the bedroom door. It creaked open silently, revealing Tasha curled beside Cookie. Her peaceful face seemed a plain contrast to the storm brewing in Tasha's eyes. Greg placed a gentle hand on Tasha's shoulder. He sank to his knees beside the bed and looked at his mother. Tears welled up as he reached out to stroke her hair.

"Mom, we're here," he murmured. "You're so beautiful, even now."

Tasha leaned into him, wrapped her arm around her brother, and squeezed his arm. Tears streamed down both their faces as they clung to each other. Pulling back slightly, Greg asked, "Did you call Sasha?"

"I tried," Tasha said in a soft low voice. "But there's no answer."

A furrow appeared between Greg's brows. "Okay,"

he resolved, wiping away a stray tear. "I'll swing by her house and see if she's there. I'll call Pop too, let him know what's happening. Maybe pick them both up. You'll be okay here until I get back, right?"

Tasha nodded, wiping at her own eyes. "Yeah, I'll be alright. I'll start making some calls to relatives and maybe look through some of Mom's paperwork. There might be things that need sorting."

Greg leaned down and kissed her forehead. "I'll be as fast as I can." He left, leaving Tasha alone in the quiet house.

***

Greg pulled at Sasha's house. Throughout the drive, he felt an unnatural feeling he had never experienced before. He knew it was due to Cookie, but there was something off about the entire situation that made it feel weird to him. His heart felt heavy, but there was nothing he could do about it at the moment.

Pulling in front of Sasha's house, he saw her car. Usually parked neatly in the driveway, it was parked in an askew, taking up two parking spots. It wasn't parked haphazardly; it was abandoned. Fear, cold and primal, snaked through him. He took a closer look at it and realized the doors were unlocked. Right then, he saw a sickening smear of blood across the pristine white leather of the driving seat he knew Sasha babied.

'Accident,' a part of his mind whispered, but the terror in his gut screamed otherwise. Dread coiled in his gut as he rushed to the front door.

"Sasha!" He called out. "Sasha, open the door!" By now, he was pounding hard on the door, almost trying to break it.

Should he break the window? But what if she was hurt...? The unanswered questions hammered into his skull. He peered through the windows, but the view was obscured by the curtains.

Panic rose in his heart. *What should I do? Oh my, where is this girl*? Endless unanswered questions clouded his mind, and terrible thoughts engulfed his brain. He couldn't take it anymore. Without thinking any further, he called the police. He then raced back to the car, grabbing a crowbar from the trunk. He pried open the rear door and slipped inside.

"Sasha? Where are you?" He called out.

Inside the house, things looked really strange. Usually, it felt cozy and welcoming, but now it was different. Thick curtains draped over all the windows, and every mirror in the house was covered, making it really dark inside, almost like twilight. It felt heavy and uncomfortable, not like Sasha's home at all. Moving through, he pushed open the door to Sasha's room, bracing himself for the unknown. Inside, he saw Sasha curled on the bed, rocking back and forth, clutching a pillow to her chest. Her eyes were vacant, distant.

"Sasha? You okay?" His voice was a strained mix of fear and concern. "What happened?"

There was no response, no flicker of recognition in her gaze. It was like looking at a stranger trapped in his sister's body.

Dread coiled in his gut, but Greg forced himself closer. He sat beside her on the bed. "Sis, I'm right here," he whispered, his voice cracking. He reached out and pulled her into a hesitant hug, mirroring her rocking motion in a desperate attempt to offer comfort.

A sharp rapping on the front door startled him. Greg leaned back, pecking a soft kiss on Sasha's forehead. "I'll be right back," he murmured before rushing to the door to answer it. "Everything will be okay."

As he swung the door open, his eyes met those of a concerned stranger.

"Hi, how are you doing? Is Sasha here?" The man asked anxiously.

"And you are?" Greg inquired, his gaze searching the man's face for any sign of familiarity.

"Rashaun. Is Sasha here?" The urgency in Rashaun's voice was tangible, and Greg felt a pang of recognition at the name. Suddenly, it clicked in Greg's mind. Sasha had mentioned Rashaun before, someone she was dating.

With a sense of relief mingled with apprehension, Greg extended his hand and shook Rashaun's firmly. "I'm Greg, Sasha's brother." Before Greg could say more, the blaring lights and sirens of the Philadelphia fire rescue approached, interrupting their conversation. Rashaun looked on, bewildered, as the first responders arrived.

"What's going on?" He asked, his brow furrowed

with concern.

"Sasha's not feeling well; come on in," Greg replied, motioning for Rashaun to enter the house. As Rashaun stepped inside, he was shocked to see the scene that greeted him - a sense of isolation and urgency permeating the air, explaining why his calls had gone unanswered.

The emergency medical service team swiftly entered the home. Their expressions were serious as they brought in a stretcher. Sasha, still withdrawn, barely acknowledged their presence. They began speaking to her in private in hushed tones, assessing the situation.

Several tense minutes passed before the lead EMS approached Greg in a grave manner. "Does she have a history of mental illness?" He asked quietly.

"No," Greg replied with conviction. The sight of his normally lively sister in such a state sent a shiver down his spine. He had no idea what had happened, but a fierce protectiveness gushed within him. "No one has heard from her in days. I came to check on her and found her like this," Greg explained as his voice choked with emotion, gesturing towards Sasha's prone form.

"She's dehydrated and has injuries to her legs. She appears to be in some kind of shock or confusion." The EMS team's assessment hit Greg like a punch to the gut. The uncertainty surrounding Sasha's condition only added to his overwhelming sense of helplessness. "We don't know if the injuries are self-inflicted or if she was attacked," the lead EMS continued. "We're going to take her to the hospital for her injuries and for her to be psychologically evaluated."

Greg wept uncontrollably as he struggled to process the gravity of the situation.

"Is there anything I can do, man?" Rashaun was laden with concern. He placed a hand on Greg's shoulder. "Do you need me to call anyone?"

"Man, our mom just died," Greg struggled to speak through his tears. "I came over to inform her; she has no idea."

Rashaun's expression softened. "Damn, man, I'm so sorry for your loss," he said sincerely. "Just tell me what you need. I got you."

Greg shook his head, feeling lost and overwhelmed. "I don't know what to do or what I need," he admitted.

Feeling Greg's distress, Rashaun suggested a plan of action. "Does your other sister know what's going on yet?" He asked.

Greg shook his head again. "No, not yet. She's with my mom now, making calls."

Rashaun nodded understandingly. "Okay, man, let's do this. I'll go to the hospital with Sasha, and you go back to be with your family. I'll keep you updated. You got me, as long as you need me."

"Is that okay?" Greg asked gently.

"Yeah," Raushan responds. "Don't worry, I'll be with Sasha," he whispered.

"Thank you, man. Thank you," Greg told him and rushed out the door.

Chapter 16

The white walls of the funeral home seemed to mock Tasha's grief. Sunlight gushed through the window, forming harsh squares across the polished wood table where she sat. Across from her, a well-meaning and cheerful funeral director, a woman with a nametag reading 'Barbara,' droned on about casket options. Tasha barely registered her words; her mind was a jumbled mess of emotion and worry.

The past few days had been a blur of phone calls, numb interactions with relatives, and a suffocating silence in her own home. Greg had tried to help, juggling between work and arrangements, but after Sasha's hospitalization, Tasha had to face everything alone.

Planning a funeral shouldn't be this lonely, she thought. She remembered Cookie's smile and comforting voice during their conversation about funeral arrangements following the passing of Cookie's dear friend, Aunt Martha, whom they both regarded as family. She recalled the lighthearted conversation about her favorite flowers and the arrangements they made together.

Tasha's lips parted, and a silent sob slipped out. This

wasn't how it was supposed to be.

Barbara cleared her throat. "Ma'am, perhaps we could take a break? Would you like some coffee?"

Tasha forced a smile. "Thank you, Barbara. That would be lovely, but maybe I would take a break outside."

Steeling her nerves, Tasha excused herself from the funeral director and stepped outside into the cool afternoon air. Looking into the distance, her mind slipped from her mother's grief to the sorrow caused by Miles. The man who she once thought to be her supposed rock had been more like a pebble, smooth and easily avoided. He'd spent most evenings 'attending to late-night church business,' returning smelling faintly of a cologne she didn't recognize. The warm hugs and reassurances were long gone now, replaced by studied politeness that prevailed whenever they were together.

Tasha's mind drifted to the events at the church a day before. Whispers and sideways glances had followed her like shadows. Parishioners who once greeted her with smiles and friendly conversation now offered hesitant nods or hurried away altogether. Even during the service, Miles had kept his distance, his gaze fixed on the podium or the congregation, never meeting hers. When she tried to reach for his hand, he subtly pulled away, a flicker of something akin to annoyance crossing his face. It was clear he was allowing the church board, and perhaps even the congregation, to believe she was the one acting distant, the jealous wife consumed by petty emotions.

Tasha could feel the frustration mounting within her. Here she was, drowning in grief and loneliness, while the man who had vowed to be by her side was absent, both physically and emotionally. A stray thought, a whisper in the back of her mind, grew louder with each passing moment. *Where was he spending all these nights?* She knew. Deep inside her heart, she knew too well, but her heart sometimes just loved to give him the benefit of the doubt or just wanted to believe him.

Suddenly, a detail from a gossip rag she'd skimmed a week ago flickered in her memory. *"Pastor Miles has been working so hard on this new community center project,"* Mrs. Henderson had chirped during a church social. *"He says they're renovating an old building in South Philly to provide after-school programs for underprivileged kids. It's such a worthy cause, isn't it?"*

Tasha had offered a polite smile, but a prickle of unease had brushed against her skin. *Renting a place in South Philly? Why would he need to be working on it at all hours of the night?* She thought. A cold dread settled in Tasha's stomach. *Could it be...? No, it couldn't be. Not Miles.* But the doubt wouldn't be silenced.

Pulling out her phone, she dialed a familiar number. It wasn't Miles. It was her friend Sarah from the neighborhood, who also happened to be a real estate agent. Both Miles and Tasha were acquainted with Sarah and knew she was highly regarded in her field. Clinging to a dwindling hope that perhaps Miles had reached out to Sarah regarding a property purchase, Tasha decided to give her a call.

Tasha took a deep breath. "Hey, Sarah," she began, her voice strained. "I need a favor. Did Pastor Miles mention anything about finding a place for some kind of church outreach program in South Philly to you?"

"Sure, I do," Sarah replied. "On Pine Street, right? Brownstone building."

Tasha's heart hammered in her chest. "Right," she forced out. "The thing is... I just wanted to confirm something. Does Miles actually own that place, or is he just renting it?"

There was a brief pause on the other end of the line. "Tasha," Sarah said slowly, "as far as I know, Miles doesn't own any property down there. But he did mention looking into buying the place. Is everything okay?"

Cold anger began to simmer alongside the grief in Tasha's gut. *Outreach program. After-school programs for underprivileged kids.* Miles had never mentioned anything about these himself. She had only heard about this place from other people's mouths. *And why would he need to rent a whole space?* The pieces were starting to fall into place, and a terrible picture was forming.

The confirmation solidified that Pastor Miles had been using the place to conduct his horrible affairs with women. Tears welled up in her eyes.

Infidelity.

Betrayal.

Those were the only words echoing in her mind. Taking a deep breath, Tasha thanked Sarah and hung up. Leaning against the cool brick wall of the funeral home, she fought back the rising tide of emotions. Grief for her mother was now intertwined with a fit of bitter anger.

Wiping her tears, Tasha straightened her shoulders. She wouldn't let Miles, or anyone else, break her. She had to be strong for her mother, for herself, and, most importantly, for Sasha.

***

A thousand eyes seemed to press down on Tasha as she sat in the front pew. Cookie's casket, adorned with a spray of lilies, stood serenely in the center of the church. Sasha remained hospitalized, still in the process of recovery, and couldn't attend. Pastor Miles, cloaked in his black robes, delivered a stirring eulogy. The forced smiles and averted gazes from the congregation did little to ease the turmoil within Tasha. Miles, she knew, had been subtly painting her as the jealous wife, the one consumed by possessiveness. He'd reactivated old insecurities from her childhood, whispering doubts about her trust in him to the deacon board. Even the church leaders started looking at her differently, believing the lies. It was like a double betrayal. Her husband was cheating on her, but he made it seem like she was the problem. He twisted the truth so people wouldn't focus on his own mistakes. And sadly, some people in the church believed him. Now, the church that once embraced her felt cold and distant.

Miles' voice boomed throughout the building. Tasha barely heard a word. Her mind was a battlefield, replaying her phone call with Sarah and the icy confirmation it brought. Yet, a sliver of awareness kept a tiny part of her mind alert, focused on the man standing at the podium.

Throughout the service, a sickening pattern emerged. The first subtle interaction occurred during a particularly moving passage in the eulogy. Miles' eyes, usually filled with a practiced sincerity, seemed to trace for a fleeting moment towards a pew on the opposite side. It was a barely perceptible movement, but Tasha caught it. Seated there, bathed in the glow of a stained-glass window, was Michele, a young woman from the church choir known for her bubbly personality and enthusiastic greetings. Michele, who always seemed to find reasons to brush past Tasha, offered a too-bright smile and a touch that lingered a beat too long.

The second instance came during a hymn. As the congregation sang, Tasha watched their reflection in the polished casket. Michele's gaze met Miles' across the room. A secret smile played on her lips, a knowing glint in her eyes before she quickly looked away with a demure flutter of her eyelashes.

The final straw came with the closing prayer. Miles' hand hovered over the podium for a moment, then reached back as if to steady himself. Tasha's peripheral vision caught a movement – Michele reached forward and squeezed his fingers briefly. The gesture was so subtle, so intimate, that only someone keenly observing would have noticed. But Tasha saw. She saw the flicker in Miles' eyes, which was something other than grief. It was confirmation. The pieces of the puzzle slammed into place and formed a picture that left her reeling.

Rage threatened to consume her. This woman, sitting smugly within the very walls of their faith, had been carrying on an affair with her husband right under her nose. The hypocrisy of it all burned. *How could Miles stand there, preaching about love and devotion, while his actions screamed betrayal?* The audacity of these two humans boggled her mind.

The anger simmered within her. Her eyes narrowed. She didn't want to cry, but the hurt consumed her heart. Michele's saccharine smile, her touch on Miles' arm, the secret exchanges - each detail replayed in her mind, fueling a white-hot rage. Taking a shuddering breath, Tasha forced her clenched fists to relax. Tears, hot and angry, welled up again. With a shaky hand, she reached into her purse, pulled out a crumpled tissue, and dabbed at her eyes.

The urge to lash out, to scream accusations and tear Michele's smug facade to shreds was crushing in her mind. A caged beast strained against the bars of her heart. Her eyes filled with tears, but this time, they were fueled by a different fire. Grief had morphed into a steely resolve. She wouldn't let Miles, or this woman, break her.

As the throng of mourners began to disperse, she stood up from her seat. The hushed conversations of people had now become a dull roar in Tasha's ears. She could see Michele lingering near the back of the church, feigning a moment of quiet reflection, but her eyes darted nervously around the room, searching for a specific face. It was a calculated move, designed to project an image of piety while subtly keeping tabs on the crowd's attention. She knew Tasha would be busy greeting condolences, and this strategic positioning allowed Michele to have some moments with Miles alone, all while maintaining a presence that might garner sympathy from any lingering onlookers.

Tasha marched towards her, thudding against the polished wood floor. Her voice, when she spoke, was a tightly leashed growl, trembling with barely contained emotion. "You have a lot of nerve showing up here," she seethed. Her eyes blazed with a fire that could rival the midday sun.

Michele caught off guard, faltered for a moment. Then, a practiced smile flashed across her face. "Oh, Tasha," she cooed in a voice dripping with sugary sympathy. "I'm so terribly sorry for your loss. Your mother was a wonderful woman."

The insincerity in Michele's voice was like a match to a tinderbox. "Don't you dare speak of my mother!" Tasha roared. "You're a woman who preys on married men! You're a woman who finds comfort in another woman's misery! You have no right to even be in the same room as her memory!"

Suddenly, Tasha spotted Miles approaching from the other side of the church. His face was a mask of forced concern, but his eyes darted nervously between Tasha and Michele. The sight of him approaching, looking like a deer caught in headlights, only intensified Tasha's rage.

"And you!" She screamed, whirling towards Miles. "Where the hell have you been? Hiding behind your pious facade while your little girlfriend here parades around like she owns the place?"

Miles stammered with panic. "Tasha, honey, what's going on here? Michele, is she alright?"

Michele's facade wavered completely. Her eyes narrowed, replacing the practiced piety. "What are you talking about, Tasha? I don't even know what you're talking about!" She protested as her voice took on a shrill edge.

Tasha leaned in her face inches from Michele's. "Don't play dumb with me," she hissed. "The way you look at him, the secret touches – I saw it all. You're the reason for the late nights, the distance between me and Miles! You're a parasite feeding off another woman's misery. You cunning homewrecker!"

Family members looked on with shock, grief and anger. Most were hesitant to get involved in Tasha's tantrum. They felt this was out of her character and she was overwhelmed with grief of her mother's passing. Whatever she was confronting must have been necessary, and she needed to handle her business.

Greg, felt the same way. He walked over toward Tasha, and placed his hand on her shoulder, not to calm her but to suggest he got her back. Not saying a word, his eyes gave Miles the look of death, daring him to disrespect his sister and warning him to walk lightly. Pastor or no pastor.

Hearing Tasha screaming, Michele bristled. "That's a lie! Miles and I are just friends, coworkers at best. You're the one who's been pushing him away, Tasha, with your jealousy and possessiveness! Don't put your misery and your lack of competitiveness to be a good wife on other people!"

Infuriated by Michele's denial, Tasha raised her hand with lightning speed and delivered a stinging slap across the woman's face. Michele's head whipped to the side as the surprise momentarily wiped the smug smirk from her face. A crimson handprint blossomed on her cheek.

The loud crack echoed through the church, and everyone's gazes turned toward the two women. A gasp rippled through the mourners, several of whom were coming toward Tasha to offer their final condolences. Eyes widened in shock, and the hushed conversations were replaced by stunned silence. The deacon, who had been on his way out, froze in his tracks. Even Miles, who had been stammering pleas for calm, seemed momentarily stunned into silence.

Tasha was screaming at the top of her lungs now. "I? NOT A GOOD WIFE? You slithered into our lives, whispered your lies, and now you think you can just sinch in here and act innocent? I see right through you, you conniving little..." Tasha's voice trailed off, not because of a lack of words but because the venom in her tone spoke volumes.

Miles, caught in the crossfire, stammered, "Both of you calm down! Tasha, there's nothing going on here, I swear. Michele, maybe you should just head hom..."

Tasha cut him off with a vicious snarl. "Shut your lying mouth, Miles! Don't you dare try to play innocent with me! I know all about your little 'outings' for church business and your 'community center' that doesn't even exist. You've been sneaking around with this woman while my mother lay dying, and now you have the audacity to stand there and act like you have no idea what's going on? You disgust me!"

Michele, sensing an advantage, seized the opportunity. A cruel smile twisted her lips. "You're delusional, Tasha. Clearly, the stress of losing your mother has made you hysterical. I've never seen someone so desperate for attention," she sneered as her voice dripped with disdain.

Hearing this, Tasha's face contorted in a mask of fury, unlike anything Michele had ever seen. This wasn't anger anymore. This was a cold, primal rage that sent shivers down Miles' spine. He had never seen Tasha so angry.

Without a second thought, Tasha lunged forward, and a primal scream ripped from her throat. Her fists clenched into tight balls of fury and swung wildly. Each blow connected with a sickening thud. Michele caught completely off guard, crumpled backward like a ragdoll. Her carefully constructed facade shattered as panic flooded her eyes. A raw, animalistic terror stripped away any pretense. The fake façade of the choir girl vanished, replaced by a trembling wreck. Her arms flailed helplessly, attempting to fend off Tasha's onslaught but failing miserably.

The spectators gasped in shock as Tasha hit Michele. "Oh my God!" A woman cried, clutching her pearls. A man stammered, "Someone stop them! This is getting out of hand!" An older woman shook her head sadly, muttering, "Did you see that? Poor Pastor Miles, having to deal with such a violent wife."

But there was nothing stopping Tasha. With each

strike, she felt a small measure of catharsis that had been building within her. It wasn't a clean or satisfying feeling, but it was cathartic. Finally, spent and her knuckles raw, Tasha stumbled back, her chest heaving like a bellows.

Michele slumped against a pew, blood trickling from a split lip and a dark bruise appearing on her cheek. Her once picture-perfect image was a grotesque parody of itself. Tasha felt no joy in her victory, only a chilling emptiness that mirrored the betrayal that had ripped a hole through her life.

"You will stay away from my family! You will stay away from Miles!" Tasha screamed. "And if I ever see you so much as glance at him again, I swear I'll rip your extensions out and shove them so far down your throat you'll choke on your own hypocrisy!"

As the stunned congregation looked on in shock, Tasha turned around. She could hear their hushed whispers, the sting of their judgment sharper than any physical wound. Walking past the people, she could hear the murmurs and the scoffs, whispering, "Always knew there was something off about her. So jealous and possessive."

With a deep breath, she strode out of the church, leaving behind a trail of shocked whispers and the wreckage of her shattered life.

Chapter 17

Sasha's hospital room seemed less daunting with Rashaun by her side. Days of beeping monitors and the scent of disinfectant had taken their toll, but the sight of his smile brought a genuine grin to her lips.

"Hey, stranger," Sasha rasped as she saw Rashaun entering the room. Her voice was weak but filled with warmth.

Rashaun pulled up a chair beside her bed, his broad form dwarfing the hospital furniture. In his hand, he cradled a bouquet of sunflowers. The bright yellow blooms seemed to radiate sunshine and added a burst of color against the stark white of the room. "Hey yourself," he said, giving her the flowers. "Doc said you finally get to escape this torture chamber today."

"About damn time," Sasha chuckled in a dry but genuine sound. "This bed is starting to feel like home, and that's not a good thing. Thanks for the flowers, Rashaun . They're beautiful."

Rashaun nodded. A drop of worry crossed his face

before he quickly masked it with a grin. "Speaking of escaping, the doctor said it's okay if you take a short walk on the hospital grounds. Wanna get some fresh air?"

The prospect of escaping the room was too tempting to resist. "Fresh air," Sasha mused, "that sounds like a dream."

With the help of a nurse, Sasha managed to stand. Her legs wobbled from disuse, weakened by the ordeal she had endured. Rashaun took her hand and placed it around his waist as he placed his around hers. His touch was warm and reassuring. They shuffled out of the room and walked past the corridor into the garden outside.

The hospital grounds were beautiful. Lush green lawns stretched before them, dotted with colorful flowerbeds. Sunlight dappled through the leaves of mature oak trees, casting shadows on the manicured lawn. A gentle breeze whispered through the branches, carrying the sweet scent of blooming flowers. Hearing the birds chirp made Sasha feel at ease after a long time.

Sasha leaned against Rashaun , taking a deep breath of fresh air. Rashaun then helped her settle on a bench beneath a sprawling oak tree. For a moment, she almost forgot the ordeal she had been through and the uncertainty that loomed ahead.

"Thanks for coming by," Sasha whispered.

Rashaun squeezed her hand gently. "No way I was letting you face this alone," he said, his voice gruff but kind.

Smiling, she lowered her head. "Should we walk a little?" She asked.

They walked in comfortable silence for a while. Over the past few days, they had formed an unspoken bond. Neither of them needed to fill the quiet of their walk with words. Just being together, sharing that stolen moment outside the confines of worry, was enough.

Finally, Sasha stopped, leaning against a lamp pole. "You know….," she said, her voice quiet but determined, "I don't know what I would have done without you."

Rashaun met her gaze. "Don't even think about it," he said firmly. "I'll always be there for you, Sasha."

Two tiny wet pearls appeared in her eyes. It wasn't just his words; it was the way he said them, the raw sincerity behind his gruff exterior. Sometimes, she thought she had found a family in Rashaun .

"You're right," she said, pulling herself together.

"You know, seeing you fight this…it reminds me of something," Rashaun said as they started walking again.

Sasha turned to him, her brow furrowed in curiosity. "What's that?"

"When I was a child, Sasha, I used to talk about wrestling all the time. I was always such a big fan. I'd devour wrestling magazines, memorize all the wrestlers' moves, and even argue with friends about who would win in a dream match."

A soft smile tugged at the corners of Sasha's lips. "Haha, that's cute! Ultimate Pain, the ferocious grappler with the iron grip. You are your dream wrestler, aren't you, Mr. Charmer!"

Rashaun chuckled. "That's me. Used to be, anyway." His smile faltered.

Sasha frowned. "What do you mean?"

"It wasn't that long ago, actually. You even came to see me fight, remember? That brutal match against The

Pulverizer? After that match, I had another. I was practicing big time for it. I was also not able to return your calls during those days because it was a tough one..."

He paused for a moment and then continued as they sat on the bench again, looking into his lap. "The day came, and we were neck and neck the whole time. The crowd was going wild.

Then, in the final moments, I went for my signature move, the Ultimate Crusher. But..." he winced slightly, his hand instinctively reaching for his lower back, "...something went wrong. I landed wrong and felt a searing pain shoot up my spine. The Pulverizer capitalized on the opening, and that was it. The ref called the match."

Sasha's eyes squinted, then widened in realization.

Rashaun nodded slowly. "The doctors diagnosed it as a herniated disc. Surgery could fix it, but the recovery time would be brutal, and there were no guarantees I'd ever get back in the ring at the same level. It was a tough decision, but ultimately, I had to listen to my body."

A heavy silence descended between them for a moment. Sasha could only imagine the disappointment

Rashaun must have felt, his wrestling dreams shattered in a single, agonizing moment. Then, she took his hands in hers and said lowly, "Rashaun, I'm so sorry to hear this."

He met her gaze, a wry smile playing on his lips. "Ummm, Yeah. Life's just like that." His eyes softened as he looked at her. "Seeing you fight through this whole ordeal, Sasha... it's like watching a champion. You're stronger than you think."

Sasha felt a warmth and burden at the same time spreading through her chest. Rashaun noticed the change in her expression and completely turned in her direction. "What happened?"

"There's something I need to tell you, too," Sasha said in a low voice that Raushan could barely hear.

"What is it, Sasha? You can tell me anything," Rashaun said, worry clearly etched on his face.

Sasha took a deep breath, steeling herself for the revelation she was about to make. "I was raped," she confessed in a trembling voice. "It happened that night..."

Rashaun 's smile faded, replaced by a look of shock and concern. He reached out, his hand hovering gently over hers. "Sasha... I'm so sorry. I had no idea. I can't even begin to imagine what you've been through."

Tears welled up in Sasha's eyes, but she forced them back. "It's okay. I'm here now, and that's what matters. But there's more..." she hesitated, then blurted out the words, "I'm pregnant."

Rashaun 's eyes widened in surprise. He stared at her for a long moment, processing the information. Then, a slow smile spread across his face.

"Wow," he breathed. "That's... that's a lot to take in. But Sasha," he squeezed her hand gently, "no matter what you decide, you have my support. One hundred percent."

Sasha squeezed his hand back. "I know," she whispered. "And I've decided. I'm keeping the baby."

Rashaun kept looking at her silently as she said the words with complete certainty. Sasha continued, "I know it's going to be hard. But I know I can do this."

Raushan put a hand on Sasha's cheek and looked right into her eyes. "You're a warrior, my love," he said in a firm yet gentle voice. "And you'll find me by your side every step of the way. It's scary, yes, but we're in this together,

Sasha. You and me, a team. And together, we can do anything."

He didn't wait for her reaction and pulled her into a protective hug.

***

The silence of her lawyer's office felt suffocating compared to the emotions churning within Tasha. The divorce papers, crisp and official, lay in her lap. She looked away from her lap and gazed outside the window. The world outside was buzzing with activity while she sat there, empty and muffled from within.

Gone was her naive belief that the church was her place of comfort. The whispers, judgmental stares, and the feeling of being ostracized had chipped away at the foundation of her faith, leaving behind a hollow shell. The very place where she made her escape from childhood trauma now felt like a source of pain.

"Are you sure about this, Tasha?" Her lawyer's voice cut through the fog, clouding her mind.

She lifted her head, her gaze flickering to the papers in her hand. "Yes," she said. "I'm sure." Each word felt like a shard of glass cutting through her throat.

The lawyer was a kind woman with weary eyes who had seen the wreckage of countless marriages. She nodded her head, understanding. "I understand this is a difficult time for you. But remember, you deserve a fresh start."

Tasha managed a ghost of a smile, but it didn't reach her eyes. *A fresh start.* The words echoed in her mind. *Did she? Could she build a new life on the ashes of the old one?*

As she signed the papers, Tasha ensured that the divorce decree would not only dissolve her marriage but also smear his clergy record irreparably. She made certain that the document bore his infidelity and abandonment, listing adultery and abandonment as the reasons for their divorce. Tasha knew the implications. It would tarnish Miles' pristine reputation, a price he would have to pay for his deceit. As she signed her name, she knew that she was holding him accountable for his actions and reclaiming her own agency in the process.

As she walked out of the office, the city lights seemed to mock her with their indifferent twinkle. The accustomed streets felt alien. The isolation, her once-feared enemy, now felt like a comforting blanket, a shield against the world's harsh gaze.

She hailed a cab and headed home…a home she built upon love and understanding. *Love…understanding…or lies?* She thought.

The house felt suffocating now. Empty spaces echoed with memories, reminding her of what she'd lost. Miles hadn't come home after that day. Tasha wandered through the rooms like a ghost in her own life.

The news of her outburst at the church had spread like wildfire, whispers and sideways glances following her like a shroud. The community now felt like a judgmental jury. Each interaction felt like a fresh betrayal, chipping away at the fragile foundation of her sanity.

Although she'd filed for divorce, it felt like a bitter pill to swallow. The church had failed her in the worst way possible. She doubted her loyalty to the church now. So, armed with the knowledge of Miles' infidelity, she ensured the divorce decree wouldn't be a clean break. The document was a stark contrast to the vows they'd exchanged years ago, cited adultery and abandonment. It was a public stain on his record, a necessary blow delivered with steely resolve.

Yet, a hollow victory couldn't fill the gaping hole in her heart. The urge to crawl back into her childhood shell, to retreat into the familiar isolation, was overwhelming. The world outside seemed a hostile place, filled with judgment and pain. Her phone remained uncharged, messages unanswered, and social media accounts deactivated. Human connection now felt like a liability. The safest place, she believed, was within the confines of her own mind, a place where the storm of emotions wouldn't be visible to the judging eyes of the world.

She settled on the couch and curled up, pulling a worn blanket around her shoulders. Sleep was nowhere near her eyes. Each closed-eye vision was a display of betrayal, hurt, and the crushing weight of disappointment. She felt hurt, angry and embarrassed. A white-hot ember still flared with every memory of Miles's deceit and burned in her gut. Every time she thought about the incident at the church, humiliation seared her skin. She was confused about whether they both even deserved her words…her anger…her tears.

Tasha knew confronting the storm raging within was the only way forward. Yet, the thought of facing the world, of rebuilding her life on the shattered foundation of her trust, filled her with a paralyzing fear.

As days went by, Tasha spent more time alone, finding comfort in being by herself. She wanted to avoid the outside world and the hurt it caused her. In her time alone, she thought a lot about herself and what she wanted. Even though she felt lonely, she believed that being by herself would help her become stronger and figure out who she really was.

***

The morning light speared through the blinds, making Tasha toss in her bed. It was an unwelcome intrusion into Tasha's numb slumber. She lay there in a crumpled heap of blankets and despair. Every muscle in her body ached. It was a dull, throbbing protest against the emotional turmoil within her. Pulling herself out of bed felt like scaling a mountain. Each step she took felt like a victory against the crushing storm within her that threatened to pin her down.

Tasha dragged herself into the bathroom. The mirror in front of her reflected a stranger. Her eyes were now hollowed out and rimmed with dark circles. Her usually bouncy curls lay limp and lifeless. The strands clung to her brush as she ran it through them. A clump of hair caught in the bristles, and a sob escaped her lips. It was a raw and guttural sound that echoed in her bathroom.

The shower water was too hot, scalding her skin, yet it provided no comfort for the fire raging within. Tears mingled with the steaming water, blurring the world around her.

Why? she screamed into the emptiness. *Why me? I followed the path I believed in! Dedicated myself fully! WHERE IS THE REWARD? Where is the explanation for this utter devastation?*

Her reflection mocked her. Gone was the woman who radiated a quiet strength. In her place stood an empty woman.

As she trudged back to her bedroom, the physical toll of her emotional chaos manifested itself. Her stomach churned, and a nauseating sensation threatened to erupt at any moment. Reaching for her sweater, a wave of dizziness washed over her, forcing her to cling to the dresser for support. The wave was so intense it felt like the room was spinning. Her heart pounded in her chest, and she gasped for breath.

Fear, cold and sharp, pricked at her. This wasn't just

sadness. This wasn't just heartbreak. This was a physical display of her misery, a warning sign she couldn't ignore. She knew she was going deeper into depression but had no idea what to do with her life anymore. Therapy felt like an admission of defeat, and meeting people was the farthest thought in her mind.

Was this what it came to? Admitting defeat, confessing that she wasn't enough?

But deep inside her heart, she knew she would have to fight back to get on her feet and reclaim her life, her purpose, on her own terms.

Chapter 18

In the dimly lit gym, the loud clang of metal reverberated, accompanied by Rashaun 's deep, guttural grunts. Sweat dripped from his brow, stinging his eyes, but he barely noticed. With every repetition, with every set, he unleashed a battle cry against the constraints his body had imposed upon him.

He pushed himself even harder, feeling the weights on the bench press lighter than they had ever been before. Or maybe it was just the cocktail of pre-workout supplements coursing through his veins – it was a concoction he'd concocted himself after exhausting every legal option to boost his performance.

Looking at his reflection in the mirror, he saw a distorted image of his former self, like a caricature. His strained t-shirt revealed bulging, defined muscles, which were a stark contrast to the leaner, more agile physique he once possessed. But the sculpted form couldn't mask the haunted look in his eyes; there was a trace of desperation battling in them with a simmering rage.

The doctor's words repeated in his head: "The

damage is permanent, Rashaun . Your wrestling career is over." Refusing to believe it, he made denial his best friend. It was a powerful emotion, this denial. It whispered in his ear, telling him that the doctor was wrong, that this couldn't be the end. It told him to keep pushing, to train even harder, to prove everyone wrong. But deep down, a tiny seed of doubt had been planted, and it gnawed at him, slowly chipping away at his confidence.

Still, he wouldn't accept it. He couldn't. Wrestling was more than just a career; it was his identity, his escape. The roar of the crowd seemed to him as the only validation of his very existence. Without it, he felt adrift, a caged lion deprived of the hunt. He was angry, not only at himself and the circumstances but at everyone else, too.

Finishing up his last reps of the day, he wiped the sweat off his forehead. The young man wiping down the benches flinched as Rashaun practically threw the towel at him, barking, "Didn't your mama teach you to clean up after yourself?" The man didn't respond and took away the towel.

Lately, he wasn't feeling like himself. He snapped at the gym staff for minor inconveniences. The girl at the front desk stammered an apology when she couldn't find his protein shake right away, earning a tirade about inefficiency and wasted time. Even the gruff weightlifter in the corner, used to the testosterone-fueled atmosphere of the gym, raised an eyebrow at Rashaun 's excessive aggression over a dropped weight plate.

But whenever Rashaun met Sasha or Greg, he didn't let them know anything about it. He joked and laughed and made sure she was okay. The charade was exhausting, but the thought of burdening them with his internal turmoil was unbearable.

One evening, he visited Sasha at the hospital. She talked about the difficulties of dealing with morning sickness during pregnancy. Out of nowhere, he felt exhausted.

"Just handle it!" He exclaimed, his voice sounding harsher than he meant it to.

Sasha's smile faded. "Rashaun ," she said. "What's wrong?"

He felt ashamed. He hadn't meant to lash out. Taking a deep breath, he forced a smile. "Nothing, just... stressed about work."

It was a flimsy excuse, but Sasha didn't pry. Later

that night, replaying the incident in his mind, he felt angry at his own self. He slammed his fist against the wall. He knew it wasn't healthy, this blind pursuit of a lost dream fueled by rage and denial. Yet, the thought of letting go, of accepting his fate, terrified him. *He was Rashaun 'The Ultimate Pain,' the wrestling champion. Without that identity, who was he?*

Staring at his reflection, a single tear rolled down his cheek. The steroid-fueled strength felt hollow, a cheap substitute for the real thing. He craved the roar of the crowd, the adrenaline rush of the fight. But most of all, he craved to feel like himself again, the man before the injury, the man Sasha saw - strong, dependable, but not consumed by bitterness.

He closed his eyes. Deep inside, he knew that he had to find a way out of this self-destructive spiral. For Sasha. For the unborn child. For himself. He didn't know how, but he had to find a way to let go of the past and embrace the uncertain future that lay ahead. But he couldn't. The image of himself, broken and defeated, on the wrestling mat was too vivid. It was a reminder of his failure. He punched his hand against the wall again, this time even harder.

***

A gentle breeze rustled the leaves outside the hospital window, making playful shadows on the white bedsheets. Sasha was no longer a prisoner of IV lines and sterile smells. She sat at the edge of the bed with a canvas tote bag filled with her belongings at her feet. She felt nervous yet excited. Today, she was going home.

Gazing out the window, she watched the world outside resume its persistent course. Cars streamed by, oblivious to the ordeal she'd endured within these walls. The past few weeks had been a blur of tests, procedures, and forced vulnerability. She thought about the day she was brought it, the numbness she felt that day. Placing a hand on her tummy, she felt the tiny life growing within her.

Just then, Rashaun bustled in with a bouquet of sunflowers – her favorite – held high. Their yellow petals brightened the room, mirroring the hopeful smile on his face. "Ready to get outta here, champ?" He boomed, brimming with enthusiasm.

Sasha chuckled a warm sound that tickled the edges of her still-healing body. "As ready as I'll ever be, I guess."

He handed her the flowers and planted a soft kiss on her forehead. "These beauties are to remind you that even through all this darkness, there's still sunshine."

"Thanks, Rashaun . They're perfect," she replied, smiling.

Raushan saw Sasha's hand unconsciously placed on her tummy. He placed his hand on top of hers and gave her a warm, gentle smile. After a moment of comfortable silence, an excited twinkle appeared in his eyes.

"Hmmm, so have you thought about names? I'm partial to something strong, like... Rocky, for a boy, or maybe Sierra, for a girl."

Sasha laughed. "Rocky? Seriously?"

"Hey, it's a classic!" Rashaun defended himself with a playful grin. "But seriously, what do you think?"

Sasha pondered for a moment. "I don't know yet. Maybe we should wait until we meet them, see what feels right."

Rashaun nodded thoughtfully. "That's fair enough. But you know, if it's a girl, I'm vetoing any names with too many frills. No princesses in this household."

Sasha swatted him playfully on the arm. "Don't

200

worry, I won't turn our child into a damsel in distress. But a little bit of femininity never hurt anyone."

Initially a shock, the news of her pregnancy settled into a quiet excitement. Even with the challenges ahead, the prospect of holding a piece of herself in her arms brought a sad smile to her lips.

The discharge nurse arrived with a list of instructions and prescriptions. Finally, the moment arrived. Rashaun carried her bags in one hand and placed his other arm around her waist as they walked out of the hospital doors.

The world outside felt overwhelming after weeks of confinement. The car horns, the chatter of pedestrians, the colors of blooming trees – it was a sensory explosion that threatened to topple her over. Yet, she felt strangely refreshed.

Taking a deep breath of fresh air, Sasha looked up at the vastness of the sky. Freedom. It was a simple concept, but it felt like a precious gift. She was finally going home.

Rashaun hailed a cab. Sasha couldn't help but lean closer to Rashaun , seeking his warmth.

He met her gaze, his eyes mirroring her own mix of

apprehension and determination.

"Ready?" He whispered.

Sasha squeezed his hand. "Ready," she whispered back.

The ride home was filled with a comfortable silence, punctuated by the occasional squeeze of Rashaun 's hand on hers. Pulling up to her house, Sasha's eyes widened in surprise. Gone were the usual bland decorations; twinkling fairy lights cascaded down the front porch. The windows of her house were gleaming from inside.

With a mischievous grin, Rashaun helped her out of the cab. As they entered, Sasha gasped. Her living room had been transformed. The pleasant smell of fragrant candles flickered on the coffee table, and a trail of rose petals led to the balcony, where a table for two awaited, adorned with a white tablecloth and her favorite china.

Tears welled up in her eyes again, this time tears of joy. "Rashaun ," she breathed, her voice thick with emotion, "this is..."

"Beautiful?" He finished, his voice laced with a nervous tremor. "Just a small token of my appreciation for the strongest woman I know."

He pulled out a chair for her, then walked to the balcony railing, his back to her for a moment. When he turned around, he held a small velvet box between his thumb and forefinger.

"Sasha," he began, his voice shaking slightly, "these past few weeks have been some of the hardest of my life. Seeing you fight, your strength, your spirit... it made me realize just how much you mean to me. You're not just a friend, Sasha. You're my rock, my confidante, my everything. And this little one we have on the way," he gestured gently to her stomach, "it fills me with a joy I never thought possible."

He knelt on one knee, his eyes filled with a love so deep it took her breath away. "Sasha," he continued, opening the velvet box to reveal a dazzling diamond ring, "Will you marry me?" He stopped for a moment and looked directly into her eyes, full of tears. Sasha was silent. He continued again. "Will you face this crazy, unpredictable journey we call life with me by my side? Will you be my wife?"

Tears streamed down Sasha's face. "Yes," she choked out, nodding her head. "Yes, Rashaun . A thousand times, yes!"

Rashaun 's face lit up with a smile that bloomed like a flower catching the morning sun. He slid the ring onto her finger. It was a perfect fit. Sasha felt like she couldn't speak. Her eyes spoke volumes of the emotional rollercoaster she'd been on.

Before she could even react, Rashaun launched himself into her arms, burying his face in her neck. The hug was fierce. Sasha wanted to cry her heart out in that moment and she did. She buried her face in her chest and felt the most protected she ever had. Rashaun held her tight as his own tears dampened her hair. They both couldn't believe they were ready to start a life together.

Chapter 19

The fluorescent light of the bathroom felt harsh against Sasha's face as she stared at the small, orange pill in her palm. She had been taking these anxiety medicines for a while now as it had settled in her chest. With a sigh, she popped the pill into her mouth.

Tonight was particularly bad. Every shadow in the house seemed to hold a lurking menace, and every creak of the floorboards sent a shiver down her spine. She traced the gentle curve of her stomach and tried to feel a subconscious reassurance that someone was there by her side. The tiny life growing there was a constant source of both wonder and fear.

Coming out of the bathroom, suddenly, a sniffle escaped her lips, catching her by surprise. The tears welled up in her eyes as she saw her reflection turn from normal to distorted into a crying face. Collapsing onto the floor, she wrapped her arms around her knees as her cries filled the small space.

WHY ME? The question played on repeat in her mind. *Why wasn't my life like the ones in the glossy magazines? Why didn't I have a picture-perfect family and happiness? Why was I raped! Why was I raped from childhood!*

Sasha could now feel her nose running. She put her head up and sniffed her nose, but the tears kept flowing. She buried her face in her hands and started crying again.

Why am I pregnant? It's like my body's holdin' onto that night! Why I gotta be walkin' this tightrope all the time, feelin' like one wrong step could send me spiralin' outta control?

As she cried, the dam holding back the memories seemed to crack. Memories played in front of her eyes like a video. Memories from her childhood…teenage… adulthood. Memories were overshadowed by the moments she was taken into the quiet room and raped several times a week while her mother knew everything. Her teenage years that were often filled with her leading down the wrong path. And then, him. The man who had violated her body and her very sense of safety.

The pill had dimmed the edge of her panic, but the raw emotions distressed her, demanding to be heard. As she cried, the carefully constructed walls of her past crumbled, revealing a lifetime of burdens.

"WHY WHY WHY! " she choked out in a voice thick with tears, "Why me? Why is my life so messed up?"

Memories flooded back like a torrent of pain threatening to drown her. She wasn't just reliving the assault, the violation that had ripped through her sense of security. It went deeper into a tangled web of experiences that had shaped her into the woman she was today.

She saw herself, a small child, cowering in the corner, trying to escape the touch of her molester.

Then, the blinding light, the deafening gunshot, the raw grief of losing her mother's boyfriend and her beloved sister, Sade, all in a single, horrific moment. The anger, the confusion, it had turned her into a bully, lashing out at anyone within reach, pushing away family and friends with a barbed tongue.

The image of Ava replayed in front of her eyes. She was her childhood friend with whom she'd sexually experimented, and to this day, she didn't know why she did that. In her teenage years, that confusion transformed into resentment and bloomed a poisonous seed that strained her relationship with Ava.

"Am I even good enough to be loved? To be a wife? To be a mother? Didn't my past, my mistakes make me unworthy of happiness?" The self-loathing whispered its cruel verdict: she didn't deserve it.

She sank to the floor once again and wrapped her arms tightly around her knees as if to contain the hurricane within. She put her head up again and looked at the ceiling. Her gaze was distant, as if not seeing the ceiling itself but looking far beyond it.

"Do I even deserve happiness? Am I even good enough to be anything to anyone?" Her cries had become louder, and now she was speaking out loud.

"I need help. I need the strength to rewrite this story. I want to be a good mother, a loving wife, a better person. I don't know if I deserve happiness, but I want a chance. I want to find it, for myself, for this child, for Rashaun !

Sasha sobbed uncontrollably as the emptiness of the room swallowed her cries. Moments ago, she'd been all over the place crying high, but now only sadness remained. A crushing guilt squeezed her chest. Cookie's face, filled with so much left unsaid, popped into her head. Sasha hadn't forgiven her before she died, and there was nothing left now except for regret. Cookie's cries that day at Miles' office echoed in her head, "Sasha, please, baby... I'm so sorry." Hearing the words in her head again and again made her tears flow even faster. The pain was unbearable. She couldn't fix the broken bond now. She was gone...gone forever. On top of everything else, the deep ache of losing her mom mixed with the waves of manic depression pulled her under a dark tide of despair.

***

The doorbell's chime sliced through the quiet of Sasha's house. Wiping her hands on a dishcloth, she hurried to the door. Peeking through the peephole, she felt relieved. It was Tasha and Greg.

"Hey guys!" Sasha forced a smile, ushering them inside. "Come in, come in. It's so good to see you both."

Tasha stepped inside, and her eyes took in the house. Gone was the usual clutter; some calm orderliness had taken its place.

"Sasha!" Tasha exclaimed, pulling her into a tight

hug. "We were so worried! How are you holding up?"

"Hey there, champ," Greg added. He handed Sasha a bouquet of sunflowers. "These are for you."

Sasha's smile widened genuinely this time. "Oh, these are beautiful, Greg. Thank you both so much for coming. It means a lot."

Greg pulled her away and looked at her. "But really, Sasha, how you doin' for real? We were worried sick about you."

"I'm... I'm gettin' there," she admitted but then tried to cut the conversation short. She then quickly ushered them inside and led them to the living room. The remnants of a half-finished puzzle lay scattered on the coffee table. "Would you guys like some coffee? Tea?"

Tasha sank onto the couch, her eyes scanning the room. "Tea sounds lovely, honey. Mind you when I say this, the place looks a lot better, Sasha!"

"Oh yeah, thanks. Just trying to organize this all a bit," she said and then added in a low voice that she could only hear herself. "...and life too, maybe."

"Sasha," Tasha spoke, feeling her unusually calm demeanor. "You are so strong. Don't you ever forget that? And don't you ever forget that we're always there for you!"

"Yeah," Greg chimed in. "You're right, Tasha. Sasha, we're here for you every step of the way. Any time you need me, just hit me up, and I'll be there."

"Thanks, guys. I really appreciate it. You know, speaking of people I need to catch up with... how's Pastor Cheater?" Sasha responded.

Tasha hesitated for a moment. Her carefree demeanor shifted into a more serious one. She exchanged a loaded glance with Greg before turning back to Sasha. Taking a deep breath, she announced, "Sasha, Greg... there's something I need to tell you both."

Greg leaned forward. Sasha sat on the sofa opposite to Tasha. "What is it?" She asked.

Tasha straightened her back. "I'm getting a divorce."

Greg, as if already expecting this to happen, placed his hand on Tasha's shoulder. Sasha's mouth opened slightly. She raised an eyebrow as if to question, "What's happening here?"

"Well," she confessed. "Remember what I told you about him last we met?"

A dawning realization spread across Sasha's face. "Wait," she exclaimed, "so, he was really..."

"Cheating on me? With someone at the church, no less?" Tasha finished the sentence as a bitter laugh escaped her lips. "Yeah, that's exactly what I think. Turns out, 'Pastor Cheater' is exactly what he is!"

Sasha's eyes blazed with fury. "That lying sack of shit!!" She roared, her fists clenching and unclenching at her sides. "How dare he do that to you, especially after everything you've been through with Mom!"

Greg reached out and placed a calming hand on Sasha's shoulder. "Woah, woah, Sasha. Easy there. We'll get through this together, alright?"

Sasha took a deep breath, trying to tamp down the urge to march right down to the church and confront Miles herself. "Greg!" She sputtered, her voice trembling with anger, "He's a pastor! Doesn't he know thou shalt not cheat on thy wife!!!"

Tasha nodded. "That's what hurts the most, Sasha.

The hypocrisy of it all. Here he was, preaching about fidelity and family up in that pulpit, all the while carryin' on with other women."

She didn't want to, but her eyes became teary. "You weren't there, Sasha, but he wasn't around much after Mom passed. Always 'attending conferences,' 'meeting with church officials,' always some excuse." She wiped away a stray tear with the back of her hand. "Turns out those conferences were just a cover for his little affairs."

"And the worst part?" She continued, dropping to a low hiss. "He wasn't even discreet about it. Found another little home in South Philly, a love nest for his little escapades. Wouldn't come home, wouldn't answer my calls... and the church board started looking at me like I was the crazy one, jealous of his 'interactions' with the other women at church."

Tasha became angry recalling everything. "He planted those seeds, you know? Made me out to be the overly possessive wife. He deflected suspicion from himself, pinning it all on me."

Greg gasped as the pieces finally clicked into place. "That's why everyone at the funeral was acting so weird towards you! I thought it was just grief..."

Tasha let out a humorless chuckle. "Grief? Honey, that was the least of my worries. There I was, at Mom's funeral, surrounded by people judging me because of his lies."

Her voice hardened with anger. "He even had the audacity to officiate the service! And all the while, he was carrying on with that... that Michele woman!" She spat out the name with disgust.

"Michele?" Sasha furrowed her brow. "Who's Michele?"

Tasha's jaw clenched tight. "His little church fling. The one who kept batting her eyelashes at him during the service, right in front of everyone! Three times, Sasha! Three times, I saw them exchanging these long, lingering glances. The nerve of those two! They thought no one would notice!"

Tasha continued. "And you know what happened when I finally confronted her? In front of everyone, no less? She had the audacity to play the innocent victim...."

Greg interrupted, finishing the story for Sasha. "And next thing I know, they were in a brawl right there in the church hall!"

Sasha winced as her eyes widened in surprise. "Oh, man! Oh, man! How I would have paid to see Tasha fighting anyone! Tasha, the ever-calm voice of reason, beating the shit outta a woman! Would have been a lovely sight indeed!"

Tasha sighed. "It was a mess, Sasha. A total mess!"

She looked at Sasha and Greg. "This divorce, it's not just about him cheating. It's about reclaiming my life, my dignity. He doesn't get to control me anymore."

Greg squeezed her hand gently. "You're right, Tasha. You're a strong woman. And you deserve so much better than him. We'll be here for you every step of the way, you hear? Whatever you need, whatever you want to do, we're behind you."

A smile touched Tasha's lips. "Thanks, Greg."

Greg paused for a moment and then tried to lighten the conversation. "So, have you guys seen the new bakery that opened up down the street? They have these amazing cinnamon rolls..."

Sasha, sensing how Greg was trying to calm them

down, tried to steer the conversation away. "Speaking of new beginnings," she said with a playful smile, "guess what?"

"What?" Sasha and Greg said in unison.

Sasha held out her hand as a smile bloomed on her face. As she wiggled her fingers, a sparkling diamond ring caught the light. "Look what I have!" She exclaimed.

Tasha's eyes widened in surprise. "Engaged? Sasha!" She stood from her couch and hugged her tightly. "Wait, is this that wrestler guy you mentioned about?"

Sasha let out a relieved laugh. "Yes! The one and only!"

Greg chuckled, scratching the back of his head. "Oh Sash! I'm so happy for you! This is fantastic news!"

Tasha felt genuinely excited for her sister. "Sasha, that sounds wonderful," she said. "I'm so happy for you. You deserve to be happy."

Her last sentence was the complete opposite of the constant train of thoughts in her head. But she didn't want them both to know anything about it, neither the anxiety nor the rape or the child. She felt a pang of guilt for not being entirely truthful, but the vulnerability of sharing her entire story, the fear of rejection, held her back. For now, this moment of joy was a much-needed oasis in the storm she was navigating.

Greg joined the hug, a wide grin spreading across his face. "Sash, throw a little engagement party, celebrate the good news!"

"We'll sure do!" Sasha responded.

After tea, they sat around the table discussing random conversations surrounding Mom's funeral when Tasha decided to reveal another piece of news. Looking at her siblings, she decided it was the best time to let them know it.

"You know," she began. "I want to dedicate my life to God. I want to help people, spread kindness…"

Sasha and Greg exchanged a surprised look, but their surprise quickly transformed into understanding support.

"Tasha," Sasha said gently. "Are you sure about this?"

Greg, on the other hand, leaned forward with a

thoughtful expression on his face. "Helping people, spreading kindness... that's something the world definitely needs more of. It doesn't have to be through a church, you know? You could volunteer, start your own initiative, find a way to connect with people on your own terms."

"Thank you guys," Tasha replied.

"That's what family's for, right?" Sasha grinned, pulling Tasha into another quick hug.

"Exactly," Greg chimed in. "Now, where were we before this whole revelation? Spill the tea, Sasha! Tell us all about this amazing fiancé of yours."

The afternoon sun dipped below the horizon as they talked and spent quality time together after ages. Tasha's phone buzzed and that's when she saw the time. She glanced at the screen, then back at her siblings.

"Wow, guys," she exclaimed. "Look at the time! I completely lost track of time."

"Well," Sasha boomed. "that settles it then. You're not going anywhere. We're ordering dinner, and you're staying put. Consider it a belated engagement celebration... family style."

Tasha hesitated for a moment, then a smile bloomed on her face. "Alright, you win," she conceded. "But you're in charge of the takeout menus!"

Chapter 20

Rashaun's mini mansion reeked of stale sweat and a metallic tang that made Rashaun wrinkle his nose. Empty beer cans littered the coffee table, and their condensation formed a sticky puddle. He slammed the cupboard shut, the sound echoing in the near-bare room. The trophies and workout posters were gone, and now there was emptiness like his own feelings.

Rashaun ran a hand through his hair. His once-thick curls were now thinning and felt dull. No reflection stared back from the grimy mirror above the sink. Just sunken cheeks and eyes that burned with a desperate hunger. The charming wrestler Sasha had fallen for was long gone. In his place stood a gaunt, jittery shell of a man with his eyes bloodshot and manic.

The steroids that once fueled his bodybuilding success now seemed like a far-off dream. He felt the need to turn to something else. The high from the cocaine was a fleeting thing and a cheap imitation of the power he used to get from steroids. But it was all he had left. The crackdown on performance enhancers had cut him off from his usual supplier, leaving him scrambling for anything to fill the void. He slammed his fist on the wall beside the mirror.

"Stupid body," he snarled at his reflection.

Coming toward the coffee table, he reached for the crumpled foil packet tucked behind the chipped mug. Cocaine. It was a cheap, desperate substitute that left him jittery and paranoid. He poured out the contents of the packet onto the already cluttered coffee table. It wasn't the soft, pharmaceutical-grade stuff he'd occasionally dabbled with before. This was rough, cut with something unknown, and a gamble every time he brought it to his nose. But the alternative - the emptiness, the constant, low-level hum of anxiety that clawed at his insides - was even more unbearable.

He tipped the packet to the edge of the coffee table, forming a small mountain. He closed his eyes as the image of his sculpted physique and the veins popping on his biceps flashed in his mind. It was a cruel reminder of what he'd lost. He took a deep breath, willing himself to ignore the metallic tang he knew was coming.

Cascading the white powder in a thin line amidst scattered cigarette butts and empty beer cans, he reached for the makeshift straw with shaking hands. But a primal need snagged at him. He glanced longingly at the half-empty bottle of whiskey by the window. *Maybe a sip, and then he could indulge in his craving?* he thought.

He stood and lunged for the table in a jerky and erratic movement. In his haste, his knee clipped the edge of the coffee table with a sickening scrape. The world seemed to tilt sideways for a horrifying moment before the carefully constructed line of powder went flying in a white dust cloud. A strangled cry escaped his lips as he watched the last of his precious escape scatter onto the stained floor. He froze as the makeshift straw dangled uselessly in his hand. The temporary high he'd craved was gone before it even arrived. It was the last of his drugs left.

Punching the wall beside the window in utter anger and desperation, he screamed but then stopped. Panic shot through him as he glanced out the window. There, huddled under the awning across the street, was Sasha. Rain plastered her hair to her face, and her clothes clung to her slender frame. *What is she doing here?* His heart hammered a frantic tattoo against his ribs. The state of his house – overflowing ashtrays, beer cans like fallen soldiers, and the stench of his desperation – was no place for her.

He scrambled to his feet. In a blur of motion, he shoved the empty beer cans into a trash bag, shoved the incriminating paraphernalia into a drawer, and yanked on a fresh shirt. He wasn't sure what story he would concoct, but he knew he couldn't let her see him like this. Not at all.

Just as he was about to close the curtains on the window, he saw Sasha walking the driveway. *She is coming!* Rashaun was now on his feet like never before. He quickly shoved his phone into his pocket and raced out the main door, catching her just as she was about to ring his doorbell.

"Sasha! What a surprise!" His voice, usually warm and inviting, emerged strained, but it would have to do. "Didn't expect to see you here tonight!"

Sasha spun around as a smile bloomed on her face. "Hey Rashaun! I was just in the neighborhood and thought I'd drop by. Actually, I was hoping to spend some quality time together, you know, just the two of us. It's been a crazy week, and I could really use some relaxing company. You in?"

Rashaun's stomach lurched. The idea of cuddling on the couch, of the intimacy it implied, sent a jolt of nervous energy through him. He wasn't exactly in the best state for cuddling. His body ached, his mind buzzed with a chaotic cocktail of drugs, and the last thing he needed was for her to see him collapse mid-cuddle.

"Uh, Sasha, that's really sweet of you," he stammered, forcing a smile that felt more like a grimace. "But, the place is kind of a mess right now, you know, with the end-of-month mess and all. Maybe another time? But hey, how about I take you out for dinner? My treat."

Sasha's smile faltered slightly. "Oh, that's sweet of you, but I don't want to put you out. It's pretty late."

"Nonsense! It's the least I can do on such a lousy night, right?" He forced a smile. "Come on, I know this great little place just a few blocks away."

Sasha hesitated for a moment, then nodded slowly. "Alright, you win. But only if you promise to let me treat you next time."

Rashaun felt relief. For a moment, he'd almost blown it. He escorted her away from the door quickly. The rain kept pouring down as they got in his car and drove away.

***

Rashaun's SUV rattled down potholed streets, the dying headlights barely illuminating the graffiti-scarred landscape of Camden, New Jersey. Rain lashed against the windshield, blurring the desolate scenery. Rashaun gripped the steering wheel so tightly that his knuckles turned white.

He pulled into a dimly lit parking lot. This wasn't his scene. He wasn't supposed to be here. Not anymore. Back in the day, he used to pass by this place to his training ground, where he'd sculpted his body into a monument of muscle. But here, in this forgotten corner of the city, he was just another desperate junkie.

A hulking figure materialized from the rain-slicked street. Rashaun recognized the man instantly - Andre. His build was like a fireplug with a shaved head that gleamed in the faint light. A gold chain, thick enough to be a tow cable, looped around his neck, and his hands, scarred and knotted, were the hands of a man who'd done his time on the streets. His eyes, however, held a disconcerting shrewdness, constantly calculating, taking Rashaun's measure in a way that sent shivers down his spine.

"Took you long enough," Andre grunted.

Rashaun forced a smile, the bravado slipping a little

easier here among those who knew his darker side. "Traffic," he lied. "You got what I need?"

Andre eyed him skeptically. "Depends. You got the cash?"

Raushan shoved a wad of cash into Andre's hand. "Got enough."

Andre grunted again as his single gold tooth glinted in the dim light. He produced a small plastic bag.

"This better be good stuff," Rashaun said, his tone laced with a hint of his usual arrogance, even in this setting. "I'm paying good money here."

Andre snorted a humorless sound. "Don't worry, pretty boy. This'll get you where you need to go." The mockery in his voice was unmistakable.

Rashaun bristled but swallowed the retort. He wasn't here to make enemies. He just needed his fix. Grabbing the bag, he tossed it onto the passenger seat.

"See you around, Rashaun," Andre said.

Rashaun mumbled a response, shoving the car into gear and peeling out of the parking lot. The rain had intensified. He reached for the bag on the passenger seat.

Back in his world, the world he presented to Sasha, he was charming and witty, the life of the party. Here, in the shadows, the mask slipped. He was a slave to his addiction, a narcissist craving attention, a man unraveling at the seams. He popped open the bag and took a long, deep look at the white powder inside.

This would last me some time, he thought as he quickly headed home.

***

Iron sharpened iron at Iron Paradise Gym. Rashaun had just finished his set of bicep curls. He dropped the dumbbells with a flourish. Sweat beaded on his forehead, but a triumphant grin stretched across his face.

Across the room, his friends, Henry and Darius, were finishing their own sets on the chest press. Henry slapped the weights down and grinned. "Damn, Rashaun! Looking swole, bro!"

Darius, the more reserved of the two, offered a hesitant thumbs up. "Yeah, good lift."

Rashaun preened, flexing his biceps again. "Just maintaining peak performance, you know? Gotta keep the ladies drooling."

Henry chuckled. "Always the charmer, aren't you?" He nudged Darius. "You think Vanessa noticed?"

Vanessa, a toned brunette with a killer smile, was doing weighted squats on the platform across from them. Every few reps, she'd steal a glance at Rashaun, then quickly look away when she caught his eye.

Rashaun smirked. "Of course she did. Can't blame the girl, can you?" He ran a hand through his hair, deliberately flexing his bicep again.

Darius snorted. "Maybe she's just admiring your...artistic talents." He gestured towards the faded motivational posters plastered on the gym walls - the ones Rashaun had insisted on putting up, all featuring impossibly ripped physiques that vaguely resembled his former self.

Rashaun's smile weakened for a brief moment, but he quickly recovered. "Hey, those posters are inspirational. What's wrong with a little artistic motivation?"

"Nothing wrong," Henry said. "As long as you

remember, most people don't have your...genetic gifts, bro."

Rashaun bristled. "Genetic gifts? Don't downplay the hard work I put in. You think anyone gets this body by sitting on their ass?"

Darius raised an eyebrow. "Well, not exactly this body anymore, Rashaun. You haven't been the same since..." he trailed off, not wanting to mention the steroid suspension.

Rashaun's jaw clenched. "Since what? Since I decided to focus on other things in life? You guys wouldn't understand. You're content with being mediocre."

Henry's grin vanished. "Mediocre? We're all putting in the work, Rashaun. Just because you used to be a walking protein shake advertisement doesn't mean everyone else here is slacking off."

Rashaun scoffed. "Look, I appreciate the pep talk, but some of us were born to be winners. You guys are just playing the participation game."

Darius rolled his eyes and went back to his workout. Henry stared at Rashaun with a mix of disappointment and anger in his eyes.

"You know what, Rashaun?" Henry finally said. "Maybe it's time you stopped looking at everyone else and focused on what you've become. Because right now, you're not the winner you think you are."

Rashaun's face flushed crimson. He opened his mouth to retort, but no words came out. Suddenly, a young woman with toned legs and a bright pink sports bra jogged onto the treadmill next to him. Ignoring Henry, Rashaun, as if on cue, grabbed the weights on his bench, making sure the clanging echoed just a little louder. He shot a glance her way, hoping to catch her eye.

Bingo. The woman looked over with a questioning eyebrow raised. Rashaun offered a dazzling smile, the one he knew melted hearts. "Rough workout?" He asked, his voice smooth as butter.

The woman, oblivious to his act, simply shrugged and returned to her jog. Rashaun cleared his throat again.

"You know," he said, "You're not doing your form any favors on that treadmill. One wrong step, and you could be out for weeks."

The woman finally stopped, and her eyes narrowed

in suspicion. "Thanks, but I think I can handle it."

"Oh, no doubt you're strong," Rashaun continued as his voice took on a patronizing tone. "But proper form is key to maximizing results. You wouldn't want all that hard work to go to waste, would you?"

The woman's jaw clenched, but she didn't want any drama. Right then, Rashaun's friend, Mark, lumbered over, oblivious to the tension.

"Dude, check out this new protein shake I found," he said, thrusting a garish neon-colored tub at Rashaun. "Tastes like freakin' candy!" Rashaun wrinkled his nose in disgust. "Seriously, Mark? You know I only use organic, all-natural supplements." He flashed a smile at the woman, clearly hoping to impress her with his health-conscious ways.

Mark, oblivious to the undercurrent, scratched his head. "Uh, right on, man. More protein for me, then." He ambled off, leaving Rashaun alone with the woman once more.

Henry and Darius watched him from afar talk about himself only. They could notice how the woman gave him a withering look and climbed off the treadmill, heading towards the locker room. But how oblivious to the reactions and how focused he was on his need for attention from everyone.

Rashaun watched the women go, and a frustrated snarl twisted his features. He slammed the weights back on the rack. His carefully constructed facade was crumbling, revealing the narcissist beneath. He craved attention and admiration, but his self-absorbed approach always backfired. Here, in the gym, the mask had slipped, leaving him exposed and alone.

***

The blended traces of sweat, spilled beer, and something far less savory wafted throughout the rickety floorboards of the club. Rashaun's designer shirt was now clinging damply to his back as he scanned the pulsating crowd. There, in a small forgotten corner of Camden, the mask he wore for Sasha melted away. He was all raw nerve endings and a primal hunger.

Around him, bodies writhed and swayed in a chaotic ballet of intoxication. Men sported gang colors and suspicious bulges in their pockets. Women, some young and naive, others hardened by the streets, wore clothes that left little to the imagination. A predatory glint entered Rashaun's eyes.

He swaggered over and exchanged greetings with a streetwise bravado that made Rashaun feel strangely alive. The night went on with cheap liquor, and with each passing moment, his lust increased. He danced with a succession of women, but a deep-seated insecurity clawed at him. His touches grew bolder, and his compliments were laced with a possessiveness that bordered on aggression.

A plastic bag full of cocaine made its rounds. Raushan grabbed it and took a sniff. Looking up, he scanned the room and saw a woman named Shana. He had been eyeing her for some time now. She was a petite firecracker with emerald green eyes. Raushan sensed that she was new to the scene, fresh off the bus from somewhere better, and her eyes still held a flicker of innocence. He saw his chance and made the move.

He downed another shot of a dubious brown liquid, the burn barely registering through the haze of cocaine that clouded his judgment. Pushing his way through the throng towards Shana, he stood right beside her. Her movements were hesitant and unsure, unlike the practiced ease of the other women.

"Hey, beautiful," he slurred. "Having a good time?"

Shana looked up, startled. Her eyes, wide and apprehensive, darted around the room before settling back on him. "Uh, yeah," she mumbled, but her voice was barely audible over the music.

He leaned in close. "You look lost," he said. "Let me show you around."

He brushed against her intentionally as the heat of her touch sent a jolt through him. Lust tore its way up his throat. It wasn't just the drugs anymore. It was the desperate need to feel something, anything, other than the hollowness that consumed him. Shana didn't flinch away. "Maybe you can," she whispered.

The response sent a shot of adrenaline through Rashaun. He grabbed her hand tightly. His grip was surprisingly strong despite his shaky limbs. Her fingers intertwined with his, which sent a delicious shiver down his spine.

"Let's get out of here," she said. "There's a quieter place around back."

He followed her through a maze of bodies. They emerged into a narrow alleyway, bathed in the pale glow of a flickering streetlamp. The air was thick with the smell of garbage and exhaust fumes, but to Rashaun, it felt charged with possibility.

Shana pressed herself against him. Her body was warm and inviting. In that dimly lit alleyway, the world outside ceased to exist for Rashaun. He forgot about everything; the only thought in his mind was to fulfill his desires, no matter how or with whom.

***

Sunlight streamed through the cracked blinds, pulling Rashaun from a restless sleep. The throbbing in his head felt like a jackhammer, and the stale taste in his mouth made him wince. He stumbled to the bathroom, wincing at the sight that greeted him in the mirror. His eyes were bloodshot, surrounded by dark circles. His jawline, once sharp, now appeared slack, and his skin seemed rough like sandpaper.

He splashed cold water on his face, feeling a jolt as it woke him up a bit. Memories of last night came rushing back - the loud music, the unknown faces, the moments with

Shana. Shame twisted in his stomach, a feeling he knew all too well.

He shuffled back into the living room. After a while, a knock at the door startled him out of his self-loathing. He scrambled to his feet, shoving the incriminating evidence out of sight before flinging the door open. It was Sasha.

"Rashaun! Hey, I was just in the neighborhood and thought I'd swing by," she chirped, stepping inside.

Rashaun forced a smile. "Hey, Sasha. Surprise! Come in, come in." He ushered her into the living room, wincing internally at the mess. "Didn't expect to see you so early."

Sasha settled on the threadbare couch. "Well, I have some news!" She announced.

Rashaun braced himself as a drop of unease crossed his features. Big news usually meant big changes, and change wasn't something he particularly craved right now. "Oh yeah? What's that?" He asked.

"I've decided to dedicate my life to God," Sasha declared.

Rashaun was taken aback, but he didn't show her. He acted to listen intently as the mask of charm slipped seamlessly back into place. He nodded encouragingly, peppering his responses with supportive phrases. But inside, a storm raged.

This new path Sasha was on clashed violently with the chaotic, drug-fueled world he was trapped in. Sasha's visit ended all too soon, and as he watched her walk away, his façade also slipped away. The silence of the house now echoed with the deafening roar of his own thoughts. He retreated to the gym, hoping the exertion would numb the disquiet troubling him. But even the clang of weights couldn't drown out the truth – he was a fraud, a man teetering on the edge of a self-made disaster.

Chapter 21

The evening sunrays dappled through the ancient oak trees, forming a mosaic of light and shadow over the impeccably landscaped gardens surrounding the venue. White chairs were neatly arranged, facing a beautiful floral arch adorned with roses, lilies, and baby's breath. Guests, dressed in their finest attire, gathered for the wedding of Sasha and Rashaun.

A gentle breeze rustled the leaves, creating a soft, calming melody. At the front of the venue, under the arch was Sasha. She was cloaked in a gown of ivory lace looking like a princess of serene elegance. By her side was Tasha, the maid of honor. She squeezed her hand reassuringly as a silent understanding passed between them for the mother Sasha missed so dearly.

"You look amazing, Sasha," Tasha whispered. "Mom would be so proud of you."

Sasha squeezed Tasha's hand back and nodded. Tasha wrapped her arm around Sasha, pulling her into a hug. Right then, Greg appeared beside her and took Sasha by her hand.

"You ready for this?" He asked.

Sasha managed a watery smile. "As ready as I'll ever be."

Taking his arm, Sasha took a deep breath and began her walk down the aisle. Her gaze was fixed on Rashaun waiting at the altar. There was a collective gasp of awe at her beauty, but it was the love in her eyes that truly captivated everyone's hearts.

Rashaun's eyes never left Sasha as he watched her approached; his gaze was filled with adoration and affection. He was all set to take in Sasha as his wife, adorning a navy blue suit. His heart was swelling with a love that defied description. He could see the flicker of grief in her eyes; he knew she missed Cookie.

As Sasha reached his side, their hands met, fingers intertwined, as Greg gently placed her hand in Rashaun's. His grip tightened as they both looked into each other's eyes. He then leaned in closer and whispered into her ear, "You look absolutely stunning, my darling."

Sasha shyly put her head down for a second, "You always know what to say, don't you?"

"Just speaking from the heart, Sasha," he replied, grinning.

Sasha leaned in closer and responded, "And that's why I love you."

Rashaun brushed his lips against her ear, "I love you too, Ma'am. Forever and always."

The officiant cleared her throat. "Whenever you guys are ready, let me know."

"Oops, yes, yes, let's proceed," Sasha responded nervously.

The officiant began the ceremony. Her voice cut through the buzzing nervousness that had threatened to consume Sasha.

When it came time for the vows, Sasha cleared her throat and began to speak, but her voice trembled slightly. "Rashaun," she began. "You came into my life when things were a mess. Dark clouds were all around me. I couldn't see clearly. But you saw it all … you saw all of me, the good, the bad, the messy parts I try to hide away. But with you, I feel safe, loved, and whole. You make me feel like I can do anything."

Tears welled up in Rashaun's eyes, mirroring her own. "Sasha," he said with emotion but rumbling with a good-natured chuckle, "You ain't gotta get all fancy on me. You know I'm your biggest fan, even when you're, well, you. You're my sunshine after the storm, the peanut butter to my jelly. You fight like a lioness, love like a dream, and laugh; well, let's just say you can light up a room like nobody's business. But the thing is, Ms. Gorgeous, I'm sticking by your side through thick and thin, sunshine and rain. We'll weather any storm together because that's what couples do."

With the exchanging of rings, Sasha and Rashaun sealed their union. Their faces were lit with happiness and smiles for all to see. The officiant then concluded the ceremony. "By the power vested in me, I now pronounce you husband and wife. You may kiss the bride."

Rashaun cupped Sasha's face in his hands. His touch still sent shivers down her spine. In Sasha's mind, the past months faded away. Here, with her loved ones, she felt only their connection. He leaned in and kissed her. She felt as if that one kiss was a promise Rashaun made to her of their love, to face any storms together, to a brighter future.

As they turned to face their cheering guests, tears streamed down Sasha's face. A single tear escaped Rashaun's eye as well, a tear not of sadness, but of happiness for the woman standing beside him, his wife, his forever. In that moment, Sasha felt a flicker of hope. A hope for a new beginning, a future built on the bedrock of love, a future where she and Rashaun would face the world, hand in hand.

***

The moving truck rumbled away, leaving a trail of dust and a bewildered Sasha standing on the manicured lawn of Rashaun's 'mini-mansion,' as he playfully called it. It was more like a sprawling ranch house, all warm brick and inviting porches.

"Wowza," Sasha breathed, taking it all in. She stood standing and staring in disbelief that the home she visited many times was now hers. "This place is huge! Are you sure you don't have a spare wing you can rent out?"

Rashaun, biceps straining under a box overflowing with picture frames, chuckled. "Maybe later, boss lady. Come on, let's get this unpacking party started."

Inside, the house was chaotic. Boxes were piled high,

furniture was draped in plastic, and sun rays made the dust motes dancing in the air even more prominent.

Sasha surveyed the scene with her hands on her hips. "Okay, so maybe 'party' is a strong word. More like an 'unpack-a-thon'?"

Rashaun grinned. "Exactly! But with pizza and terrible unpacking jokes. You in?"

Sasha laughed. "Wouldn't miss it for the world. Now, where do we start? Kitchen first, obviously. A woman can't live on takeout alone, even if it's her amazing husband bringing it home."

Rashaun feigned a dramatic gasp. "Husband? Since when? We just said 'I do' two days ago!"

"Technically," Sasha countered, already attacking a box labeled 'Utensils.' "We're married now. So spill the beans, Mr. Husband, where's your secret stash of takeout menus?"

Rashaun mock-offended and pretended to search the room. "Hmm, can't seem to find any. Maybe you married a takeout-challenged husband?"

Sasha swatted him playfully with a spatula. "Oh no, you don't! You're not getting out of this that easily. We're making a grocery list after this. Team effort, remember?"

Rashaun laughed. "Okay, Okay! You know what? I have an idea. We can dedicate a whole shelf in the living room to our coupledom. We can fill it with hilarious photos, concert tickets, and maybe even that giant plastic spork you won at the county fair. What do you say?"

Sasha snorted, digging through a box of mismatched mugs. "The spork? Seriously, Rashaun? You're lucky I still talk to you after that questionable shrimp-eating incident."

Rashaun winced dramatically. "Hey, it was a learning experience! Besides, that spork symbolizes our commitment...to questionable life choices." He winked, pulling out a chipped ceramic mug with a faded cartoon cat. "Speaking of questionable, is this REALLY yours?"

Sasha snatched the mug as a blush crept up her neck. "Don't judge! It was a high school phase, okay? And besides, I still love it!"

Rashaun burst out laughing. "Well, love it or not, it's definitely going on our coupledom shelf. Right next to the picture of you with braces and those questionable bangs."

Sasha shoved him playfully. "Hey! No fair! You promised no wedding blackmail!"

Rashaun threw his hands up in mock surrender. "Alright, alright! You win. Now, Sasha, let's order something first, please. I'm starving!"

Hours flew by in a whirlwind of unpacking, playful banter, and stolen kisses. By the time the pizza arrived (courtesy of Rashaun, who miraculously remembered the takeout menus after all), they were both exhausted but glowing with contentment.

"This is actually kind of fun," Sasha admitted, taking a bite of pizza. "Who knew unpacking could be so...romantic?"

Rashaun raised an eyebrow playfully. "You mean unpacking with your incredibly handsome husband couldn't be romantic?"

Sasha rolled her eyes. "Oh, stop it. But seriously, this place is starting to feel like home to me already."

Rashaun pulled her close and wrapped his arms

around her. "It is your home, Sasha. As long as you're here, wherever we are, it's home."

Sasha leaned into him, feeling peace engulfing her heart.

***

The bass throbbed on the floor, vibrating the shaky table where Sasha sat. Across from her, Rashaun was a blur of movement, his head bobbing with the music, eyes gleaming with a manic energy that sent shivers down her spine. He hadn't touched his drink - a clear, non-alcoholic concoction for show - but the edge to his behavior was unmistakable. Months of this charade were wearing Sasha thin.

"Yo, you good over there, girl?" Rashaun leaned over. His voice was strained and high-pitched.

"Yeah, I'm fine," Sasha forced a smile. Her gaze flitted across the crowded dance floor. She spotted a guy, a couple of drinks in, blatantly leering at her. He was a few tables over, but his gaze was fixed. His eyes remained on the curve of her hips as she shifted in her seat, then traveled suggestively up her body, taking in the way her dress hugged her figure. Sasha's obvious protruding belly did not alter his lustful attraction towards her. A smirk played on his lips, and he nudged the guy next to him, both of them erupting in laughter. Sasha felt a prickle of unease crawl up her spine. This wasn't the first time tonight a stranger's gaze had made her skin crawl, and with Rashaun acting wired, she felt particularly vulnerable.

Rashaun's gaze snapped to the other guy, catching the tail end of the smirk. It was a look he knew all too well - a look that dismissed Sasha, a look that objectified her. It fueled a fire in his gut, a primal urge to protect his territory, even if his perception was warped by the drugs coursing through his veins. His mind raced. *'Damn it,'* he thought, *'Why does this girl gotta dress like that, flaunting herself for every jackass here? She knows it makes me uncomfortable.'*

Suddenly, Rashaun's hand whipped out, slapping the back of her head with a loud crack. "What's got your attention! Eyes on yo man!" He slurred with a possessive glint in his eyes. Sasha's head snapped forward as the world momentarily went white. Pain exploded in her skull, a searing counterpoint to the humiliation that burned in her throat. Sasha's jaw clenched. Humiliation burned in her throat. "Rashaun, what the hell was that for?" She hissed, her voice barely audible over the music.

"You was lookin' at him," he spat back, his words thick with accusation. "I told you, you gotta show these fools who you belong to."

Tears welled up in Sasha's eyes. *Belonged to?* It felt more like she was being caged. "I wasn't looking at anyone," she mumbled, pushing her untouched drink away.

Rashaun scoffed. "Yeah, right. You always gotta be the center of attention." He stood up abruptly as his body swayed precariously. "C'mon, let's hit the floor." He grabbed her hand, pulling her toward the dance floor with surprising strength.

Sasha's breath hitched. The sting of the blow to her head was eclipsed by a gush of anger and embarrassment. She yanked her hand free. "I need some air," she said. Before Rashaun could respond, she pushed past him and hurried towards the back of the club. She found the restroom, which was comparatively quieter than the continuous throbbing music outside. Splashing cold water on her face, she tried to calm her racing heart. Tears welled up in her eyes, blurring her vision. This wasn't how things were supposed to be.

After a few minutes, she emerged from the restroom, hoping to find Rashaun and maybe, just maybe, salvage the night. But he was gone. An empty beer bottle sat abandoned on their table, and their belongings were scattered haphazardly across the sticky surface. Panic groped at her throat. *Where has he gone? Had he found someone else to party with?* The thought sent a fresh wave of nausea washing over her. This wasn't the life she signed up for. With shaking hands, she called an Uber.

Finally, at 3 am, an Uber pulled up outside the club. Sasha slipped out as the cool night air brushed against her skin. As she drove away, the image of Rashaun, lost in a haze of his own making, burned into her memory.

Back at home, now feeling more like a gilded cage, Sasha let herself in. She knew Rashaun wouldn't be back for hours, if at all. This had been an ongoing thing. Months had blurred by in a haze. With each passing day, Rashaun's playful demeanor had morphed into something darker. The nights that used to be filled with laughter were now punctuated by an edge, a hair-trigger temper fueled by a white, powdery substance Sasha found stashed in a drawer one morning.

Exhaustion and a deep sense of loneliness washed over her. Upstairs, in the vast emptiness of their bedroom, Sasha finally let the tears fall.

***

The stale smell of burnt was lingering across the breakfast bar. Sasha sat hunched over a lukewarm cup of coffee; the classifieds splayed out before her like a battlefield map. Across from her, Rashaun was slumped on the plush leather couch with a bottle of whiskey in one hand and a stack of unpaid bills in the other. In front of him was his laptop, where he had just received another rejection email from yet another company.

Sasha's tolerance was reaching its limits. Trying to control her emotions, she asked gently, "Rashaun, have you heard back from any of the job applications you sent out?"

Rashaun's shoulders slumped even further as he shook his head and sniggered a bitter laugh.

"Nah, ain't nobody hirin' a washed-up wrestler with a busted back," Rashaun muttered.

Sasha's heart ached at the defeat in his voice. She knew how hard Rashaun had been trying to find work, but the rejection letters kept piling up. Each rejection only served to be a blow to his already fragile ego.

Sasha stood from her stool and walked toward him. Taking the bottle from his hand, she sat beside him. "Maybe it's time to consider other options, Rashaun. There's gotta be something else you can do," she said.

But Rashaun's pride won't let him entertain the thought of giving up on his dreams. He clung to the last shreds of his former glory, refusing to accept the reality of his situation.

As the days stretched into weeks, Rashaun's financial woes had only worsened. His endorsement sponsor contracts that were once a lucrative source of income began to dry up one by one. With each contract lost, Rashaun's desperation grew, driving him deeper into a cycle of self-medication and denial.

Sasha watched helplessly as Rashaun took another swig of whiskey. "Rashaun, this ain't the answer. Maybe you should try something new?"

Rashaun scoffed. "New? Like what? Flipping burgers? That ain't me, Sasha. I gotta be in the spotlight."

He reached into his pocket and pulled out a crumpled wad of bills. He slapped it down on the table. "Look, I got this. Don't you worry your pretty little head about it?"

Sasha stared at the money. It wasn't from a job. The bills were all high denominations, the kind that came from their dwindling savings or...something darker.

"Rashaun," she began. "Where did you get that money?"

He avoided her gaze, picking at a non-existent flake of paint on the table. "Just...a little somethin' somethin' to hold us over."

But Sasha knew better. The telltale signs – the dilated pupils, the forced bravado – were all too familiar.

"Oh no, Rashaun," she pleaded. "Don't you even think about going there or doing something like this?"

The anger simmering beneath the surface finally boiled over. He slammed his fist on the table, rattling the cutlery. "Don't you nag me, Sasha! It's all I can do to keep a roof over our heads and food on the table, and you wanna judge me?"

His outburst left Sasha in tears. Her heart was beating faster, and now she felt scared of him...scared of the person she loved and thought would protect her. Rashaun stormed out of the room, leaving Sasha alone with the wreckage of their breakfast and a gnawing fear that the future she had envisioned was slipping through her fingers like sand.

Rashaun went into their bedroom and sat down at the edge of the bed. His mind was clouded by the numbing grip of alcohol, and his pride was too stubborn to admit defeat. Since the wedding, the playful banter had been replaced by a tense silence. The late nights out and the empty promises of "I'll get the job" all fueled the white powder that was his dirty little secret.

Reaching into the drawer of the coffee table, he brushed his fingers against the cold, familiar metal of his stash tin. Temptation crashed over him, and the thought of oblivion rang a siren song in his ears. As soon as he popped the lid, the acrid scent filled his nostrils.

Just a little to take the edge off, he rationalized in his head. *Just to forget about the bills, the emails, the way Sasha looked at him lately, a mixture of pity and something he couldn't quite decipher.*

He wanted to lash out, blame the world, blame his injury, blame Sasha for that worried look in her eyes. Scooping a small pile onto a credit card, he ignored the nagging voice of reason in his head. *I ain't a bad guy*, he convinced himself. *Just a guy down on his luck.* A snort later, the world swirled around him, and the sharp edges of his anxieties softened into a hazy fog.

***

Sasha was busy stirring the simmering stew, which smelled great. In between, she glanced at the clock anxiously. It was well past nine, and Rashaun, who usually grumbled about dinner being late, hadn't shown up.

Suddenly, the front door slammed shut. Rashaun stalked in, his face looking like a thundercloud. He tossed his keys on the counter with a clatter.

"Hey babe," Sasha greeted with cautious optimism. "Dinner's almost ready. How was your day?"

Rashaun grunted, avoiding her gaze. He shuffled past her, heading straight for the living room, where he flopped onto the couch, burying his face in his phone.

Sasha frowned as a knot of unease tightened in her

stomach. This wasn't unusual lately. His once carefree spirit had been replaced by a dark, brooding demeanor.

"Honey," she began tentatively. "Is everything okay?"

Rashaun didn't reply; he just scrolled through his phone with a monotonous swipe of his thumb.

Sasha sighed as her smile faded. Lately, it felt like she was walking on eggshells around him. She sat down at the table alone, but her appetite waned with every passing minute. The phone buzzed again, this time with a notification from a local news website.

"Hey, babe," she started again with a flicker of excitement in her voice, "Guess what? They're doing a feature on the community center project I've been working on! It could be great publicity."

Rashaun remained glued to his phone. A barely audible "huh" was the only response she received. Sasha felt hurt. Every attempt at conversation seemed to be met with a wall of indifference.

Sasha finished her meager dinner alone, pushing the food around the plate more than eating it. The silence stretched on, punctuated only by the rhythmic tapping of Rashaun's thumbs and the occasional frustrated groan escaping his lips.

Just then, her phone rang. A smile bloomed on her face as she saw Tasha's name on the screen.

"Hey, Tasha!" She answered. "How are you?"

"I'm perfectly alright. What's going on with you, how's everything going?

"Listen, you won't believe what just happened! They're doing a feature on the community center project! Remember how much work I've put into that? I can't believe it!" Sasha told her excitedly.

Tasha's voice crackled through the phone, filled with genuine excitement. "Oh my gosh, Sasha, that's amazing! I always knew you could do it. So, when's the feature coming out? I'm gonna tell everybody!"

Sasha beamed. "It's supposed to be in tomorrow's paper! I know, right? It's crazy! This could be a game-changer for the center, you know? Maybe we can finally get that funding for the new wing."

"That's fantastic, Sasha! I'm so proud of you," Tasha exclaimed. "You've been working so hard on this, and it's finally paying off. What are they going to say in the article?"

Sasha's smile widened. "They're going to do a whole profile on the center and the impact it's having on the community. They might even interview some of the kids who participate in the after-school programs."

"Oh my gosh, that's even better!" Tasha cheered. "This is going to be huge. You could be a real inspiration to other people."

As they chatted for a while longer, Sasha filled in Tasha with the details. Sasha lit up, recounting the news with animated gestures. Rashaun, still glued to his phone, couldn't help but steal glances at her. Her joy seemed to irritate him as a dark scowl creased his forehead. He let out a frustrated sigh. As they wrapped up the call, Sasha could feel Rashaun's eyes boring into her from across the room. His expression seemed to darken with jealousy. Sasha tried to ignore it, focusing instead on the conversation at hand, but she knew he was annoyed.

Suddenly, Rashaun rose from his seat abruptly. Without a word, he stormed out of the house again, leaving

Sasha feeling bewildered and hurt.

Hours passed, but Rashaun still hadn't returned home. Sasha lay awake in bed as her mind raced with worry. She knews this pattern all too well – Rashaun's jealousy manifesting in silent treatment and disappearing acts.

As the clock ticked past midnight, Sasha's frustration boiled over. The glow of her phone was the only light illuminating the room. She stared at the screen, willing it to light up with a message or call from Rashaun, but it remained silent.

She picked up her phone again and dialed Rashaun's number for the umpteenth time, but it went straight to voicemail.

She decided to leave a voicemail. "Rashaun, where are you? This isn't fair. We need to talk about this." But her pleas fall on deaf ears.

Rashaun had gone to the bar and surrounded himself with people who seemed to fuel his ego. He laughed and joked as if nothing was wrong. He relished in the attention, soaking up the admiration and validation from those around him.

Later that night, the city outside hummed with the restless energy of 5 am. Sasha's sleep had abandoned her long ago. She knelt beside the bed and murmured a prayer. When she finished, a quiet sigh escaped her lips, and she looked up to find Rashaun silhouetted in the doorway, his gaze filled with bitterness and contempt.

"What are you doing?" He scoffed with bitterness.

Sasha flinched. "Just...praying," she mumbled, feeling strangely defensive.

He let out a humorless snort. "Yeah, right. Like that's gonna solve anything."

Sasha rose to her feet as tears pricked her eyes. "What's gotten into you, Rashaun? This isn't you."

He shot her a look that could curdle milk. "Maybe it is now. You happy?" His voice was laced with a veiled accusation.

Sasha furrowed her brows in confusion. "Happy about what?"

"About being Miss Perfect all the time," he spat as his words dripped with sarcasm. "About having your little prayer sessions and your perfect phone calls with your goody-two-shoes family."

Sasha's jaw clenched. "My family? What's wrong with you? They love you!"

"Yeah, well, maybe I don't need their love right now," he snapped. "Maybe all I need is a wife who doesn't act like a saint all the time!"

Sasha stared at him. This wasn't about her family or her prayers. This was about something deeper, something she couldn't quite grasp. But one thing was clear: his jealousy had boiled over, twisting his perception of her into a distorted caricature.

"Is that really what you think?" She asked in a trembling voice. "That I put on some kind of act for everyone else?

He didn't answer; he just turned away from her and went into the living room. As the morning light slowly crept in, Sasha sat on the edge of the bed. Rashaun hadn't returned to their room. She stood and went into the living room only to find him sprawled on the couch with the TV on droning in the background and a half-empty bottle of something amber clutched in his hand. He pulled the covers over himself, creating a self-imposed exile within their shared space.

***

Sasha diligently cleaned the living room with a dusting cloth. The bright morning light illuminated the neglected state of the once-gleaming room. Coffee cups overflowed on the end table, clothes draped haphazardly over furniture, and a telltale haze drooped in the air.

Reaching for the ashtray overflowing with cigarette butts and what looked like...cannabis roaches. Sasha's stomach lurched. This wasn't new, and her past taste for the herb wont allow her to pass judgement, but the blatant disregard for their home concerned her. She sighed, grabbed the ashtray, and headed for the kitchen.

Suddenly, a vice grip clamped down on her wrist. "What the hell are you doing?" Rashaun snarled.

Sasha yelped in surprise, dropping the ashtray with a clatter. Burnt remnants scattered across the hardwood floor. "Rashaun! I was just cleaning!"

He shoved her back against the wall. His breath reeked of stale smoke and something sharper, metallic. "Cleaning what? You trying to steal my stuff?" His voice was a low growl laced with paranoia.

"Steal? It's an ashtray full of…stuff! This place is a mess!" Sasha stammered as fear prickled her skin. He'd never really been physically violent before, but he was esculating and its becoming more frequent.

Rashaun's eyes narrowed. He scanned the floor, and as his gaze fell on the scattered remains of the blunt, his face contorted in rage. "That was the last of it! You're lying! You knew exactly what you were doing! You're always trying to ruin everything for me! You did this on purpose, didn't you?"

"The last of what? Rashaun, I had no idea there was anything in that ashtray besides cigarette butts!"

Sasha felt panicked. This wasn't weed. She knew the signs. Cocaine. He was using cocaine.

His face twisted into a cruel expression. "Liar!" He lunged at her, and his hand connected with a sickening slap across her cheek. He then grabbed Sasha by her neck.

Sasha cried out at the immediate sting. Tears welled up in her eyes. The world seemed to slow down. The only sound she could hear was the ragged gasps escaping her lips and his heavy breathing.

"What is wrong with you, Rashaun?!" She screamed, more out of defiance than anything. "This isn't you! You need help!"

Rashaun's face contorted further, and his voice dripped with venom. "Shut the fuck up, bitch! Rashaun thrusted her body backward as he released her neck. You know exactly what you're doing, don't touch my shit! You can't control me! You want to control or wanna touch something, touch this dick like you suppose too. You don't control shit," he continued. "When I want that good-good, trust, I get it and you ain't got nothin' to do with it."

"What the hell is wrong with you!" Sasha screamed.

Rashaun eyes blazed with a manic intensity. He raised his hand again, but this time, Sasha ducked. With a burst of adrenaline, she shoved him back, sending him stumbling against the coffee table.

"Don't you touch me!" She yelled.

Rashaun glared at her, his face contorted with a mix of rage and something akin to surprise.

His jaw clenched so tight it seemed like it might snap. He stepped closer to her, his breath hot against her face, reeking of alcohol and aggression. For a tense moment, they stood locked in a silent showdown.

Then, with a roar that rattled the walls, Rashaun unleashed a string of curses that would make even the toughest of sailors blush. Finally, with a guttural curse, Rashaun stormed out of the room, slamming the front door behind him with a deafening boom.

Sasha collapsed to the floor, her body trembling with adrenaline and shock. Her cheek throbbed where Rashaun's hand had struck her. This wasn't the life she signed up for. This wasn't the love she deserved.

***

The kitchen was brimming with activity. Sizzling sausages filled the air with a delicious aroma. Plates piled up high with potato salad and baked beans crowded the counter. Sasha and Tasha hustled around, arranging things with practiced ease while Greg and Rashaun engaged in conversations in the backyard.

Sasha and Tasha sat at the table, and they all began to eat

together. Patting Sasha's hand affectionately, Tasha began, "You've really outdone yourself with this barbecue, Sasha. Everything tastes delicious!"

"Thanks, Sis. I'm just glad you guys could make it," Sasha responded, smiling.

As they chatted and enjoyed the food, Rashaun took center stage and continued his efforts to be the center of attention, telling his stories and self-praises.

"And then, I swear, the fish was THIS big! You should've seen it. I practically wrestled it out of the lake myself!" Rashaun gestured dramatically.

Greg began to laugh, enjoying Rashaun's animated storytelling.

Sasha, smiling but slightly embarrassed, said, "Rashaun, maybe you're exaggerating just a little bit..."

"Nah, babe, you know me. I never let the truth get in the way of a good story!" Rashaun grinned as if nothing was wrong between them.

Sasha's smile faded slightly as she exchanged a knowing glance with her sister. Rashaun's tendency to exaggerate and steal the spotlight was becoming a source of frustration for Sasha.

Later, after the barbecue had ended and the family had left, Sasha sat at the kitchen table. The remnants of the meal were scattered around her. She knew she had to talk to Rashaun.

Taking a deep breath, she called out, "Rashaun? Are you in the living room?"

He sauntered in, a beer already in his hand. "Yep, just catching the game."

"Can we talk?" Sasha asked.

Rashaun sighed dramatically. "About what? The glorious display of my fishing skills everyone seemed to enjoy?"

Sasha forced a smile. "No, about… your recent arrest."

His smile vanished. He took a long swig of his beer as his eyes hardened. "What about it? It's just a bump in the road."

Tentative but determined, Sasha finally said what had been in her mind for a long time. "Rashaun, I've been thinking...maybe it would be a good idea for you to see a therapist. You're drinking every night, and it's affecting your health and our relationship. Especially after your recent

DUI."

Rashaun slammed his beer can on the table. "Therapy? Are you kidding me, Sasha? I don't need some shrink telling me what's wrong with me and who you think you are, huh? You don't get to tell me how to live my life!"

"I'm your partner, Rashaun. I care about you, and I'm worried about what this is doing to you, Rashaun. It's about getting the help you need to work through your issues," Sasha replied gently.

Rashaun shook his head. "I don't give two shits about your feelings, Sasha. And I sure as hell don't need your nagging!"

Sasha's heart sank at his callous words, but she refused to let him intimidate her. "This isn't about me, Rashaun. It's about you and your well-being."

Rashaun's face twisted with rage. "I said I don't care, Sasha! You're not my mother, and you don't get to tell me what to do!"

"I'm not trying to control you, Rashaun. I just want you to get help before it's too late," Sasha stood her ground.

Rashaun raised his voice, trying to drown hers. "I DON'T

NEED ANYONE'S HELP, SASHA! My recovery, if you want to call it that, is between me and God. I don't believe in paying someone to tell me what I already know. "

He then closed in on her, raising his index finger right at her nose. "And maybe you should think about fixing your own little mistakes rather than telling me to visit some crappy ol' shrink!"

Sasha's stomach lurched as she braced herself for what she knew was coming next.

"If you weren't out there running those Mise money runs, maybe you wouldn't have gotten this little surprise in your belly right now."

Sasha winced as Rashaun threw her past back in her face. She fought to fight back her tears. She began to pray silently in her head, in attempts to soften the blow.

"And what about your mother, huh? You were too busy with your own life to be there for her when she needed you the most!"

Sasha's heart clenched at the mention of her mother. That was one of the most painful and sensitive topics she had confided in him, and that's exactly where he hit her.

"Please…stop," Sasha mumbled slowly as Rashaun was now inches away from her face, his finger almost touching the tip of her nose.

"What? What did you say, huh? I couldn't hear you," Rashaun closed his ear to her mouth in a dramatic manner, changing his voice.

"I know I wasn't there, Rashaun, but I've been regretful. Can't we focus on moving forward instead of dredging up the past?"

Rashaun's anger swelled. His need to make her feel small consumed his entire being. He let out a cruel laugh and then said coldly, "Maybe if you had been there for your mother, she wouldn't have died feeling so alone and abandoned."

Sasha recoiled as if slapped. The pain of Rashaun's words cut her to the core. She couldn't believe what she had heard. Her heart sank as she knew he said it all to hurt her conscious. She knew that without professional help, his cycle of addiction and destructive behavior would continue unchecked, but convincing him to seek help seemed like an impossible task.

Chapter 22

Sasha hadn't imagined this day when she refused to attend Cookie's baptism. She hadn't thought a day would come when she would stand in the same place as her mother with the same atmosphere. She imagined Cookie's body and face when her head was down in the water. It was for mere seconds, but she saw her. She saw her face, the same face that she witnessed that day through the glass-stained window of the Church from afar. There she was, standing, her eyes looking for Sasha. Little did she know that her daughter was right behind, having experienced an unthinkable nightmare.

Sasha had just reached home from the Church after her baptism. It was after a while that her entire family was present. Tasha and Greg followed closely behind.

"Thanks for coming home with me, guys," Sasha said.

Tasha reached out and squeezed Sasha's hand reassuringly. "Of course, sis. We're here for you."

Greg nodded in agreement, his expression solemn. "Yeah, whatever you need, we've got your back."

Sasha couldn't help but smirk at Greg's earnestness. "Even if I need you to fight off a horde of zombies?"

Greg chuckled, playing along. "Absolutely. I'll be

the first in line with a baseball bat and a battle cry."

Tasha rolled her eyes playfully. "You two are ridiculous."

"But you love us anyway," Sasha teased, nudging her sister with a grin.

Tasha sighed dramatically. "Unfortunately, yes. I'm stuck with you two."

Just then, the sound of footsteps came from the hallway, and Rashaun appeared in the doorway. His eyes flickered briefly to Sasha before he turned his attention to Tasha and Greg.

"What's up, y'all?" Rashaun said, his voice cheerful but strained. "Sorry, I'm late, got held up on the way back from the church."

"That's okay. Oh, I could smell some delicious aroma in here. What's cookin' Sasha?" Tasha asked.

Sasha smiled. "Just threw together a little something for lunch. Got some mac and cheese baking in the oven and some fried chicken on the stove."

Greg's eyes lit up. "Fried chicken? Now you're speaking my language!"

Tasha chuckled. "You and your love for fried food, Greg. You're worse than a kid sometimes."

Rashaun nodded, though his gaze lingered on Sasha for a moment longer than necessary. "Sounds good, Sasha. I'll take some of that fried chicken."

Sasha nodded. "Sure thing, Rashaun. Plates are in the cupboard."

As Sasha bustled about the kitchen, serving up lunch for everyone, Rashaun remained silent, his usual jovial facade slipping for just a moment. But as soon as Tasha and Greg began chatting about their plans for the rest of the day, Rashaun joined in as if nothing were amiss. She felt a pang of sadness, knowing that the man she loved was capable of such deception, even in front of their own family.

As the days passed, Sasha noticed a change in Rashaun's demeanor. He grew increasingly irritable, especially when Sasha played gospel music while cleaning or cooking. It seemed to grate on his nerves like never before, his reactions bordering on explosive.

One evening, Sasha hummed along to a gospel tune as she washed the dishes after dinner. Rashaun, sitting at the kitchen table with a scowl on his face, couldn't contain his frustration any longer.

"Can you turn that crap off already?" He snapped.

Sasha paused, surprised by the sudden outburst. "I'm sorry, Rashaun. I didn't realize it bothered you."

"Well, it does. I'm sick of hearing that all the time," he retorted.

Sasha bit her lip as her fingers tightened around the dishcloth. This wasn't the first time this had happened. Lately, anything remotely religious seemed to set Rashaun off.

"It helps me clean faster," she mumbled, desperately trying to appease him.

He slammed his hand against the table, making Sasha jump. "Doesn't matter. Turn it off, Sasha. Now."

His voice, dripping with icy finality, left no room for argument. A lump formed in Sasha's throat, and she choked back a sob of frustration. She switched off the radio.

Rashaun grunted in satisfaction and left the kitchen. Tears welled up in Sasha's eyes, blurring her vision. She slumped against the counter, her reflection staring back at her – a shell of the woman she once was.

Later that night, after Sasha had gone to bed, Rashaun sat alone in the dimly lit living room. His shoulders were slumped, his head bowed low. Tears that hadn't flowed glistened in his eyes. He was thinking about everything he had been doing lately. Seeing Sasha flinch had been a punch to the gut. The way she'd shrunk back, the tears he knew were welling up behind those brave brown eyes... that wasn't right.

He wasn't a monster. At least, he tried not to be. Shame began to creep in. He slumped onto the couch, burying his face in his hands. A single, dismayed sniffle escaped his mouth, raw and unexpected. It wasn't the first time. His anger, his need for control – it was suffocating them both. He knew it.

But changing was hard. Scary. What if she didn't like the real him, the one who felt threatened by her simple joys? The one who craved her but pushed her away in the same breath?

Another sob wracked his body, a silent plea for a way out of the tangled mess he'd created. He yearned to apologize, to bridge the chasm his insecurity had built. But the words wouldn't come. Not yet. For now, he was left with his guilt.

***

Rain tapped against the window as Sasha looked outside, standing firm. She then turned around and crossed her arms. Rashaun was pacing before her. His face flushed with a mix of anger and something that looked suspiciously like desperation.

"Come on, Sasha," he pleaded. "It's just a quick errand. I can't wait for a cab in this weather."

Sasha's gaze held his. "No, Rashaun. You were swerving all over the road last night. I can't let you take my car again, not until you're sober."

Rashaun scoffed. "I barely had anything to drink! I'm fine now."

"Barely is not nothing," Sasha countered. "It's not safe for you or anyone else on the road."

His frustration boiled over. "Don't you trust me?" He yelled.

"It's not about trust," Sasha said, her voice calm despite the rising storm in her chest. "It's about being responsible."

He slammed his fist against the wall as a tremor ran through the picture hanging above it. Sasha recoiled. This wasn't the Rashaun she fell in love with.

"Fine," he spat, storming towards the door. "I'll figure something else out."

The slam of the door rattled the windows. Sasha sank onto the couch. She held her head in her hands, not believing what he was going to do.

The night stretched on. No call, no text. Finally, with the first rays of dawn filtering through the window, the sound of a sputtering engine crushed the silence.

Sasha rushed to the window with her heart pounding. There, parked haphazardly in the driveway, was her car. A deep scrape ran along the passenger side door. Fury bubbled up within alongside the lingering fear.

He stumbled out of the car, his clothes rumpled, hair a mess. His eyes met hers with a drop of shame, battling defiance. Sasha ran down and confronted him right outside. "What happened to my car, Rashaun? And where have you been all night?"

Rashaun avoided her gaze, his demeanor defensive. "It's nothing, Sasha. Just a little accident. And I crashed at a friend's place, that's all."

But Sasha wasn't buying his excuses. "You took my car against my wishes, drove under the influence, and now look what's happened. You could have killed someone, Rashaun! Or even yourself!"

Rashaun was too high to even respond. He mumbled a weak apology so lowly she could barely hear. He went inside the house, leaving Sasha alone with her damaged car in the driveway.

Later that day, Sasha called Emily, a friend with whom Sasha had always felt a deep connection. Sasha sat across from her friend in the cozy corner of their favorite café.

Emily listened intently as Sasha poured her heart out, tears streaming down her cheeks.

"I just don't know what to do anymore, Emily," Sasha confessed. "I keep praying for things to get better, but it feels like I'm stuck in this endless cycle of pain and disappointment."

Emily reached out and gently squeezed Sasha's hand, offering her a comforting smile. "I know it's hard, Sasha. But remember, everything is going to be alright one day, even in the midst of these struggles."

Sasha nodded. "I know, Emily. And I want to believe that things will work out in the end. But sometimes, it feels like I'm fighting a losing battle."

"It's okay to not have all the answers, Sasha. Marriage is hard work, and sometimes, even with faith, the road gets bumpy," Emily reassured.

Sasha leaned into Emily's touch, taking a shaky breath. "But how bumpy is 'bumpy'? This constant fear, this walking on eggshells around him... this is not what I intended for marriage!" Emily sighed. "There's a difference between working through challenges and living in endless turmoil. I, of course, wouldn't want to see you live your life like this, being fearful even in your own home."

"But what if giving up is the easy way out? What if I'm supposed to persevere, no matter how bad it gets?" Sasha said as she sniffled. Emily squeezed her hand gently again. "True strength lies not just in enduring hardship but in knowing when to seek help. Have you talked to Rashaun about how his behavior affects you?"

Sasha shook her head. "Sometimes he acts so nice I almost feel like there is something wrong with me and not him, and sometimes..." she trailed off as the events of the past few months replayed in her head.

"Sometimes nights like last night happen," she continued, wiping her tears. "And I can't help but wonder... what in hell is going to happen next?"

A tear escaped her eyes again, tracing a path down her cheek. "Maybe I'm being naive, Emily. Maybe this isn't the marriage I thought it would be. Maybe this is just... hell."

Emily didn't flinch. "Sometimes, using the right words can be the first step towards healing, Sasha. It's okay to feel angry, hurt, and scared."

"I just feel like I can't do it anymore!" Sasha buried her face in her hands as Emily stood and sat right next to her now, hugging her sideways.

"Maybe... maybe this is some kind of payback," Sasha sniffled. "Maybe I am put into this situation because of how I put others through in the past."

Emily's hand tightened on Sasha's shoulders. "It's easy to fall into the trap of 'what ifs' and past hurts, Sasha. Forgive yourself, my love. This might be a chance for you to grow, to learn about yourself and what you deserve in a relationship."

Sasha considered her words. "But what if I'm just clinging to something that's broken?"

"Only you can decide that, Sasha. But before you make any decisions, you deserve to feel safe. You deserve a partner who respects you and your boundaries," Emily reminded her.

Sasha simply nodded as she grabbed a napkin and cleaned her soaked face.

"Actually, Sasha, I have an extra car sitting unused. It's a bit older, but it runs perfectly. If you need something reliable while yours gets fixed..."

Sasha's eyes widened. The kindness in Emily's offer was overwhelming. "Emily, I don't know what to say. Thank you from the bottom of my heart."

"No need for thanks, honey," Emily said. "You're strong, Sasha. Stronger than you think. And you deserve to be happy. Just promise to take care of yourself, okay?"

Sasha nodded.

With a supportive hug and a promise to stay in touch, Sasha left the café that day feeling a little light. She couldn't help but feel grateful for the small moments of light that helped her through the darkness in her life.

Chapter 23

Tasha scrolled mindlessly through Facebook, sitting by the window. Her attention was divided between the screen of her phone and the world beyond the glass. The afternoon sun was slanting through the window and warming her neck. These days, she always noticed when the sun made her feel warm. As she swiped up and down on her phone, looking at posts and pictures from friends, she couldn't help but feel the sunlight on her skin. It felt nice, like a gentle hug from nature.

Suddenly, a chipper tune from her phone jolted her. It was the church's weekly newsletter notification. With a grimace, she clicked it open, bracing herself for another picture of Pastor Miles beaming next to a platter of charity bake sale cookies.

Her breath hitched. There, splashed across the top banner, was a wedding announcement. Miles, in a rented tux that strained across his widening midsection, stood next to a woman with a blinding smile. But it wasn't just any woman. It was Michele.

Beneath the picture, a caption screamed at her:

"Congratulations to Pastor Miles and Michele on their upcoming nuptials!"

The world dissolved into a blur. Michele. The woman who'd wormed her way into their lives, dripping with fake piety. The woman who'd stolen kisses from Miles. Tasha recalled that this woman had stopped attending services after Tasha's public confrontation for a few months. Now, it all clicked into a sickeningly clear picture.

The memory of that fight played in front of Tasha's eyes. How dare they? How dare Michele, the woman who'd poisoned their marriage with her sly smiles and forced hugs, parade her victory in front of the entire congregation?

The world seemed to tilt on its axis. Michele…the very same Michele who used to be a fixture in the front pew, her blonde curls bouncing as she sang hymns a little too loudly. The one who always gave Tasha those suffocating hugs and said, "God bless you, honey," with a saccharine smile that never quite reached her eyes.

A bitter laugh escaped Tasha's lips, but the hypocrisy of it all burned. Michele, the woman who'd feigned piety while carrying on an affair with a married man, was now getting married in the very church she'd stopped attending out of… guilt? Convenience?

Tasha slammed her phone shut, the plastic digging into her palm. Her stomach churned with a cocktail of anger, betrayal, and a strange, hollow feeling. Miles, the man who preached forgiveness and fidelity, was a walking contradiction. And Michele, the woman who'd fooled everyone, including Tasha, was now the 'blessed' bride.

The irony, huh? Tasha thought. *The mistress gets promoted to wife, all under the veil of forgiveness. Maybe forgiveness applies to adultery, but what about betrayal? Does that get a free pass, too? Apparently, in the eyes of the church, some sins are more forgivable than others, especially if they come with a pretty face and a younger body.*

She looked out at the blooming cherry tree in her backyard. A single, tear-shaped drop fell onto the windowsill. She didn't know what to do. She turned on her phone and reopened the picture of Miles and Michele. Their faces radiated a sickeningly smug joy, the kind that thrives on public validation. But what stung most was the silence from the church community.

There were no concerned calls, no visits to see if she was alright. The whispers that had swirled around her during the difficult months of the divorce seemed to have solidified into a disapproving hum. Tasha, the wronged wife, somehow became the topic of hushed conversations and sideways glances.

Michele was the woman who'd not only betrayed her but also been ostracized by the very church that now welcomed her back with open arms. It was a slap in the face, a public declaration that her pain didn't matter.

The final straw came a Sunday morning. As Tasha walked in, the usual greetings were absent. Heads were dipped, and whispers rippled through the pews. Even Pastor Williams, who had been close to Sasha and had been like a friend, offered a tight-lipped nod instead of his usual warm smile.

During the sermon, Pastor Williams spoke of forgiveness and starting anew. But every word felt pointed toward a justification for Michele's actions and a condemnation of Tasha's outburst at the funeral. The congregation seemed to nod along, passing looks of judgment toward her way.

Later, at the fellowship hall, the usual potluck buzz was muted. People clustered together, avoiding eye contact with Tasha. Even Sarah, who'd been a close friend, offered a smile from across the room, then quickly retreated into a conversation with someone else.

Michele, however, was the centerpiece. Adorned in a smile and a suspiciously familiar dress (the same one Tasha vaguely remembered her wearing on a 'church retreat' that Miles had conveniently attended), she was surrounded by well-wishers. The women who'd once confided in Tasha about their own marital troubles now cooed over Michele, offering congratulations and praising her "strength."

One particularly enthusiastic woman, Brenda, a woman who'd tearfully confessed to Tasha about her husband's gambling addiction just months ago, gushed, "Michele, you look absolutely stunning! And marrying Miles, what a wonderful new chapter! You two are just meant to be."

Michele fluttered her eyelashes modestly. "Thank you, Brenda, that's so kind of you to say. It's been a difficult journey, but we were meant to be together."

Brenda leaned in conspiratorially. "Yes, of course, my dear. But some people just couldn't move on. Some people hold onto grudges forever."

"It's a sad situation," Sarah agreed with faux sympathy. "But Michele, we wish you nothing but a good

286

future!"

Tears welled in Tasha's eyes. This wasn't just about Miles; it was about a community that had failed her. They were happy to forgive the homewrecker, the woman who'd broken their sacred vows, but Tasha, the wronged wife who'd reacted out of pain, was left ostracized.

With a clenched jaw, Tasha set down her untouched plate. This church no longer felt like a place she felt comfortable in. It was a place that perpetuated hypocrisy and punished the victims. She didn't touch the food and stood up to leave when a voice stopped her.

It was Natalie. She was a quiet woman who usually sat in the back pews. "Tasha," she said. "I may not understand everything, but I see your pain. You deserve better."

Tasha's heart skipped a beat. In that one sentence, Natalie offered more comfort than the entire congregation had all morning. It was a small gesture, but in that moment, it was a lifeline.

***

The sterile white of the ceiling pressed down on Tasha. Four walls had become her world. The bed felt like a solitary raft adrift in a stormy sea. Every cough that wracked her thin frame resonated in the oppressive silence. She knew she wasn't feeling well but didn't want to do anything about it.

The fight had drained her. Not just the physical one, the desperate struggle against Michele at her mother's funeral, but the emotional war that had raged ever since the infidelity began. The migraines, a continuous dull throb behind her eyes, seemed a fitting punishment for daring to feel. The only thought in her mind that echoed was… *you weren't strong enough. You weren't good enough.*

Her hair littered the pillow like fallen soldiers. The mirror on the dresser, usually ignored, mocked her with a gaunt reflection. The woman staring back had hollow eyes. Food now brought only nausea. The metallic tang of bile rose in her throat with every attempt to swallow. Her once-toned body had become a skeletal frame, draped in clothes that hung loosely.

Tasha traced the outline of a palm tree on the worn bedspread, a relic from a happier time, a family vacation to a sunny beach. *Escape.* The word screamed in the emptiness of the room. Maybe a new place, a blank canvas, could offer a chance to start anew. A place where the whispers wouldn't follow, where the judgmental stares wouldn't pierce her soul.

This sterile prison couldn't hold her forever. She had to get out and vanish into a world where Miles and Michele and their self-righteous church didn't exist. A new place, the only chance to outrun the memories, to silence the accusing whispers in her head. She imagined herself on a plane, soaring above the clouds, leaving the wreckage of her old life behind. A new city, bustling and anonymous, promised the anonymity she craved. She could reinvent herself and become someone untainted by their betrayal.

But the journey there seemed insurmountable. The thought of packing a single bag, of uprooting herself from the only life she'd ever known, felt heavy. A sob escaped her lips, a choked, pathetic sound. *Am I strong enough? Can I rebuild alone on the shifting sands of a new beginning?*

A wave of nausea rolled through her. She scrambled out of bed, her legs weak and wobbly, and rushed to the bathroom. The porcelain bowl was there, waiting for her to throw up again.

Back in bed, the tears came, silent and hot, tracking salty trails down her cheeks. "Mom," she rasped. Her mom, the person who had always been there for her, was gone. Now, facing the wreckage of her marriage and the judgmental whispers of her former church community,

Tasha felt completely alone.

Suddenly, the phone on the nightstand buzzed, a jarring intrusion into her self-imposed isolation. It was Jessica, one of the women who had fawned over Michele at the wedding. Tasha debated ignoring it. Her fake kindness felt awful. But a tiny bit of hope, a need to talk to someone, made her pick up.

"Tasha, honey, how are you doing?" Jessica's voice was all happy and worried, different from the mean whispers that still bothered Tasha.

"Just peachy," Tasha mumbled, her voice flat. It wasn't true.

"We're all so worried about you," Sarah continued, oblivious to Tasha's sarcasm. "Pastor Miles and Michele have been sending their love."

The names scraped raw against Tasha's already frayed nerves. "Please," she choked out, the single word laced with a world of hurt.

"We're having a potluck next week. You should come," Sarah chirped, seemingly undeterred.

Tasha let out a humorless laugh. The thought of facing the congregation, a gauntlet of pitying looks and veiled barbs, felt overwhelming. "Maybe next time," she lied again, the effort exhausting.

"Well, honey, don't be a stranger," Sarah chirped before ending the call. Tasha stared at the phone, feeling even more alone. Their niceness felt fake, not like the real help she needed.

Right then, her phone lit up again. It was Greg. After the conversation with Jessica, she didn't want to talk to anyone. She let it be and put her phone on the nightstand again. Burying herself in the comforter, she closed her eyes, hoping to sleep, but sleep was nowhere in sight.

Just then, a knock on the door startled her. "Tasha? You alright?" It was Greg.

Tasha didn't respond, the mere thought of conversation draining the last vestiges of her energy. But the doorknob rattled, and then, with a creak, Greg entered. He had come into the house with the spare key he had. He hovered near the doorway with his normally boisterous demeanor subdued.

"Hey," he mumbled. "You didn't pick up your phone."

Tasha cracked open one eye, the fluorescent light

from the hallway assaulting her. "I wasn't feeling up to it." Her voice came out hoarse, a mere rasp.

Greg winced. "Yeah, I figured. Sasha told me you haven't been…" he trailed off, searching for the right words.

"Eating?" Tasha finished for him, a bitter laugh escaping her lips. "Not much. Everything tastes… wrong."

She hated being so weak and needing to be taken care of. Greg sighed with a sound heavy of helplessness. He walked towards the dresser. "Well, I brought you some chicken noodle soup. Mom used to make it for you whenever you were sick."

A lump formed in Tasha's throat. The mention of her mother was a fresh wound, a gaping hole in a life already shattered. She wanted to lash out, to scream at the unfairness of it all, but the energy just wasn't there.

"I don't think I can stomach it, Greg," she rasped, closing her eyes again.

He placed a steaming bowl on the nightstand anyway. "Just try a few bites, okay? You need your strength."

Tasha didn't respond, the thought of food turning her stomach.

"Look," Greg finally said. "I know things are tough right now. But you can't just shut yourself away like this. You're going to get sick."

Tears welled up in Tasha's eyes, spilling over onto the pillow. "Everyone's already turned their backs on me," she choked out.

Greg sat down on the edge of the bed. "Am I not there for you? Is Sasha not there for you? Aren't we family supposed to take care of each other? Nobody wants you to shut yourself in. We're worried sick about you."

"I feel like I can't stay here anymore, Greg. Not with all the memories…" she said.

Greg reached out, his hand hovering awkwardly above hers. "Then don't. You could come and stay with me for a while. A change of scene might do you good."

The thought of leaving the place where she'd built a life with Miles was daunting. But the alternative, drowning in her grief, seemed even worse.

"I… I don't know," she stammered, her voice weak.

"Just think about it, okay?" Greg squeezed her hand gently. "In the meantime, you need to take care of yourself. Eat some soup, even if it's just a few bites. You need your strength, Tasha. You're going to get through this, I promise."

He paused for a while, then continued. "You're not giving up, Tasha. You're taking back control. You rebuild on your own terms, somewhere you feel safe and happy. But it's your choice, okay? No pressure."

He kissed her on the forehead gently and then handed her the bowl to eat. "C'mon now, don't be a baby. You wouldn't want me to spill over this on your shirt while spoon feeding you, now would you?"

The endearment brought a fresh wave of tears to Tasha's eyes. This time, however, they were tears of gratitude. With a weak smile, she opened her mouth and had some soup. She had her brother, and that, for now, was enough.

Later that night, Tasha sat in the quiet of her room, her thoughts heavy with unspoken prayers. She didn't have the right words to articulate her feelings. Tasha stared into nothingness with confusion and anger. Words failed Tasha. She tried to speak from her heart to God but found no words to worship or pray. She suddenly felt overthrown with the feeling of rebellion and darkness. She yelled aloud as if someone was in the room.

I want to be angry, and yes, I want revenge! Why do

I have to be strong all the time? she rhetorically asked herself. Now, Tasha was yelling at the top of her lungs.

I have been obedient to the Bible for years over top of years, just to be condemned to this hell my whole entire life!

I submitted myself... just to be the center of everyone's joke? I look so stupid!

What do I do? What is being required of me!?

What is the purpose of putting me in this hell?

As her cries faded, tears streamed down her cheeks, carrying with them the weight of her emotions and desires. She just hoped that perhaps even in the quiet roar of her broken heart, her cries were heard.

Chapter 24

The digital clock on the nightstand flickered at 3:37 am, casting the room in an eerie green glow. Sasha lay sprawled on her back, sheets tangled around her ankles, breathing in slow, even breaths. A faint thump from downstairs throbbed through the floorboards, barely registering over her deep sleep.

The bedroom door creaked open a sliver, then swung wider with a silent push. Rashaun, his usually steady gait replaced by an erratic shuffle, slipped into the room. His pupils were dilated as pinpricks against the whites of his eyes. A crimson rim around the irises betrayed a night of indulgence. Sweat plastered his short curls to his forehead, and a dark ring circled his flushed face. A manic energy crackled around him. His face was frozen in a predatory leer. His lips, cracked and chapped, were pulled back in a snarl, revealing gritted teeth. The stale scent of alcohol and cigarettes lingered in his breath.

He hovered near the bed and fixed his gaze on Sasha. He then trailed his eyes down. She lay sprawled, and her form barely concealed by the thin sheets that draped over her. Despite her protruding pregnant belly, her legs were half-exposed, enticing Raushan. His eyes trailed along the curves of Sasha's body, his breath hitching as he drank in her beauty. Despite the changes her body had undergone during her pregnancy, he found himself drawn to her with an intensity that surprised him. He dismissed the thoughts of her belly or her need for intimacy and softness. All he could think in that moment was his own lust and desire.

With a quick and impulsive movement, Raushan threw the covers back off Sasha, revealing her fully to his hungry eyes. His hands reached out, fingers curling around and digging into her supple thighs as he pulled her towards him with a possessive force. Sasha gasped as her eyes widened in surprise as she found herself being tugged towards the edge of the bed, unable to resist his determined advance.

Sasha's pulse got faster as her breath came in shallow gasps. She saw his red eyes and smelled the alcohol. She knew where he came from. His touch and force told her he was lustfully horny. He then wrapped her legs around him, pushing her underwear to the side, and fumbled his penis around her entryway and penetrated her. He didn't wait for her to self-lubricate.

His movements were harsh and rough. Not even

looking at her face or giving her a kiss, he focused on finishing off, each push getting stronger by the minute. Sasha could feel the pain between her legs but kept herself tight-lipped. Despite her attempts, she couldn't contain her groans from pain as the dryness made it even more difficult. A single tear rolled from her eyes to the sides and fell on the sheets. A swirl of conflicting emotions clouded her mind. She knew it was her duty as a wife to fulfill his needs and be there for him in every sense, so she didn't speak. But beneath the surface of her compliance, there brewed a deep sense of dissatisfaction, a feeling of being used, of being nothing more than an object to satisfy his desires.

Her thoughts drifted to the countless times she had caught him in his indiscretions, the evidence of his infidelity leaving scars on her heart. Yet, despite the pain, there was a glimmer of relief that he came home to her, fulfilling his desires for his wife rather than in the arms of another woman or in the darkness of a strip club. As she endured the bangs and rough intimacy, Sasha couldn't help but cling to the fragile hope that maybe, just maybe, his return signaled a flicker of commitment, a desire to choose her over his fleeting temptations, but deep down, she knew it wasn't true. She felt nothing but an object to him.

Rashaun kept on going till he finished off. He then

abruptly fell on Sasha, his entire weight catching his breath. She immediately pushed him aside. Her hand protectively cradled her swollen belly and shot Rashaun a reproachful look. He then crawled his way up the bed with his shoes on and lay on his stomach, immediately falling asleep. Lost in her own thoughts, Sasha traced the patterns of the ceiling with her eyes as tears rolled down her cheek as she dragged herself to the bathroom.

***

The sun beat down on Sasha's back, turning the morning cool into a clinging heat. She cradled the ceramic mug, the coffee lukewarm and forgotten. The remnants of the night, the unwelcome weight of Rashaun, left her body sore and her spirit colder.

Her gaze drifted across the shimmering expanse of the pool. It was glistening in the glow of the sun's rays, almost like a jewel. Suddenly, the light blue of the pool turned red. She gasped and blinked her eyes twice. It was blue again. She had seen Miste's blood in her thoughts. His body hanging from above came in front of her eyes, and she couldn't help but feel like throwing up.

Putting the coffee mug on the floor, she dipped her feet in the cool water of the pool. A pang, sharp and unexpected, ripped through her. The baby. The tiny life growing inside her. It was a constant reminder of the path she didn't know if she wanted to embark on. Love and hate battled within. The joy of motherhood and the fear of the upcoming haunted her like nothing else. The white walls of a doctor's office, the cold gel on her belly, the grainy image on the screen – she couldn't face it yet. The thought of seeing that tiny form, a physical manifestation of her conflicting emotions, was too much to bear.

Sasha closed her eyes. She needed a decision, a path forward. But all she saw was a tangled mess of betrayal, longing, and a tiny, unseen life that depended on her. The coffee remained untouched as she thought of all the chaos going on in her life.

Just then, the back door slammed like a gunshot, ripping away the peace of the morning. Rashaun stumbled into the kitchen. His face was a picture of sleep and barely contained annoyance. He tossed a pack of cigarettes onto the counter with a loud clatter, completely ignoring Sasha where she sat by the pool. This silent treatment, his usual way of starting the day, was now a routine for Sasha.

She tried to smile, but it came out weak and forced, like a cracked vase. "Coffee?" She offered, already knowing the answer.

He grunted, brushing past her on his way to the fridge. Sasha watched him go. Her smile collapsed into a frown. He came back with a carton of milk. As he poured himself a glass, a tiny spark of something - defiance, perhaps? - flickered to life inside her.

Sasha came inside and entered the kitchen. "Would you like some eggs with breakfast?" She asked in a calm voice.

Rashaun slammed the fridge door shut, the sound making the whole kitchen vibrate. "I just woke up, woman! Of course, I'm hungry," he snapped, his voice thick with sleep and an underlying anger that had nothing to do with her question. "If you're gonna make breakfast, then make it! Don't ask dumb questions!"

His words stung like a slap. Sasha flinched at the venom in his tone. She fought to maintain her composure, swallowing the lump in her throat as she turned away to resume her cooking.

In the silence that followed, broken only by the sizzle of eggs in the pan, Sasha wondered how they had arrived at this point, where simple gestures of kindness were met with such hostility. And as she continued to cook, her thoughts drifted to a distant hope. But for now, all she could do was endure, clinging to the fragile hope that one day, things might be different.

The day wore on, and Sasha stewed in her silence. The drone of the pool filter became a mocking soundtrack to her thoughts. Rashaun, true to form, had disappeared into his man cave, likely shrouded in a haze she refused to acknowledge. She knew he was getting high, and there was nothing she could do to stop him. If she said something, he wouldn't stop; instead, he would get even more hyper and even beat her up. She went out and sat by the pool again. This time, she thought about the good memories she had with Rashaun, especially before their marriage and in the early days after their union. A memory of Rashaun, laughing, eyes crinkled with joy, as they chased each other around that same pool crossed her mind. The man she fell in love with, the man who seemed to have vanished.

It wasn't until later in the evening that Rashaun emerged from his man cave. His eyes glazed with a distant gaze that hinted at the lingering effects of his indulgence. But despite the haze that surrounded him, there was a spark of familiarity in his smile, a glimpse of the man Sasha had once fallen in love with.

"Hey there, beautiful," he said, his voice surprisingly warm. Sasha stared at him, unsure of this sudden transformation. He extended a hand towards her with a playful glint in his eyes.

"Come on, let's go for a swim. The sun's setting, perfect time for a dip."

He wasn't the man she'd woken up to that morning. This was Rashaun before the addiction, the man she'd fallen in love with – funny, charming, with a genuine twinkle in his eyes. For a fleeting moment, the anger and resentment that had been churning within her softened. A memory surfaced: a younger Sasha, laughing with this same man by the pool.

Hesitantly, she took his hand. "You sure you're up for it?" She asked, her voice cautious.

He squeezed her hand, his touch sending a jolt through her. "Never been more sure," he replied, his voice warm. "Come on, let's race to the other side!"

A ghost of a smile touched her lips. "You're on," she said, a playful glint mirroring his own in her eyes.

They ran towards the pool, his laughter echoing in the now-golden evening light. As they reached the edge, Sasha sat down. Rashaun playfully pushed her in with a gentle shove.

"Hey!" She shrieked, a surprised laugh escaping her lips. She sputtered and surfaced, shaking water from her hair.

Rashaun was already halfway across the pool, a triumphant grin on his face. "Come on, slowpoke!" He called out.

Sasha kicked her legs, powering through the water. The cool water washed away some of the tension that had been coiled tight within her. For a moment, all that existed was the race, the feel of the water against her skin, and the sound of their laughter blending with the chirping crickets.

She reached the other side, gasping for breath. Rashaun was already there, leaning against the pool wall, a bouncy glint in his eyes.

"Well, well," he said, feigning surprise. "Looks like the old lady still has some moves."

Sasha swatted him playfully on the arm. "Oh, it's on," she declared as a competitive fire reignited within her. "Next time, you're going down."

As they walked back inside, the playful energy lingered. She snuck a glance at Rashaun, his smile genuine, his eyes clear. A sliver of hope, fragile as a spiderweb, began to spin in her chest. This was the Rashaun she'd married, the man she loved. But the memory of his withdrawal, the cold, manipulative stranger he became under the influence of the drug, was a harsh counterpoint to this hopeful moment.

She yearned for this to be real, for him to be truly present, not just a fleeting glimpse of the man he could be. She wanted to believe in the possibility of change so that they could rebuild their fractured relationship. But the path wouldn't be easy. It would require honesty, commitment, and a willingness to face the demons that haunted him. And most importantly, it would require him to choose her, to choose their family, every single day.

They changed and sat down on the couch in the living room. Sitting there, Sasha got lost in her own thoughts. *Would this playful interlude last? Was it a genuine reconnection or just another cruel trick of his addiction?* Only time will tell. But for now, she allowed herself to be swept away by the warmth of his behavior. She wanted to indulge in the moment and not think anything negative.

"What would you like to have for dinner?" Rashaun asked casually, pulling her closer to himself.

Sasha was taken aback. *Was she listening to things on her own, or was Rashaun really asking her this question?*

"Ummm…I don't know," Sasha replied hesitantly.

"Oh well, don't worry about it," he replied. He then stood up and went into the kitchen. He grabbed the Salmon from the fridge and started preparing for dinner. Soon enough, the house smelled of grilled salmon and roasted vegetables. It was a welcome change from the usual fare of takeout boxes Sasha had grown accustomed to. Rashaun set the table. He'd even remembered her love for extra lemon wedges.

An awkward silence seemed to exist between the two of them as a residue of the tension from the morning. But Rashaun seemed determined to bridge the gap.

"Hey, did I ever tell you about that time with Mr. Henderson next door?" Rashaun asked, setting down a plate with a flourish. Sasha raised an eyebrow, intrigued.

"Mr. Henderson? The grumpy old man with the perfect lawn?" She asked, a smile playing on her lips.

Rashaun chuckled. "Exactly! So, the other day, I'm out mowing the front yard, right? And this squirrel darts out from under the bushes, carrying this giant acorn in its mouth. It runs straight for Mr. Henderson's rose bushes, and I'm thinking, 'Uh oh, this isn't going to end well.'"

Sasha snorted with laughter. "Oh no, what happened?"

"Well, the squirrel gets halfway there, and this acorn just pops out of its mouth and thwacks Mr. Henderson right on the head! He jumps back like he's been shot, yelling at the top of his lungs. The squirrel just stared at him for a second, then went off like nothing happened."

Rashaun doubled over with laughter. Sasha couldn't help but join in, the memory of the grumpy Mr. Henderson and his startled reaction conjuring a genuine smile on her face. This was the Rashaun she'd missed, the one who could draw her into easy conversation.

Sasha felt a sliver of hope, a fragile thing that she cradled carefully. *Could this be a new beginning? Perhaps, with effort, they could rebuild what had been fractured.*

As they finished the last bites of dessert, a comfortable silence settled between them. Rashaun excused himself, heading towards the shower. Sasha cleared the table. *Maybe, just maybe, this façade of normalcy could become something real.*

The sound of the shower cutting off shattered the hopeful atmosphere. A moment later, Rashaun reappeared, towel slung around his waist with a devil-may-care grin on his face.

"Hey," he began, a hint of hesitation in his voice, "Do you mind if I borrow the car? Need to run a quick errand."

Sasha's heart stuttered. The hopeful warmth that had bloomed within her chest began to shrivel. This – this casual request for the car – was a test, a subtle attempt to gauge how far his manipulation could reach after his manufactured good mood. Letting him take the borrowed car after his night of indulgence felt reckless and irresponsible.

She met his gaze, her voice devoid of the playful lilt from moments ago. "Actually," she started, choosing her words carefully, "I wouldn't feel comfortable with that. It's a borrowed car, and you…" She trailed off, searching for the right way to phrase her concern.

Rashaun's smile vanished completely, replaced by a flicker of annoyance. "Come on, Sasha," he said, his voice dripping with condescension. "It's just a quick errand. What's the big deal?"

The way he spoke to her, the dismissal in his voice, solidified her suspicions. This wasn't a genuine request; it was a power play. He was testing the boundaries he himself had blurred, hoping to see how much control he still wielded.

Taking a deep breath, Sasha stood her ground. "The big deal is," she said, her voice firm, "you were… indisposed last night. I can't let you take the car when I'm not confident you're fit to drive."

Rashaun's face contorted in anger. "Indisposed? You make it sound like I was out partying all night! I just needed to unwind a little."

"Unwind a little," she repeated, the bitterness evident in her voice. "That's what you call it? Look, I appreciate the effort you're making…"

"Effort?" He spat back, interrupting her. "Don't patronize me, Sasha."

The anger in his voice was a complete reminder of the volatile man he could become. Sasha took a step back, her hope for a genuine connection dashed against the reality of his addiction. Here it was again, the cycle restarting. The loving facade, the manipulation, the anger.

"Maybe," she said, her voice calm but firm, "we need to talk about something more important than erran…"

The words died on her lips as Rashaun sucked his teeth with a theatrical puff of air. He didn't even bother to retort as his frustration simmered just beneath the surface.

With a final, angry slam of the bedroom door, he stormed out.

Moments ticked by, filled with a tense silence. Sasha tried to focus on the hum of the refrigerator, anything to dispel the unease creeping into her gut. But then, a different sound descended – it was the sound of the garage door opening where his truck resided.

A chill ran down her spine. She peeked through the blinds, her heart sinking as she saw only the empty driveway bathed in the cool moonlight. She saw just two receding red brake lights at the end of the street, the car moving backward as it pulled out.

Panic seized her. Rashaun hadn't just stormed out; he'd stolen the car. The carefully constructed facade, the charming dinner, the laughter – it had all been a calculated ploy, a smokescreen for his manipulative agenda.

Fury burned in her chest, a white-hot rage that replaced the fragile hope she'd dared to hold onto. She raced to the bedroom, ripping open her purse. Empty. He'd taken her keys too.

"The bastard," she seethed, the bitter truth hitting her like a physical blow. She'd seen this play before, fallen for his deceptive calm only to be left cleaning up the mess. But not this time. Not anymore.

This wasn't just about the car. It was about respect, about boundaries. He was treating her like a pawn, someone whose trust and well-being meant nothing. And she, fool that she was, had let him.

Adrenaline replaced her panic. She bombarded his phone with texts, desperate pleas for him to bring the car back. But her messages were met with a deafening silence. It was a confirmation of her worst fears.

Should I report the car stolen? The thought flashed across her mind but quickly died. She knew him all too well. He wouldn't hesitate to use it against her, to paint her as the hysterical wife. But she threatened him anyway in a text message that she would report the car stolen, but she knew that Raushaun knew she wouldn't do it to avoid social embarrassment.

Rashaun needed a wake-up call, a taste of his own frustration. He needed to understand that he couldn't control her anymore. A daring plan took root in her mind. Let him miss her for a change.

With a new resolve, Sasha dialed Nikkay's number. "Hey girl," she said, her voice firm, "can you pick me up? I need a weekend getaway."

"Is everything alright?" Nikkay asked.

"Yes, just need a place to stay for two days," she told her.

"Alright, I'll come pick you up."

Nikkay came, and as they pulled away from the house, Sasha glanced back at the empty driveway, a strange mix of fear and defiance warring within her. Her plan was risky, a leap into the unknown. But one thing was certain – she wouldn't sit at home fretting, waiting for the inevitable storm.

The road ahead was uncertain. As they sped into the night, Sasha vowed to never again fall for the illusion of peace that Rashaun offered. She was done being his doormat. It was time for him to face the consequences of his actions, and it was time for her to do something to make him realize the stress and heartbreak he caused her.

Chapter 25

Nikkay had served herself as a lifeline for Sasha. Sasha knew the moment the plan hatched that Nikkay wouldn't bat an eyelash before whisking her away. True to form, Nikkay arrived with a car and a pre-planned itinerary that reflected serenity and, most importantly, girl time.

Sasha clutched Nikkay's hand as they walked down the busy sidewalk. This wasn't just a getaway; it was a reunion with a part of herself she'd neglected. She walked into the café, and to her surprise, Nikkay had organized a brunch with their childhood friends, the 'Chocolate Diamonds' as they called themselves – a group of Black women Sasha hadn't seen in years.

The brunch spot buzzed with energy. For a moment, all Sasha could hear was the laughter and the clinking of glasses as her friends and associates piled into a corner booth.

"Hey Sasha, over here!" Called out Maya, waving her hand enthusiastically.

Sasha's lips curled into a smile as she made her way over to the table. "Hey everyone, it's so good to see you all!"

A whirlwind of hugs and exclamations erupted the moment Sasha walked in. Sasha settled into her seat, feeling a sense of belonging wash over her in the presence of her closest friends. Years melted away as they reminisced about childhood escapades.

"Remember that time we snuck out to see New Edition?" Simone giggled as her eyes sparkled with nostalgia.

"And how about that science project that went hilariously wrong?" Chimed Aisha, pulling out her phone to share a grainy picture of a volcano erupting all over the classroom floor.

They shrieked with laughter, the memory vivid even after all these years. The conversation then shifted to their careers.

"Okay, spill the tea. What's been going on with everyone?" Sasha asked, eager to catch up on the latest gossip and news.

Nikkay had landed a promotion at her advertising firm. Maya was showcasing her work at a local gallery. Aisha had landed her dream job as an engineer. As they shared their triumphs, Sasha couldn't help but feel a pang of envy. Her life had become consumed by the ever-present needs of her husband and their unborn child.

"Girl, you look amazing!" Simone exclaimed, snapping Sasha out of her reverie. "Seriously, motherhood agrees with you."

Sasha offered a weak smile. "Thanks, Simone. It's… a lot."

"We hear you," Aisha said, reaching across the table to squeeze Sasha's hand. "But motherhood doesn't have to mean sacrificing yourself. You're still Sasha, that fierce, independent woman we all know and love."

Sasha's heart swelled with a forgotten warmth. These were the women who knew her, who had seen her before the world had dimmed her light.

The conversation inevitably turned to relationships. Nikkay launched into a passionate diatribe about self-worth and independence.

"Girl," she declared, her voice ringing with conviction, "we are Black queens! We don't need some man to complete us. We built our own empires, climbed our own ladders, and ain't nobody gonna walk all over us!"

A chorus of agreement echoed around the table. Sasha listened, but a tug-of-war raged within her. She wholeheartedly agreed with their message. Black women had a fierce strength, a capacity for resilience and self-reliance that was unparalleled. But a quiet voice within her heart whispered of the attributes of a virtuous wife. Something that spoke of the loyalty of a woman who supported her husband no matter the struggle.

Sasha wasn't one to share her inner turmoil, especially not in that moment when she could become the target of everybody's judgment. Instead, she offered a weak smile, nodding along as the others shared stories of their strong, independent lives. Their words reminded her of the woman she could be, the woman she was before her world became so focused on Rashaun.

Later, as they strolled through the park, the afternoon sun dappling the green pathway, Sasha caught Nikkay's knowing gaze.

"Something on your mind, girl?" Nikkay asked gently.

Sasha hesitated, her voice low. "It's Rashaun," she admitted.

Nikkay stopped, her arm wrapping around Sasha's shoulder in a silent display of support. Sasha poured out her story, the frustration, the hurt, the suffocating feeling of being used. Nikkay listened patiently.

"Girl," Nikkay said when Sasha finished. "You deserve better. There's a difference between supporting your husband and being his doormat. You can be strong, independent, and still be a loving wife, but not if he doesn't respect you."

Sasha pondered Nikkay's words. There was a seed of truth taking root within her. Maybe there was another way. Maybe her strength, her independence, wouldn't be a rejection of her vows but a way to reclaim her own sense of self, the woman she'd almost forgotten.

The next morning, Sasha stretched luxuriously as the stress of yesterday melted away with each languid movement. Yesterday's brunch with her friends had rekindled a spark within her. She continuously thought about the independent woman she was before life narrowed her focus to Rashaun and her impending child.

However, guilt gnawed at the edges of her peace. For the first time in their marriage, she'd abandoned Rashaun without a trace. The stolen car… the silence from him – it painted a picture of a situation spiraling further out of control. A small part of her worried. A maternal instinct was urging her to return and face the consequences, no matter how unpleasant.

But another, stronger voice rose within her. *'Rashaun can't keep walking all over me,'* she thought. *'He messed up, taking the car, disappearing like that! He needs to learn that his actions have consequences. He couldn't manipulate me with his feigned charm and disappearances only to return expecting everything to be back to normal.'* A flicker of anger sparked within her. *'And besides,'* she continued in her internal dialogue, *'this weekend is exactly what I needed. A chance to remember who I am, to take care of myself. A strong Sasha is a better Sasha for everyone, Rashaun included.'*

Determined to make the most of her remaining time, Sasha booked a spa day at a nearby resort. Luxury robes and soothing music greeted her as she entered. Expert hands kneaded away the tension knots in her shoulders while cucumber slices cooled her puffy eyes. For a few blissful hours, she surrendered to the pampering, the worries of home and Rashaun fading into the background.

As she emerged from the final treatment, feeling refreshed and rejuvenated, the guilt returned with a vengeance. The image of Rashaun, alone and frustrated, filled her mind. Here she was, indulging in self-care while he… well, who knew what trouble he might have gotten himself into. The stolen car and his unpredictable nature were a cocktail for disaster.

Sasha debated cutting the day short, returning home to face whatever awaited her. But then, Nikkay's words echoed in her mind: "You can be strong, independent, and still be a loving wife, but not if he doesn't respect you." Nikkay was right. Taking care of herself wasn't a betrayal; it was a necessity. A strong, healthy Sasha was better equipped to deal with Rashaun and whatever challenges their future held.

With a deep breath, Sasha pushed the guilt aside. She deserved this time for herself. She deserved to feel beautiful and strong. Maybe, just maybe, this self-care wouldn't just benefit her, but their relationship as a whole. She might return with a renewed perspective, a new strength to face whatever awaited her back home.

The rest of the day passed in a blur of manicures, pedicures, and a delicious lunch overlooking a cascading waterfall. Sasha savored every moment. But as the sun began its descent, a pang of longing tugged at her heart. She missed him and wanted to be a good wife, no matter what he did to her. The conflicting thoughts were driving her mind crazy.

At this point, she felt like she didn't even know what she wanted.

***

The flickering streetlamp cast an eerie radiance through the living room window, illuminating the trail of destruction Rashaun left in his wake. An overturned chair lay sprawled on the floor, a half-eaten bag of chips sat abandoned on the coffee table, and the air was full of the stale scent of cigarettes. It was 3 AM, and Rashaun had just stumbled through the front door. His body was a symphony of aches, and his mind a swirling vortex of confusion.

The initial euphoria of the night had long since evaporated, replaced by a gnawing emptiness that settled in his gut like a stone. He scanned the room as his bloodshot eyes searched for a sign, anything, to explain Sasha's absence. She used to wait for him in the living room whenever he had been out or would come running down from the room upon his arrival. But she was nowhere. The cold, empty silence ridiculed him, confirming his worst fears. She was gone.

A primal rage surged through him as a gush of anger threatened to consume him. *How dare she disappear? Doesn't she understand I need her?* But the anger was quickly overshadowed by a suffocating wave of worry. *Where is she? Is she safe?* These questions hammered in his head like a persistent drumbeat against the backdrop of his throbbing skull.

He slumped onto the couch as the anger dissipated into a hollow frustration. *I should be furious*, he thought, enraged by her defiance. But a strange sense of emptiness held him captive. He craved the accustomed sting of her disapproval, the way her concern, even her anger, had always been a tether to his sanity. Now, there was only silence, a deafening void where her presence should be.

A desperate plea welled up from the depths of his being. He lurched to his knees as his head pounded. "God," he rasped. "Help me. Fix me. I… I don't know what to do." A sob escaped his eyes as he put his head down on the floor. The wreckage of his own making came before his eyes. "I'm thankful for Sasha and for everything she does for me. Help me be the man she deserves," he said aloud in a muffled scream as he covered his mouth with both hands, kneeling down on the floor, his head touching the ground.

'I don't deserve her, not in this state,' he thought, but the idea of her leaving, of losing her altogether, terrified him. The path ahead was uncertain, but a single, fragile hope

flickered in the darkness of his mind – a hope for redemption, for a future where he was worthy of Sasha's love and where she wouldn't have to disappear to be seen.

Rashaun struggled back and forth with reality and demonic emotions. The terror that he felt from the thought of losing her, frighteningly, did not overpower his pride for reconciliation. He still refused to call her or render questions to family and friends about her whereabouts. He felt the need for Sasha to feel her disappearing act had no effect on him. This will prevent her from trying this stunt in the future. Rashaun could not help but perceive that by not showing care for Sasha's feelings, he would be fully in control as a man, as anything less would be a sign of weakness.

Exhausted by the emotional chaos, in a few moments, he was deep in slumber, sprawled on the very floor.

***

The tendrils of sleep began to loosen their grip on Rashaun, pulling him from the oblivion he'd sought. But instead of the harsh reality of the living room floor, he found himself bathed in the warm glow of the bedroom. Sasha stood before him.

A wave of relief washed over him, so intense it took

his breath away. She looked amazing. Her hair, usually pulled back in a practical braid, cascaded down her shoulders in a halo of soft curls. The worry that had etched lines on her face had vanished, replaced by a gentle serenity. In the dim light, her warm brown eyes shone with a depth that melted the ice around his heart. She looked beautiful, not just in the way that turned heads on the street, but with a beauty that radiated from within.

Tears welled up in his eyes, blurring the image of her. She was here, safe, home. He reached out, his hand trembling as it grasped hers. It was warm, solid, a lifeline in the storm he'd created.

"Sasha," he croaked in a thick voice. "I... I'm so sorry." The words tumbled out in a flow of apologies for his actions, for the hurt he'd caused her. He laid bare his vulnerability, the fear of losing her a raw, exposed nerve.

Sasha's eyes mirrored his own, glistening with tears. But they weren't tears of anger this time. They were tears of relief. A soft cry escaped her lips as she pulled him into a tight hug.

"Oh, Rashaun," she whispered. "I was so worried. But I'm here now. And we'll get through this together."

A laugh, shaky but genuine, escaped her lips. It was

the sound of hope, a melody that chased away the oppressive silence that had haunted him. He held her tighter, clinging to her like a lifeline. This was his wake-up call, a glimpse of what he could lose. He wouldn't take it for granted again.

Then, with a jolt, he awoke. The hard floor of the living room greeted him. The warmness of Sasha's embrace was replaced by the cold floor. His hand, still clutching at empty air, ached with the phantom touch of hers.

It had all been a dream, a cruel trick his subconscious had played on him. A reminder of what he was on the verge of losing. He lay there on his belly as the weight of his actions pressed down on him.

A single tear traced a path down his cheek. He knew what he had to do. He had to fight for himself, for Sasha, and for the future he'd glimpsed in his dreams, but would he be able to? Only time will tell.

Chapter 26

The tan SUV rolled to a stop in the driveway. Sasha's apprehension was palpable as she gazed at her home from the back seat. The sight of the borrowed car, snatched by her husband three nights ago, only added to her unease.

"Thank you for putting up with me," she murmured, her gratitude tinged with guilt, before slipping out of the car without waiting for Nikay or Torri's response.

Nikay's forced "Anytime, girl," earned a strained smile from Sasha, though inside, she seethed at their judgment.

'To hell with both of y'all for judging me,' she thought bitterly, closing the rear passenger's door behind her.

With a heavy heart, she unloaded her plastic shopping bags and the Gucci duffle bag overflowing with clothes as the trunk popped open.

Entering her house, Sasha punched in the front door code, praying that no drama lurked beyond the unlocked threshold. Stepping into the grand living room, she took in the neatly arranged furniture, a stark contrast to the chaos within her mind. As she deposited her bags in a corner, the sounds of her husband's slumber echoed from the master bedroom - a sleeping bear, temporarily at peace.

Moving through the house, Sasha entered the kitchen, surprised to find the Friday night dinner dishes cleared away. His act of cleaning hinted at a rare moment of respite from their turbulent emotions, stirring a mix of hope and apprehension within her.

Quietly slipping off her shoes, Sasha tiptoed towards the bedroom, her heart heavy with the weight of shame and guilt. With cautious steps, she sought confirmation of his slumber, hoping for a reprieve from the storm brewing within them both.

There he lay, stretched out, his stocking cap snug on his head, one hand nestled inside his sweatpants, finding solace in each rumbling breath. Sasha returned to the living room, her gaze falling on the disorganized bags. Tears welled in her eyes as she realized she couldn't risk unpacking, fearing what might transpire if he woke.

"Okay, now what?" She whispered to herself, the weight of uncertainty pressing down on her. Suddenly, she remembered the urgency of finding the car key. With cautious steps, she ventured into the master bedroom, craning her neck to peek around.

Nothing.

She hurried downstairs to the second guest bedroom, heart racing. As she entered, a mix of confusion and disbelief washed over her. The room was adorned with her stepchildren's baby photographs, meticulously placed on the dressers. His shoes stood in regimented lines against the wall as if he had claimed the space as his own. Sasha's emotions swirled, torn between anger at his calculated detachment and a flicker of relief at the prospect of reclaiming a fragment of autonomy.

Regardless of her conflicting feelings, the scene before her defied description. It was a tableau of manipulation and estrangement, where words failed to capture the depth of emotion. Only sharp, dagger-like words could pierce through the layers, reaching the heart of the matter.

With a sudden movement, the key caught Sasha's eye, perched at the edge of the dresser as if forgotten in haste. Snatching it up like a prized possession, she searched for a hiding spot, already bracing herself for the tumultuous aftermath. The coat pocket seemed a safe bet—inside it went, hanging innocuously in the closet. If he searched, he wouldn't suspect the coat she rarely wore, and if he found it, a plausible explanation could be conjured to quell his potential rage and insults.

Taking a deep breath, Sasha attempted to navigate the whirlwind of thoughts swirling in her mind. A hot bath seemed like a sanctuary, a gesture to signal her desire to avoid conflict. With determined steps, she retraced her path to the master bedroom, only to find the once-open door now firmly shut.

She turned the doorknob - *locked.*

Frustration boiled within her as she headed to the adjoining office room, hoping for an alternative route into the master bedroom. But as she tried the door to the master bathroom, her agitation peaked - *locked.*

"What the fuck?" She exclaimed, her voice tinged with a mix of anger and desperation, trapped in a maze of closed doors and unanswered questions.

"He has got some nerve," Sasha muttered under her breath as she knocked on the door, a humble request for him to unlock it.

But after three rounds of consecutive knocks, the volume on the flat-screen television spiked, signaling the onset of the silent treatment. Recognizing the futility of her attempts to gain his attention, Sasha retreated to the study, choosing silence over further confrontation.

Seated in the quiet confines of the study, Sasha wrestled with the bewildering cascade of emotions triggered by his passive-aggressive reaction.

What did I do wrong to deserve this treatment yet again?

Her mind drifted back to the day she had left and the conflicting thoughts she suffered. Now that she thought about it, she was still confused about all that was happening and what the future awaited.

Right then, Sasha realized that she needed to confront the situation head-on instead of allowing herself to be manipulated by her husband's behavior. She resolved to address the issues at hand and take control of the situation.

Leaving the study, Sasha decided to take a different approach. She marched back to the master bedroom door and knocked firmly out, "Open the door, Rashaun. We need to talk."

Silence greeted her once more, but this time, Sasha refused to be deterred. She continued to knock.

"I won't let you shut me out like this," she asserted.

After what felt like an eternity, she heard the click of the lock, and the door slowly swung open to reveal Rashaun standing there with a guarded expression.

"We need to talk," Sasha repeated, stepping into the room without waiting for an invitation.

Tension crackled in the air like electricity, and it didn't take long for sparks to fly.

"What the hell?" Sasha's voice trembled with a mix of anger and frustration. "You can't just lock me out and ignore me whenever you feel like it!"

Rashaun's eyes flashed with defiance.

"I can do whatever I want in my own damn house!" He shot back, his voice laced with bitterness. "You're the one who ran off like a coward, leaving me to clean up your mess."

Sasha scoffed, eyes narrowing. "Clean up my mess? You're the mess, Rashaun! A pathetic excuse for a husband!"

Rashaun's face turned red with fury. "Watch your mouth, you ungrateful b****! You don't know good you've got it."

"Good? Ha! More like trapped," Sasha spat back, her voice dripping with disdain. "You suffocate me with your control freak bullshit. You spend all your money, then take mine until I am unable to pay the bills, and you don't care! You get mad at me every time I am on the phone, whether I am speaking to family or mutual friends! You are emotionally immature! You give your famous silent treatment whenever a hard conversation must be had, and lately, you even avoid conversing about the baby! You keep me walking on eggshells without shoes!" Sasha paused to catch her breath.

"And should I go on about how you make me feel victimized when you come in the house five in the morning high and physically forcing sex on me? I don't even know where you have been or who you've been with, nor do you answer the questions when I ask! Who do you think you are Rashaun? Then, you choose to ignore me for days as if I have done something to you! I am the one holding us down and creating the illusion of a great relationship, just so you can look good from the outside!"

Rashaun knew all she was saying was true, but his wall of delusional defense would not allow him to be humble and face his reality. His true emotions made him feel like a failure yet again, and of course it's all Sasha's fault.

Rashaun's hands trembled. He felt a mix of jealousy

and insecurity as he looked at Sasha, his mind consumed by the gnawing feeling of being played and disrespected. Every glance, every word from Sasha felt like a dagger to his wounded pride, amplifying his sense of inadequacy and emasculation.

His voice grew louder, booming with anger. "You want space? Fine! Go ahead and disappear! I'll be better off without you!"

Sasha's hands balled into fists at her sides. "I left because I couldn't take it anymore!" She exclaimed. "You're suffocating me!"

Suddenly, Rashaun came closer and grabbed Sasha by the neck so tightly she almost choked.

"Suffocating, huh! Now, I'll tell you what suffocation actually means!" Rashaun spat in a low, cruel growl as he tightened his grip on her neck.

Sasha's eyes widened in terror as Rashaun's grip tightened around her neck, cutting off her air supply. Panic surged through her veins, and she struggled against his iron hold, clawing desperately at his fingers in a futile attempt to break free.

"Rashaun, stop!" She gasped, her voice strained and

hoarse. "You're hurting me!"

But Rashaun's eyes were wild and furious, and his face contorted into a mask of pure rage.

"You think you can talk back to me, you little bitch?" He snarled, his voice dripping with malice. "You want to know what suffocation feels like? I'll show you!"

With a vicious twist of his hand, Rashaun exerted even more pressure on Sasha's throat, his fingers digging into her flesh like vise grips. The world around her began to spin as darkness encroached on the edges of her vision, her lungs burning for air that refused to come.

Terror gripped Sasha's heart as she realized the extent of Rashaun's brutality. She kicked and thrashed, desperation lending her strength as she fought for her very survival.

But just as she felt herself slipping into unconsciousness, a sudden surge of adrenaline coursed through her veins, fueling her determination to break free from Rashaun's deadly grip.

Summoning every ounce of strength she possessed, Sasha delivered a swift, powerful blow to Rashaun's abdomen, causing him to double over in pain and release his hold on her neck.

Gasping for air, Sasha collapsed to the ground, coughing, and wheezing as she struggled to fill her lungs with oxygen. Tears streamed down her cheeks as she stared up at Rashaun.

Rashaun staggered back, clutching his stomach in agony. "You little bitch," he growled, his voice low and dangerous. "You'll pay for that!"

Unable to contain the raging storm of emotions within him, Rashaun's anger erupted into a violent outburst. He lashed out at Sasha with a ferocity fueled by his own insecurities, his fists raining down upon her with unbridled fury.

"You think you can make a fool out of me?" He roared. "You think I don't see through your lies?"

Sasha recoiled from the onslaught, her body battered and bruised by Rashaun's persistent assault. Tears mingled with blood as she pleaded for mercy.

"Rashaun, please," she begged, her words barely audible through the haze of agony. "I didn't do anything wrong. Please, just stop!"

But Rashaun's jealousy blinded him to reason. His

mind was consumed by a toxic cocktail of rage and insecurity. He continued to rain down blows upon Sasha.

"You think you can disrespect me and get away with it?" He snarled as his fists clenched in a white-knuckled grip. "You're mine, Sasha. Mine!"

"*Shut up! Stop!*" Sasha yelled at him, trying to save herself.

Right then, Rashaun's already wounded pride, his simmering jealousy, and feelings of inadequacy erupted into a violent frenzy. Without a moment's hesitation, he lunged at her as his hands closed around her throat with a vice-like grip once again.

"You think you can make me feel less than a man?" He snarled. "I'll show you what happens when you disrespect *me*!"

Rashaun's fingers tightened around her neck. He then threw her on the floor once again like a ragged doll and grabbed her hair. He tightened his grip on her roots as if they were a rope and, with a brutal force, dragged her through the study, the bedroom, and into the living room. His grip never loosened as he unleashed his pent-up rage upon her.

Rashaun's eyes narrowed with a predatory glint as

they fell upon the old broken shoe rack in the corner of the living room. With a menacing grin, he stalked toward it.

"This'll teach you a lesson, you worthless piece of trash," he spat out, his voice dripping with venomous disdain.

Sasha watched in terror as Rashaun approached the broken rack, her heart pounding in her chest with a sickening mixture of dread and despair.

"Please, Rashaun, don't," she pleaded. "You don't have to do this."

But Rashaun's laughter was cruel and mocking as he seized the makeshift weapon, the jagged edges of the wooden slats glinting in the dim light of the room.

"Oh, but I do," he sneered, his eyes alight with sadistic pleasure. "Shut your mouth, you pathetic excuse for a woman! You think you can talk back to me? You think you're better than me?"

With a savage snarl, Rashaun swung the broken shoe rack through the air, the sound of splintering wood echoing through the room like a crack of thunder. Sasha's screams filled the air as the weapon rained down upon her.

"You brought this upon yourself!" Rashaun growled.

"You made me do this."

Each blow from the shoe rack felt like a sledgehammer against Sasha's fragile frame, the pain searing through her body with agonizing intensity. She cried out in anguish, her pleas for mercy drowned out by Rashaun's deafening roar of fury.

"You want to play games with me?" He roared. "I'll show you what happens when you disrespect me!" He said as he hit her head, which was bloodied now.

"You think you're better than me?" He bellowed, his voice echoing off the walls as he continued his relentless assault. "You're nothing without me, Sasha. Nothing!"

As Sasha lay battered and broken on the floor, Rashaun's rage reached a fever pitch. With a savage snarl, he seized a belt from the nearby dresser, wrapping it around Sasha's throat with a cruel and merciless force.

"You want to play games with me?" He hissed, his eyes ablaze with a feral intensity. "I'll make sure you never forget who's in control!"

Sasha's world spun into darkness. The relentless blows from the broken shoe rack left her face a bloody, battered mess, and her left eye was swollen shut. Her skin was marred by deep gashes and bruises. And now, with the belt around her neck, she could barely see or breathe.

Tears mingled with blood as Sasha's screams filled the air, each cry a desperate plea for mercy and salvation. But Rashaun's rage knew no bounds, his assault relentless and unforgiving.

"You like that, huh?" He jeered, his voice dripping with sadistic delight. "You thought you could defy me? Now look at you, begging for mercy like the pathetic w**** you are."

Suddenly, as Rashaun loosened his grip on her neck, Sasha's heart seized with a new wave of horror as she felt the warm stickiness of blood saturating her virginal area and running down her legs. A sickening sense of violation washed over her, mingling with the searing pain of her injuries to form a suffocating cloak of despair. Tears streamed down Sasha's cheeks as she struggled to make sense of the nightmare unfolding around her.

"Rashaun, please, stop!" Sasha begged.

"Oh, but seeing you like this makes me feel like such a man." Rashaun moaned.

Sasha felt sick. Before she could gather any strength

to move, Rashaun grabbed her hair in a fist and started dragging her.

He dragged her to the nearby kept couch, and threw her on it in a way that her back was to his front. Then, he undressed himself.

"I'm going to take you like this today. Your face is disgusting me right now." Sasha heard Rashaun grunt.

She felt Rashaun grab her neck from behind, and with much strength, she managed to open her right eye, but only half way.

He eyes fell on the small coffee table in front of her, but what caught her gaze was Rashaun's gun thrown carelessly on it.

Seeing herself being treated like such trash, she had enough. In that moment, she realized that she didn't give a f***k of the consequences. She wanted revenge now. She wanted to be rid of this man, and there was only one way.

With trembling fingers, she wrapped her hand around the cold metal, her grip tightening with resolve.

As Rashaun loomed over her from behind, ready to take her dignity again, time seemed to stand still for Sasha. In that moment of clarity, amidst the chaos and violence, a series of faces flashed before her eyes - her mother, Cookie, her brother, John, her sister, Sade, her friend, Mise', and the haunting memory of the rape she had endured.

"Protection," Sasha heard Rashaun mumble and felt cool air hit her as Rashaun left to get what he needed.

In that moment of spiritual awakening, Sasha found the answer she had been subconsciously seeking. She realized that she could no longer allow herself to be a victim of Rashaun's brutality, nor could she continue to perpetuate the cycle of violence and abuse.

Gathering all her strength, she stood up and turned around with the gun now firmly gripped in her hand. With a slight smile of determination playing on her lips, she looked up at the approaching figure of Rashaun.

"No more," she whispered, her voice filled with a newfound strength, a smile on her face. "May God forgive us both."

And then, with unwavering resolve, Sasha pulled the trigger, the deafening sound of the gunshot reverberating through the room like a thunderclap. In that moment, Sasha knew that she had taken control of her own destiny, breaking free from the chains of abuse and reclaiming her power.

Time seemed to freeze as Rashaun's eyes widened in shock and disbelief. But Sasha's smile remained intact. Tears streamed down her cheeks but that smile—*that content smile*—remained unwavering.

Chapter 27

The room was heavy with tension, the aftermath of the gunshot still lingering in the air like a palpable weight. Amidst the silence, the ring of a phone shattered the stillness, its urgent tone cutting through the chaos like a beacon of hope.

With trembling hands, the caller reached for the phone, their heart racing with a mixture of fear and desperation. As they lifted the receiver to their ear, their breath got caught in their throat, their mind racing with a thousand thoughts.

"911, what's your emergency?" Came the voice on the other end of the line, calm and professional.

The caller hesitated for a moment, their pulse pounding in their ears.

"I... there's been a shooting," they managed to stammer, their voice barely above a whisper. "Please, you have to send help."

The operator's voice remained steady, reassuring. "Can you tell me your location?"

The caller swallowed hard, their mind struggling to

process the events unfolding around them. "I... I'm at 437 Oak Street," they replied, their voice trembling with uncertainty. "Please, hurry."

"Can you tell me what happened?" The operator asked.

"I don't know…" The caller trailed of.

"I need you to keep talking to me. Can you do that?" The operator tried to calm the caller.

"Yes, I think…?"

"Okay, tell me what is happening around you right now?"

The caller looked around and all that could be seen was blood.

"Blood. There's a lot of it. Blood…" The caller whispered, traumatized.

As the 911 operator tried to keep the caller on the line, they could hear the tremor in their voice, the palpable fear and trauma seeping through the receiver.

Despite the operator's soothing words and reassurances, the caller's breaths came in ragged gasps, each one a struggle against the overwhelming tide of emotions threatening to engulf them.

"Stay with me," the operator urged gently, their voice a lifeline in the darkness. "Help is on the way. You're not alone."

But the caller's responses grew more disjointed, their words choked with tears and anguish. They tried to articulate the events that had unfolded, the terror of the gunshot still ringing in their ears, but the words caught in their throat like a bitter pill.

"I... I can't..." the caller managed to whisper, their voice barely audible over the din of sirens in the distance. "I loved..."

The operator's heart ached for the caller, their own sense of helplessness mirrored in the silence that followed. They knew that all they could do was stay on the line, offering whatever small comfort they could until help arrived.

"Take deep breaths," the operator encouraged gently, their voice a steady anchor in the storm. "You're doing great. Help is almost there."

But as the moments stretched on, the caller's breathing grew more erratic, their sobs echoing through the line like a haunting refrain. The operator tried to maintain their composure, their own heart heavy with the weight of the caller's pain.

"Please," the caller pleaded, their voice raw with emotion. "I can't... I can't do this anymore."

But even as the caller's words trailed off into silence, the operator stayed on the line, their presence a silent promise of support and solidarity.

And as the sound of approaching sirens grew louder, the operator prayed silently for the caller's safety, their heart heavy with the knowledge that some wounds would take far longer to heal than others.

Outside, the scene was a flurry of activity as police cruisers and emergency vehicles descended upon the quiet suburban street. The flashing lights cast an eerie glow over the surrounding houses, illuminating the darkness with a kaleidoscope of red and blue.

Police officers leaped from their vehicles, their movements swift and purposeful as they took up positions around the perimeter of the house. They were armed and ready, their training kicking in as they assessed the situation and prepared to respond to whatever awaited them inside.

Fire rescue personnel followed closely behind, their faces grim with determination as they readied themselves for the task ahead. They carried medical equipment and stretchers, their minds focused on the possibility of casualties and the need for swift intervention.

As the officers and rescue workers approached the house, they were met with an eerie silence that hung heavy in the air. The only sound was the distant wail of sirens, a haunting reminder of the urgency of their mission.

With a sense of gravity weighing on their shoulders, the officers and rescue workers took their positions, forming a tight perimeter around the house. They communicated silently with hand signals and nods, their eyes scanning the windows and doors for any sign of movement.

Inside the house, the tension reached a fever pitch as the caller waited in agonizing silence, their breaths coming in shallow gasps as they listened for the sound outside the house.

As the officers and rescue workers maintained their tight perimeter around the house, the caller's senses heightened and their nerves on edge, inside the house, the tension reached a fever pitch.

The caller's heart pounded in their chest, their breaths shallow and labored as they clutched the bloodied gun in their trembling hand.

With each passing moment, the weight of their actions bore down upon them, a heavy burden they could no longer bear. In a haze of desperation and despair, they stumbled to their feet and made their way to the main door, the gun a cold and heavy presence in their hand.

They waited until the main door burst open. Finally, the caller's eyes met those of the officers gathered outside, their expressions a mix of concern and determination. The air crackled with tension as the caller lifted the gun, their movements slow and deliberate, the weight of their decision hanging heavy in the air.

"Drop the weapon!" One of the officers shouted, their voice firm and commanding.

But the caller's grip on the gun remained steady, their gaze unwavering as they lifted the weapon towards the officers, a silent plea for release from the agony that consumed them.

In an instant, the air was filled with the sound of gunfire as the officers responded to the imminent threat before them. The caller's body jerked back with the force of the bullets, their grip on the gun loosening as they crumpled to the ground, the weight of their pain finally lifted.

Outside, the street fell silent once more, the echoes

of the gunfire fading into the night as the officers approached the fallen figure in the doorway.

With heavy hearts and solemn expressions, they surveyed the scene before them, knowing that they had done what they could to bring the situation to a close.

But as they looked upon the lifeless form of the caller, a sense of sorrow washed over them, a poignant reminder of the human cost of their profession.

One of the officers approached the fallen caller, their footsteps slow and deliberate as they knelt beside the lifeless form. Gently, they reached out to check for a pulse, their fingers searching for any sign of life, but their efforts were in vain. With a solemn nod, he rose to his feet and turned to his colleagues.

"No pulse," he announced quietly, his voice thick with emotion. "Time of death—5:53."

The other officers exchanged somber nods, their expressions reflecting the weight of the moment. In unspoken solidarity, they signaled to one another to continue their search of the house, knowing that their duty was far from over.

Amidst the chaos and tension, the police officers

carefully combed through the rooms of the house, their eyes trained to detect any sign of movement or danger. As they moved through the living room, their gaze fell upon the devastating sight of another fallen figure, hidden in the shadows.

With a sense of dread weighing heavily upon him, one of the officers approached the bloody body, his heart pounding with trepidation. Carefully, he knelt beside the prone form, his trained eyes scanning for any sign of life amidst the grim tableau of tragedy.

With gentle precision, the officer placed his fingers on the pulse point of the body, his touch light yet purposeful. His breath caught in his throat as he waited, praying for the faintest flicker of a heartbeat beneath his fingertips.

Seconds stretched into eternity as he held his breath, his senses heightened to the slightest movement or sound. And then, a moment of relief washed over him as he felt the faint thud of a pulse beneath his fingers, weak but unmistakable.

Heart racing with a mixture of hope and urgency, the officer wasted no time. With steady hands, he reached for his radio, his movements swift and decisive as he relayed the critical information to dispatch.

"We have a pulse," he announced, his voice filled with a sense of urgency. "Requesting immediate medical assistance. Female victim, pregnant, gunshot wound, barely alive. Send paramedics to our location, over."

With the message relayed, the officer remained by the side of the injured individual, his thoughts consumed by the gravity of the situation. He could only pray that help would arrive swiftly, knowing that every moment counted in the race to save a life.

Sasha, her pregnant form lying motionless on the floor. A gunshot wound to her head told a harrowing tale of violence, yet despite the severity of her injuries, Sasha still clung to a faint thread of life.

An EMS first responder from fire rescue swiftly arrived on the scene, their trained eyes assessing the situation with a practiced gaze. With a heavy heart, they knelt beside Sasha's prone form, their hands moving swiftly to check for vital signs.

"She's barely hanging on," the first responder announced, his voice filled with solemnity. "We need to get her to the hospital. Now!"

Without hesitation, the officers and first responders worked together to carefully lift Sasha onto a stretcher, their movements gentle yet urgent. With each passing moment, the urgency of their task weighed heavily upon them, knowing that not only Sasha's, but a baby's life hung in the balance too.

Outside, the flashing lights of emergency vehicles illuminated the darkened street, casting an eerie glow over the somber scene. Police officers maintained their vigil around the perimeter of the house, their eyes scanning the surroundings for any sign of danger.

The other emergency responders gathered, their expressions reflecting the weight of the moment. With a sense of respect for the lives that had been lost, they prepared to transport both Sasha and Rashaun from the scene, their hearts heavy with the knowledge of the devastation that had occurred within the walls of the house.

And as the ambulance pulled away, its sirens wailing into the night, the officers and first responders remained behind, their thoughts with Sasha as she fought for her life, and with Rashaun as he embarked on his final journey.

Chapter 28

As Sasha was rushed into the operating room, the hospital corridors buzzed with urgency and tension. Medical staff moved with purpose, their steps quick and efficient as they prepared for the life-saving procedure ahead.

In the waiting area outside the operating room, Sasha's family and friends gathered, their faces etched with worry and fear. Greg. Vick, and Ava, sat with tears in their eyes, their hands clasped tightly together in silent prayer.

In the midst of the group stood Pastor Miles, a pillar of strength and solace in times of crisis. His presence brought a sense of calm amidst the chaos, his words of reassurance offering a glimmer of hope to those gathered.

Together, they formed a united front, bound together by their love and concern for Sasha and her unborn child. As they waited anxiously for news from the operating room, their thoughts and prayers were with Sasha, willing her to pull through the ordeal and emerge safely on the other side.

Inside the operating room, the medical team worked with precision and determination, their focus unwavering as they battled to save both Sasha and her unborn child. Every second was precious, every decision critical as they fought to stem the tide of tragedy and bring about a miracle of healing.

As the minutes ticked by, the tension in the air was palpable, a silent reminder of the high stakes at play. And amidst the flurry of activity, one thing remained clear: Sasha was not alone. She was surrounded by a circle of love and support that stretched far beyond the walls of the hospital, a testament to the strength of the bonds that held her close.

Amidst the chaos, Tasha walked into the hospital. Her steps were mechanical, her movements devoid of purpose as she navigated the sterile corridors of the hospital. Her mind was numb, her thoughts a jumbled mess of confusion and disbelief. She couldn't feel any emotions, couldn't process the magnitude of what was happening.

As she walked, Tasha barely registered the concerned looks from hospital staff, their attempts to stop her lost in the fog of her mind. She was on autopilot, her gaze fixed ahead as she moved inexorably toward the source of her anguish.

And then, she saw it.

In the triage area, amidst the flurry of activity, Tasha's eyes fell upon Sasha's clothing and jewelry, saturated in blood. Her heart lurched in her chest, a wave of nausea washing over her as the reality of the situation crashed down upon her like a tidal wave.

For a moment, she stood frozen in place, her mind unable to comprehend the sight before her. Sasha, her beloved sister, lay somewhere beyond that curtain, fighting for her life.

With trembling hands, Tasha reached out, her fingers tracing the outline of Sasha's belongings as if seeking solace in their familiar touch. Tears welled in her eyes, but she couldn't bring herself to cry. The pain was too raw, too overwhelming to be contained in mere tears.

And so, with a heavy heart, Tasha turned away from the triage area, her footsteps faltering as she stumbled blindly down the hallway. She didn't know where she was going, didn't know what she would do when she got there. All she knew was that she couldn't bear to see Sasha like this, couldn't face the reality of her sister's suffering.

Lost in her grief, Tasha continued to walk, her mind consumed by a whirlwind of emotions that threatened to engulf her completely. She didn't notice the concerned glances from passersby, didn't hear the murmured words of comfort offered by sympathetic strangers. All she could think about was Sasha, lying alone in that hospital bed, fighting for her life with every breath she took.

As the clock ticked relentlessly in the dimly lit hospital waiting room, Greg, Ava, Vic, Tasha, and Pastor Miles endured an excruciating vigil, their collective anxiety mounting with each passing minute. The sterile scent of antiseptic hung in the air, mingling with the palpable tension that gripped the room like a vise.

Tasha paced back and forth like a caged animal, her movements agitated and restless. Her hands clenched and unclenched at her sides, her heart pounding in her chest as she grappled with the uncertainty of Sasha's fate. She couldn't bear to sit still, couldn't bear to confront the possibility that she might lose her sister, her confidante, her rock.

Greg sat hunched over in a chair, his face buried in his hands. He felt utterly powerless, consumed by a gnawing sense of guilt and regret. If only he had been there to protect her, to shield her from harm. But now, all he could do was wait, his mind tortured by thoughts of what might have been.

Vick sat beside Greg, her eyes red-rimmed with tears. She reached out a trembling hand to grasp his, offering what little comfort she could in the face of their shared grief. The weight of Sasha's absence hung heavy between them, a gaping void that threatened to swallow them whole.

Ava sat in a corner of the room, her arms wrapped tightly around herself. She felt numb disconnected from the world around her as she tried to make sense of the nightmare unfolding before her eyes. Sasha couldn't be gone, couldn't be lost to them forever. It simply wasn't possible.

Pastor Miles stood quietly in the corner, his hands clasped in silent prayer. His heart ached for Sasha and her loved ones, his faith tested by the enormity of their suffering. He knew that in times like these, there were no easy answers, no quick fixes. All they could do was lean on each other and cling to hope.

As the minutes turned into hours, the tension in the waiting room became almost unbearable. Every sound, every movement felt magnified, amplified by the suffocating weight of uncertainty. Time seemed to stretch on endlessly, each moment dragging by with agonizing slowness.

And then, finally, the door to the waiting room swung open, and a doctor emerged, his expression grave and solemn. The room fell silent, every eye fixed on the doctor as they braced themselves for the news they dreaded to hear.

The doctor took a deep breath, steeling themselves for the difficult task ahead.

"I'm sorry," he began, his words hanging heavily in the air. "We did everything we could, but... Sasha didn't make it."

A collective gasp of disbelief rippled through the room, followed by anguished cries of grief and despair.

Tasha's legs gave out beneath her, and she collapsed to the floor, her sobs echoing through the room as she struggled to come to terms with the devastating loss of her sister.

Greg sat frozen in shock, his hands trembling as he reached out for support, his face a mask of disbelief and anguish. Tears streamed down his cheeks as he tried to process the crushing weight of grief that threatened to engulf him. He let out a gut-wrenching wail of anguish, his grief raw and unfiltered as he grappled with the reality of losing his sister.

Vick collapsed into the nearest chair, her tears flowing freely as she mourned the loss.

Ava wrapped her arms around her family members, offering what little comfort she could amidst the overwhelming tide of grief that threatened to consume them all.

Pastor Miles bowed his head in silent prayer, his words a whispered plea for strength and solace in the face of unimaginable loss.

But amidst the darkness, a faint glimmer of hope emerged. The doctor's next words cut through the sorrow like a ray of light in the darkness.

"But we were able to preserve the pregnancy. The babies were delivered via emergency C-section." He announced. "They are in the Neonatal Intensive Care Unit, where they are receiving the care and attention they need to thrive."

For a moment, the room fell silent, the weight of the doctor's words sinking in as the family grappled with the bittersweet reality of new life amidst the shadow of death. Tears mingled with smiles as they held onto the fragile thread of hope, knowing that even in their darkest hour, there was still a beacon of light to guide them through the darkness.

Meanwhile, Tasha remained on the floor, her body wracked with sobs as she mourned the loss of her sister.

Greg knelt beside her, his arms wrapped tightly around her as he whispered words of comfort and solace. Vick and Ava joined them, forming a tight-knit circle of support as they navigated the turbulent waters of grief together.

Pastor Miles offered a silent prayer for Sasha's soul, his heart heavy with sorrow but buoyed by the knowledge that she was at peace. He knew that in the days and weeks to come, Sasha's family would need all the love and support they could get as they grieved the loss of their beloved sister, and friend.

As the doctor's words hung in the air, a heavy silence descended upon the waiting room, broken only by the soft sound of Greg's whispered plea. His voice trembled with emotion as he spoke, the weight of his grief evident in every syllable.

"Can I see my sister?" Greg's words were barely a whisper, but they echoed through the room like a mournful lament. His heartache was palpable, his longing for one last glimpse of Sasha etched into the lines of his face.

Without waiting for a response, Greg rose from his seat and made his way to the door of the operating room, his steps heavy with the weight of anticipation and dread.

Everyone followed suit, their faces drawn and solemn as they prepared to confront the reality of their loss.

As they entered the operating room, a wave of emotion washed over them, threatening to drown them in its intensity. The sight of Sasha lying motionless on the operating table sent a shiver down their spines, her peaceful expression belying the tragedy of her untimely passing.

Greg approached Sasha's bedside with a mixture of trepidation and longing, his heart pounding in his chest as he reached out to touch her cold, lifeless hand. His fingers lingered on her skin, tracing the contours of her face with a gentle touch as he whispered words of love and sorrow into the silent void.

Tasha stood beside Greg, her eyes brimming with tears as she looked upon their sister's still form. The sight of Sasha lying there, so small and vulnerable, tore at her heartstrings, filling her with a profound sense of loss and regret. She reached out to touch Sasha's cheek, her fingers trembling with emotion as she whispered a silent prayer for peace and rest.

Vick and Ava stood nearby, their faces streaked with tears as they struggled to come to terms with the enormity of their grief. They exchanged a glance, their shared pain evident in the depths of their sorrow-filled eyes. Together, they approached Sasha's bedside, their hands clasped tightly together as they sought solace in each other's presence.

Pastor Miles stood at the foot of Sasha's bed, his hands clasped in silent prayer as he offered a final blessing for her soul. His heart ached for Sasha and her loved ones, his faith tested by the magnitude of their suffering. But even in the face of such profound loss, he clung to the hope that Sasha had found peace in the arms of the divine.

As each member of Sasha's family said their final farewells, the room was filled with a profound sense of sorrow and longing. Raw, unfiltered emotions poured forth like a flood, washing over them with a force that threatened to consume them whole.

Greg's grief was raw and visceral, his tears falling freely as he held Sasha's lifeless hand in his own. He whispered words of love and regret, his voice choked with emotion as he struggled to come to terms with the reality of her passing.

Tasha's grief was a silent scream, her tears flowing unchecked as she leaned over Sasha's bedside, her heart breaking with each passing moment.

She wished she could turn back time, erase the events that had led them to this moment, but she knew that such wishes were futile in the face of fate.

Vick's grief was a heavy weight upon her shoulders, threatening to crush her beneath its unbearable burden. She clung to Ava for support, her tears mingling with hers as they shared in the collective pain of their loss.

Ava's grief was a silent sob, her body racked with tremors as she struggled to contain the tidal wave of emotion threatening to overwhelm her. She reached out to touch Sasha's face one last time, her fingers lingering on her skin as she whispered a final goodbye.

Pastor Miles's grief was a silent prayer, his heart heavy with sorrow as he bowed his head in reverence for Sasha's departed soul. He offered a final blessing for her journey into the afterlife, knowing that she would be welcomed with open arms into the loving embrace of the divine.

As everyone gathered around her bedside, they found solace in each other's presence, drawing strength from their shared grief and the love that bound them together. In the midst of their pain, they found comfort in the knowledge that Sasha's spirit would live on in their hearts forever, guiding them through the darkness with the light of her memory.

And so, as they said their final farewells to Sasha, they knew that her legacy would endure, a testament to the power of love and the resilience of the human spirit.

And even as they mourned her passing, they found solace in the knowledge that she would always be with them, watching over them from above with a love that knew no bounds.

Not being able to breathe inside, Tasha ran out. But the second she stepped out of the room, a nurse called for her.

"Miss Tasha? You are the sister, right?" Asked the nurse.

"Yes?" Tasha answered in a trembling

"Follow me, please." Requested the nurse.

As Tasha was guided through the labyrinthine corridors of the hospital, her steps felt heavy, as if she were dragging an anchor behind her. The nurse's gentle touch on her arm was a lifeline in the sea of despair that threatened to engulf her.

Together, they made their way to the Neonatal Intensive Care Unit (NICU), where the delicate cries of newborns mingled with the steady hum of machines.

Entering the NICU, Tasha's eyes were met with the sight of two tiny figures swaddled in blankets, their little forms nestled snugly in incubators. They were beautiful. Their innocence was palpable, a stark contrast to the grief that weighed heavily on Tasha's heart.

The nurse approached the incubators, her movements gentle and reverent as she lifted the blankets to reveal the sleeping babies within. Tasha's breath caught in her throat at the sight of them, their tiny features so perfect and delicate that she feared they might shatter at the slightest touch.

"These are your nieces," the nurse said softly, her voice a soothing balm against the raw edges of Tasha's grief. "They're fighters, just like their mother."

Tasha nodded numbly, her mind struggling to process the enormity of what lay before her. These tiny beings were Sasha's legacy, a living testament to the love and life she had brought into the world.

For what felt like hours, Tasha remained rooted to the spot, her eyes fixed on the two sleeping infants before her. She was in a daze, her mind a jumble of conflicting emotions as she tried to reconcile the joy of new life with the crushing weight of loss.

As the minutes stretched into hours, the nurse gently approached Tasha, her presence a silent reminder that she was not alone in her grief. She offered Tasha a sympathetic smile, her eyes filled with understanding.

"It's time to give them names," the nurse said gently, her voice breaking through the fog of Tasha's thoughts.

"What would you like to call them?"

As the nurse's words cut through the fog of Tasha's thoughts, a sudden wave of clarity washed over her, sweeping away the numbness and despair that had clouded her mind.

In that moment, she felt a surge of emotion unlike anything she had ever experienced before—a profound sense of relief and gratitude, tinged with a bittersweet longing for what could have been.

For so long, Tasha had been adrift in a sea of grief, lost in the tumultuous currents of sorrow and despair.

But now, standing before the incubators that cradled her sister's babies, she felt a glimmer of hope stirring within her—a flicker of light amidst the darkness.

These babies were more than just Sasha's daughters; they were a gift—a second chance at life, a chance to start anew. In their tiny faces, Tasha saw the promise of a future filled with love and possibility, a future that had once seemed impossibly distant.

With trembling hands, Tasha reached out to touch the glass of the incubators, her heart overflowing with love and longing. Tears welled in her eyes as she gazed upon the sleeping infants, their peaceful expressions a stark contrast to the turmoil raging within her own heart.

And then, as if guided by an unseen hand, Tasha felt a sense of clarity wash over her—a deep knowing that these babies were meant to be hers, meant to fill the void left by Sasha's untimely passing. In that moment, she knew with unwavering certainty that she had found her purpose, her assignment from God.

With newfound resolve, Tasha turned to the nurse, her voice steady despite the tears that threatened to spill from her eyes.

"Their names are Sasha Wright and Sade Wright," she said, her words a whispered prayer of gratitude and hope.

The nurse nodded, her smile radiant with understanding. She could see the transformation that had taken place within Tasha, the shift from grief to acceptance, from despair to hope. In that moment, she knew that Tasha was ready to embrace the challenges and blessings that lay ahead.

"Beautiful names," she murmured, her words a

gentle reminder that even in the darkest of times, there was still beauty to be found.

And so, with hearts full of love and determination, Tasha and the nurse set about filling out the paperwork, each letter of their names a testament to the love that would forever bind them together.

Tasha couldn't understand why her loving sister, the strongest person she had ever known, would take her own life. Suddenly, this very question seemed to give her the answer. "She died thinking that we could live again." She thought of Tasha, Sasha and Sade.

Tasha closed her eyes and smiled as she made a vow to Ssaha, "We will live and honor you. You can rest now, sister."

Information

Narcissistic Personality Disorders are known for their patterns of grandiosity, need for admiration, and lack of empathy for others. It often presents itself as being impaired to maintain relationships and work. The disorder causes one's behavior to be overly emotional and unpredictable. When combined with any substance abuse, the individual can become very violent and dangerous.

Experts say the developmental stage of NPD is harmful. The examples given that may contribute to NPD are being rejected as a child and having a fragile ego during early childhood. However, the belief that a child may have extraordinary abilities and given excessive praise may lead to NPD.

There are basically two types of NPD: Overt Grandiose, which presents aggression, and boldness.

Vulnerable Grandiose subtype presents hypersensitivity and defensiveness. This can often be missed.

Below are some pervasive patterns of grandiosity (behaviors or fantasy). Experts say possessing at least five can be an indication of NPD by the very early stages of adulthood.

- Has a grandiose sense of self-importance (e.g., exaggerates achievements, expects to be recognized as superior without actually completing the achievements)
- It is preoccupied with fantasies of success, power, brilliance, beauty, or perfect love.
- They believe they are "special" and can only be understood by or should only associate with other special people (or institutions).
- It requires excessive admiration.
- Has a sense of entitlement, such as an unreasonable expectation of favorable treatment or compliance with his or her expectations).
- It is exploitative and takes advantage of others to achieve their own ends.
- Lacks empathy and is unwilling to identify with the needs of others.
- Is often envious of others or believes that others are envious of them.
- Shows arrogant, haughty behaviors and attitudes.

"Persons with an antisocial personality disorder would show a lack of morals compared to persons with NPD and have a past diagnosis of conduct disorder."

Take a conscious note and study. Other disorders, such as antisocial personality disorder, bipolar, depression, and anxiety, are just as important.

If you are struggling, seek refuge for good mental health. Please contact the National Alliance on Mental Illness.

Nami.org

National Hotline for Mental Health Crises and Suicide Prevention 1 800 273 Talk (8255) Or text "Helpline" to 62640.